BENEATH CRUEL WATERS

BOOKS BY JON BASSOFF

The Disassembled Man

Corrosion

Factory Town

The Incurables

The Blade This Time

The Lantern Man

The Drive-Thru Crematorium

Captain Clive's Dreamworld

Beneath Cruel Waters

BENEATH CRUEL WATERS

JON BASSOFF

BLACK
STONE
PUBLISHING

Published in 2022 by Blackstone Publishing
Cover and book design by Kathryn Galloway English

Printed in the United States of America

First edition: 2022
ISBN 978-1-7999-3888-0
Fiction / Thrillers / Psychological

Version 1

CIP data for this book is available
from the Library of Congress

Blackstone Publishing
31 Mistletoe Rd.
Ashland, OR 97520

www.BlackstonePublishing.com

For Anna and Noah

We were therefore buried with him through baptism into death in order that, just as Christ was raised from the dead through the glory of the Father, we too may live a new life.

—Romans 6:4

God gave Noah the rainbow sign
No more water, but fire next time
Pharaoh's army got drowned
Oh Mary don't you weep

—"Oh, Mary, Don't You Weep"
(traditional)

PROLOGUE

1984–2018

Except for the lines of cottonwoods and willows nestled against the banks of the South Platte River, the landscape surrounding the town of Thompsonville, Colorado, was mainly desolation and starkness. Golden-brown buffalo grass, interrupted by a grain-field expanse, sloped gently to the west, while cloudless blue skies transformed into swirling grays and lightning storms before returning, just as abruptly, to that foreboding calm. Highway 53, its asphalt worn and splintered, stretched north and south, and parallel to it were some signs of life, or at least as much life as eastern Colorado could muster: railroad tracks and telephone poles and feed elevators and tire cemeteries. Away from the highway was the occasional dairy farm, maybe a horse ranch or two. And that was about it.

Three miles east of the town stood an old brick grange, long since abandoned but still marked with a dirty sign that read "Liberty Hall: Service and Friendship." On this evening, a broken-down Lincoln Continental, its windshield broken, its tires flat, was parked out front, as if it had been waiting for some community dance that would never materialize. Just past the grange there was a gathering of gnarled and leafless cottonwoods, and then, just past that, a dilapidated farmhouse, its white paint peeling to brown, its windows boarded-up, its porch sagging toward an eventual grave. Car parts and empty beer cans were strewn on a dirt lawn decorated with weeds. A Gadsden flag hung from the house—"Don't Tread on Me"—snapping to attention in the cool evening breeze. The porch light was flickering.

Inside the house, things didn't look much better. A small television set rested in the corner of the living room, rabbit ears wrapped in tinfoil. *The A-Team* was on, but nobody was there to watch it. The only furniture was a wooden chair and a whiskey crate, which served as a makeshift table. On the crate there was unopened mail, a school photograph of a girl with pigtails, and a pocketknife. A narrow hallway led toward the kitchen, the wooden floor warped and filthy. In the middle of the kitchen there was a round metal table, and on the table was a package of Salems, an ashtray with a half dozen cigarettes crushed out, a bottle of Old Crow, mostly empty, and a juice glass with only a taste of whiskey remaining.

Surrounding the table were three folding chairs, and sitting in one of the chairs was a man, probably in his early thirties, his head shaved and his jaw clenched. He wore a white T-shirt that was too small for his thick chest. Both of his arms were covered with tattoos, but the ink was fading. His most prominent tattoo was the one on his neck: a rose, blood dripping from its petals. He reached for a pack of cigarettes, pulled out a crooked one, and stuck it into the center of his mouth. He flicked open a flame and lit it. His eyes narrowed, and smoke trickled from his nostrils. For several minutes, he barely moved, only occasionally lifting his calloused hand to his mouth to suck down more smoke.

The cigarette was almost down to the filter when the man's head jerked to the right and his eye twitched. From the living room the sound of the front door creaking open and then footsteps on the hardwood floor. Still, he remained seated, unmoving.

A moment later, a woman appeared, stopping in the doorframe. She was tall and thin and pretty. She had black hair, piled high on her head, and cornflower blue eyes. She wore lipstick but no other makeup. A white dress fell just below her calves. A red purse dangled from her shoulder. The man gazed at the woman, and his mouth curled into a grin.

"And now she's here," he said, and his voice was harsh, as if he hadn't used it in many months. "I kind of always figured you'd come back."

The woman didn't answer, just remained in the doorway, her shoulders rising up and down, her lower lip trembling.

"Come on, then," he said. "Have a seat. Have a drink."

She shook her head, said, "I'm not thirsty." She took a step forward, and then another. Her eyes were darting around, and her hand was rubbing up and down her purse.

The man crushed out his cigarette and rose to his feet. "Fine. No drink. Then come give me a kiss."

"No," she said, forcefully. "No." After a moment's hesitation, she reached into her purse. She pulled out a small pistol.

The man nodded at her, said, "That for me?"

She cocked the weapon and waved it vaguely in his direction. "You should have left us alone," she said. "You shouldn't have done what you did."

"I don't know what you're talking about. I didn't do a damn thing. But I do know that you're not gonna use that little pistol."

The woman laughed, and it was a high-pitched, desperate laugh. Without saying another word, she closed one eye and aimed the gun at his chest. Then she squeezed the trigger, once, twice, three times.

The explosions echoed loudly in the kitchen. One of the bullets hit the man in the stomach, the other two in the chest. He slammed against the wall, groaning. He remained upright for a moment, as if trying to make up his mind whether to live or die, but life drained quickly, and he slid to the floor, blood smearing the wall behind him. For some time, he sat in that scarlet puddle, shoulders rising, breath rattling in his throat. Soon the rattling stopped, his eyes glazed over, and he was still.

The woman stayed where she was, the gun still raised and still trembling in her hand. Finally, she lowered the weapon. With a deep sigh, she studied the man, the man that she had killed, and then took stock of the kitchen, perhaps making sure she hadn't left any evidence behind.

She placed the gun back into her purse, and now she pulled out something else: an old Polaroid camera. She got down on one knee and focused the camera on the dead man. She pressed the button, and the camera clicked and whirred. A photograph, still blank, lowered from the bottom. The woman held the photograph in front of her and shook it a few times. After a couple of minutes, the image became visible, first dull and ghostly and then vivid and grotesque.

"Dead," she whispered. And then, once again, "Dead."

She placed the camera and photo into her purse. Then she turned and walked out of the kitchen, where blood was still spreading slowly across the floor. Her footsteps got softer and softer, and soon the front door opened and slammed shut. And then everything was quiet again, everything but the muffled screams coming from the television set. Time passed, but the man remained slumped against the wall, shirt soaked with blood, mouth parted, eyes bulging.

Over the next couple of days, nothing happened. That is, nobody entered the old farmhouse behind Liberty Grange. The man's body cooled and then stiffened. His skin blistered and turned green. His tongue protruded from his mouth and his eyes from their sockets. The stink overwhelmed the house.

On the third day following the murder, midmorning, a fat woman wearing an oversized flower dress stepped out from her car and walked toward the house. With each step she took, she muttered about how there was shit everywhere on the lawn and about how she never should have let this motherfucker rent the house in the first place. "Nothing but trouble," she said. "Nothing but a pain in my ass." In one hand, she was holding a paper with the words "Eviction Notice" stamped across the top.

She knocked on the front door a few times, her glasses falling to the tip of her nose, but there was no answer. She moved toward a window and pressed her face against the glass, trying to peer inside. The lights were all on, the TV flickering, but there was no movement.

"I know you're in there, Mr. Ray," she said loud enough for only her to hear. "Not going to leave without my money."

Back to the front door. More knocking, but no footsteps from inside. She tried the door handle. It was unlocked. She stepped inside and stood in the doorframe. Her expression immediately turned to a grimace, and she pinched her nose. She took another few steps forward, cleared her throat.

"Mr. Ray? Are you here? It's your landlord, Janet Dovoavich. Hello?"

The stench was overwhelming. Ms. Dovoavich covered her mouth with the crook of her arm. Still she moved forward—curious, perhaps, as to what the smell was. Curious, perhaps, as to who was dead. When she arrived in the kitchen and saw the corpse—blood-soaked and bloated, foam leaking from its mouth and nose—Ms. Dovoavich didn't gasp, didn't scream, didn't make a sound at all, at least not right away. She dropped the eviction notice, and it fluttered to the floor. She backed up a few steps and steadied herself against the wall, her shoulders heaving up and down. Her gaze remained on the grotesque corpse, flies buzzing by its torso.

Ms. Dovoavich's mouth opened, and now she finally made a sound. It was a shriek of terror that might have lasted for a second. She remained in the kitchen for another moment or two, and then she stumbled away, through the hallway and out the front door.

Less than thirty minutes later, the muted sounds of sirens could be heard, occasionally washed away by the wind. When they arrived, it was the whole cavalry. Police cars (two), ambulances (two), and a firetruck (one). The vehicles crowded onto the dirt road, and the men stepped out of vehicles and hurried across the lawn. Kaleidoscope lights flashed from the top of the vehicles, and radios buzzed.

A pair of police officers were the first to enter the house. One of them had a thick black mustache and a pockmarked face. The other had red hair and looked too young to be a police officer. Upon entering, they both covered their mouths with the crooks of their arms, just like the old landlady had done. The man with the mustache looked at his partner and shook his head. They walked slowly through the house, observing minutia as police officers are taught to do. See the unopened mail on the whiskey cart? What about the photo of the girl? And this check, from the meatpacking plant, uncashed?

When they got to the kitchen and peered inside, the redhead turned pale. He placed his hands on his knees and leaned forward as if he was going to be sick. He didn't vomit, however. His partner ignored him, instead peering around the kitchen, at the floor, at the wall, at the ceiling.

A few minutes later, two other men entered the house, one tall, one short, both in shirts and ties, sleeves rolled up to the elbows. They wore latex gloves on their hands and coverings on their shoes. When the tall one saw the body, he muttered, "Fuck," and then moved closer and got down on his haunches. He said "Fuck" again.

The short man said, "You know him, Lieutenant?"

The lieutenant nodded his head. "I do. I paid him a visit not so long ago. Had a little talk with him. Gave him a warning. But I guess my warning didn't stick."

"Enemy also paid him a visit, huh?"

"Yeah, maybe. Or a real bad friend."

The short man grunted.

After that, the lieutenant and the short man barely talked to each other. They spent the next thirty minutes speaking into tape recorders, writing down notes, and bagging evidence. Other officials—all men—entered the house. One of them dusted the walls and counters, searching for fingerprints. Another took photographs. But most of them were only there for a short time, peeking their heads into the kitchen and then leaving.

Eventually, the coroner arrived. He was a hefty man with thick gray sideburns. The perspiration glistened on his forehead. A couple of his assistants, perhaps his sons, placed plastic over the body and then moved it to a stretcher. They counted to three and then lifted. Just like that, the body was gone.

The lieutenant and his partner remained in the house for another hour or two, and then they left. They didn't come back. The house was empty again.

Over the next several weeks, a handful of people entered the house. One man, a locksmith, changed the locks on the door. Another group of workers, dressed in hazmat uniforms, cleaned the walls and floor of blood and skin and tissue. A woman and a man, carrying a transistor radio playing top forty music—"When Doves Cry," "Dancing in the Dark," "What's Love Got to Do with It," "Jump"—packed up the remaining items in the house, which weren't all that many. Some dishes. Some clothes. Some towels. Some toiletries. A toolbox. It didn't take them long, maybe an hour. And then they left.

The house was quiet again. Nobody would come back, not for a long time.

Months passed, and then years. A new president was elected and then another. Styles began to change. Leg warmers and neon colors turned to flannels and ripped jeans. At one point, there was a For Sale sign outside the property. It stayed up for three months and then came down. Nobody bought the house.

The snowy winters and dry summers took their toll. The wood began to rot, causing the house to sway in the wind. Animals—rabbits, coyotes, owls, bats—found shelter there. People stayed away, except for the occasional teenagers who would sneak onto the property to drink or screw.

And then, on the eve of the new millennium, as the snow fell in every direction and the temperature toppled below zero, an old man with a yellowing beard pushed through the front door and set up camp in what used to be the living room. He huddled inside his sleeping bag, a pink-and-yellow pompom hat pulled below his ears, and ate from a can of sardines. When he finished the sardines, he took a long chug from his bottle of Four Roses and wiped his whiskered lips with his gloved hand. Then he curled up in his bag and slept for twenty hours straight, snoring heavily, his body barely moving. When he finally woke, he sat up without stretching and reached for the bottle of whiskey again. This time he drank four, five, six, seven chugs before dropping the bottle and spilling whiskey across the floor. He lit a cheap cigar and smoked, all the while singing a song of nonsense. After ten minutes, he dropped the nub of the still-burning cigar and sang some more, his eyes bloodshot and wild.

Soon the song ended and the conversation began, a conversation with somebody not there, somebody named Margaret. He was angry that she had cheated on him, angry that she had left him. The conversation lasted several minutes and didn't stop until he noticed that the floor was on fire. Even then the old man didn't move, although he stared, his eyes nearly bulging from their sockets. The shelves ignited and then the walls. Finally, he broke from his stupor and stumbled to his feet. As the room became engulfed in fire, his filthy face glowed like some devil.

"Margaret!" he hollered through smoke-induced hacks. He managed to burst through the fiery doorframe outside into a snowdrift, where he rolled around for a few seconds and used his hands to mash snow against his face and neck. He turned around and watched as the house transformed into a hellish inferno, the black smoke sucked toward the sky.

Windows turned red. The door collapsed forward. The roof caught fire. The old man struggled to his feet and staggered down the dirt road, past the towering cottonwood, and then he was gone.

By the time the firefighters arrived, there was nothing much they could do. They managed to wash the fire away, but all that was left was a charred skeleton of a structure collapsing onto scalded earth.

So what do you do with a burned house that nobody owns? You let it sit there, an eyesore to anybody who ventures off the two-lane highway and decides to drive past the old grange.

Another decade passed and then most of the next one. The earth healed, regenerated, but not the house. At some point, a group of men wearing hardhats walked around the skeletal house, taking photographs and writing notes. They talked about razing the structure, discussed cost analysis.

They came back two more times.

The structure remained.

It was late fall, 2018, and most of the leaves had fallen from the cottonwoods, a sad breeze dragging them across the dirt. An old Ford moved deliberately down the dirt road, barely visible because of all the dead leaves and broken branches. The car slowed and then stopped, fifty yards from the charred house. For several minutes the car remained idle, the engine still running. Eventually, the engine shut off, but nobody got out.

Ten minutes. More. The door finally opened and a leg appeared, a black dress falling nearly to the ankle. Moments later, the other leg, and then a woman. She was stooped at the shoulders, either from age or sorrow. Her white hair was thin and disheveled. But behind creased lids her eyes were lovely and lively, and cornflower blue. It was the same woman who had entered this house years ago, the same woman who had pulled a pistol from her purse and shot and killed a man while he smoked in his kitchen.

The woman walked slowly toward the burned and rotted house, her lower lip trembling, her dress swaying in the breeze. In her right hand she held a Bible, its cover battered. She shuffled through the structure and took in the blackened boards, the remains of the floor. She stood where the kitchen had once been. There was ash, shattered glass, and twisted scraps of metal, perhaps remnants of the oven or refrigerator.

The woman got down on her knees, her dress spreading beneath her, and placed the Bible on the ground. She opened the cover, and a breeze through the missing windows fluttered the pages. She licked her finger and flipped through the book until she arrived at the page she was searching for. She read silently, her lips moving almost imperceptibly. Then she squeezed her eyes shut and began rocking back and forth. Eventually, she closed the Bible, rose to her feet, and trudged through the house toward the front.

The Bible was left behind.

Outside, the sky had begun to darken, and the air was getting cooler. The sound of a train's ghostly whistle echoed through the autumn air. The woman edged around the perimeter of the burned-out structure, leaves floating past her, toward a water well, long since abandoned. It was made of crumbling brick and covered by a few wooden planks bolted lazily into the brickwork. Crossing herself, the woman bent at the knees, grabbed ahold of one of those planks, and yanked. The wood was rotted and came away easily. She got down on her knees, placed her hands on the brick opening, and peered down the darkened tunnel.

There was no bucket, no water. Only blackness. And yet, as the minutes passed, she continued to gaze into that blackness, and then she began to sob, her wails echoing against the brick walls. When she finally rose to her feet, tears wetted her wrinkled cheeks. She wiped them away with the back of her hand.

Eventually, she left the abandoned well and returned to her car, dead leaves collecting on the windshield. From the trunk, she removed a rope and a step ladder. Then she walked toward a bare cottonwood, gnarled branches jutting from the trunk.

She placed the ladder a foot or so from the tree and climbed it slowly. She found a thick branch and yanked on it with her free hand. Despite her frailty, she managed to tie and tighten the loose end of the rope around the branch. She then placed the other end—already secured in a noose—around her neck and tightened it. A soft breeze blew. She took a deep breath and closed her eyes. Five seconds, ten. Then she kicked the ladder away. It wobbled slightly before crashing to the ground.

For a few moments—as her body convulsed, eyes bulging from a distorted face—the woman's arms became perpendicular to her torso, and she resembled a grotesque mockery of Christ. But then her hands fell to her sides, and she twisted and kicked and jerked in silence.

And so the woman died, her body still swaying gently from the crooked tree as the sky darkened, and lightened, and darkened again.

PART I

2018

CHAPTER 1

The motel was nothing special. Bed, nightstand, dresser. One photograph of a horse in a meadow. Another photograph of a red barn. The girl was nothing special either. She had bleach-blond hair, pale blue eyes, and a plain, white face. Holt had met her the night before and had liked the way she poured his coffee, had liked the way she hummed that nameless tune, had liked the way she laughed. Happiness sometimes begins that way. She had told him her name, but he hadn't listened. They shared some drinks and a few laughs. Later, he got a little rough with her, but she didn't seem to mind. Some girls are just like that. Now they were lying inside this cheap motel, and he felt like he was dead.

"I don't usually do this kind of thing," she said, stroking his chest, but he figured she was lying. He figured she did it all the time.

In the room next to theirs, a baby started crying, shrieking really, and Holt worried that it'd never stop. He felt panicked and wanted to leave, but he couldn't seem to move. That happened to him from time to time. A paralysis of will.

The girl wanted to make conversation. "Do you live here in Deerfield?"

Holt shook his head no. He had no intention of providing his life story. He had no intention of providing anything at all.

"Where do you live then?"

"Around. Topeka area."

The girl smiled. She had a gap between her front teeth, and Holt figured that she hadn't been blessed with very much. Not looks or intelligence or even a decent car. A girl like her could only get what she could get. And he guessed that was him.

She said, "So why were you in the café last night?"

He placed his hands behind his head, shrugged. "I don't know. Sometimes I go driving to clear my mind. That's what I did last night. And then I got hungry. Spotted the café. The pie was good."

"Yeah, well. Best in Deerfield, anyway. I'm glad you found me. But why you got to clear your mind? You got worries or something?"

He glanced at her quickly and then glanced away. "Don't we all?"

She laughed. "Yeah. I guess we do. My husband's a worry, for one thing. Fat bastard." And now she winked. "Jealous too."

Holt didn't care that she was married. They didn't arrest you for adultery anymore. He stared at the ceiling. It was cracked in several places, and the white enamel was peeling. They were letting this place die. Just like everything.

"You got a job?" she asked.

"Yup."

"Well, what kind?"

"I fight fires. Rescue cats from trees. That sort of thing."

"No shit? You're a firefighter? That's so exciting. I thought that's what you looked like when I first saw you. Honest, I did." She pointed to his wrist, which was scarred, the skin pink, fibrous, and raised. "That's how you burned yourself?"

He didn't answer, not right away. Instead, he touched the wound and closed his eyes. And just like that he remembered the flames and smoke and sirens and screams. The mother and the child, huddled in the closet. The mother was dead, face frozen in agony, but somehow the baby was alive—

Holt opened his eyes and nodded his head. "Yeah. That's how I burned myself."

For a few weeks, Holt had been a hero. There had been an article in the local newspaper, with a picture of him lowering the baby down the ladder. FIREMAN SAVES BABY. He'd thrown it away.

She asked more questions, and they floated in and out of his consciousness: *You ever been married? Do you think I'm pretty? You got a girl?* Holt answered with nods and grunts, all the while calculating how many more minutes he had to stay.

His phone vibrated on the nightstand, and he reached across the girl's flattened breasts to grab it. He didn't recognize the number, but he did recognize the area code: his hometown, Thompsonville, Colorado. His stomach tightened.

He brought the phone to his ear. "Yeah?"

It was Joyce Brandt, his mother's best friend, the one who had been married to the police lieutenant. Holt hadn't heard Joyce's voice in a decade at least. She asked how he was doing, and he answered vaguely. Then she started speaking quickly, as if someone else were waiting to use the phone. *Down by Liberty Grange . . . a couple of kids found her . . . been there a week or more . . . can't imagine why . . . nobody knows what to do . . . a hell of a thing . . .* Holt only caught phrases instead of the whole monologue—his brain couldn't quite catch up to the words—but her meaning was clear.

"Thanks for telling me," he said, and hung up.

After that he just lay there, staring at the ceiling, the cell phone resting on his bare chest. But the girl wouldn't let him be.

"Who was that?" She touched his stomach.

"Just some woman," he said. "A friend of my mother's."

"And what did she need to tell you?"

Holt rolled over to his side, his back to the girl.

"She needed to tell me about my mother. She needed to tell me how she killed herself."

The girl tried comforting him, and he appreciated the effort, but it was really no use. Eventually, he got out of bed and got dressed. The girl asked if he'd call her soon, and he told her maybe, and he figured she knew what that meant.

Ten minutes later, he stood in the hotel parking lot, hands buried in his pockets, as the sun rose over the nearby refinery plant. He gazed at a destitute man, just across the lot, leaning against his truck, crushing out a cigarette with his boot. The air smelled like hog shit.

Holt got into his car and drove, feeling even more lonely than usual. He hadn't been close to his mother in a long time, but somehow knowing she was gone made him hurt. He thought about the words he'd never said, and the ones he wished he hadn't. He pressed hard on the gas down Highway 42, getting the old Ford up to seventy, eighty, before letting up again, but he decided it was no good, you can't escape from yourself, no matter how fast you drive. No matter how far you go.

And then, as the radio crackled, he felt that familiar urge, the one that had been plaguing him ever since he'd saved that baby from the flames. Ten or fifteen miles outside of Deerfield, just south of Topeka, there was a nameless lake, all brown with mud. He'd been there on a few occasions, the last time a month or so ago after struggling through another bout of insomnia. Nobody was ever there, nobody but him.

Now he pulled off the highway and drove down a dirt path toward the water, his car lurching over unseen holes and bumps, and parked near a shallow gully. He killed the engine and stepped out of the car.

That urge, that urge.

Soon he was standing on the shore and staring at the murky water, surrounded by cottonwoods and yesterday's sins. Nobody was there, so he stripped his clothes and stepped in. He closed his eyes. "Just as Christ was raised from the dead, by the glory of the Father, so we too might walk in newness of life," he whispered. The water was icy cold, and despite the mildness of the day, he couldn't stop shivering.

He wandered farther in, until the water reached his knees, then his thighs, then his chest. From somewhere he could hear the screeching of an animal, and then he took a deep breath and dropped beneath the surface. He kept his eyes open, and as he kicked deeper into the water, he wondered if it was possible to drown yourself by pure will, or if the human drive to survive, to live, was too strong.

Pretty soon his chest was aching, and bubbles trickled from his mouth. He thought of his mother, he thought of the baby, and soon he came floating upward until his face was out of the water and he was gasping for air.

CHAPTER 2

It had been more than twenty years since Holt had filled a couple of duffel bags with clothes and toiletries and some worthless souvenirs and stuck out his thumb, looking to get as far away from Thompsonville, Colorado—as far away from his mother—as possible. In all those years he'd never been back to his hometown, not once, although his mother had visited him in Topeka five or six times, and each time he had immediately longed for her to leave.

As a young child, however, things had been different. As a young child, he had relied on her presence and became panicked when she wasn't within earshot, cried when she didn't get home before dark. His father had skipped town months before he was born, and so she had been Holt's only protector. He used to sleep with his door open a crack, so that whenever he opened his eyes he could see the corner of her bedroom and would know that she was nearby. Mornings, after the sunlight woke him from forgotten dreams, he would tiptoe through the hallway and climb into his mother's bed, where she would hold him tight, listening to every breath he took. Evenings, they would eat dinner together at the kitchen table, telling stories and laughing. After putting the dishes away, they danced to Elvis and the Beatles with his older sister, Ophelia, clapping and stomping her feet all the while.

If only he could ever feel that safe again.

After Ophelia was taken away by those men in white, his mother had changed. Or maybe it had been before that, his memory of that time was unclear, foggy. Now when he came into her bed on those early mornings, she didn't pull him close, she didn't listen to him breathing. Instead she would roll over, her back toward him, and pull her knees toward her chest and softly sob. At dinner there was no laughter, no stories. She would sit upright, stare straight ahead, and chew her food slowly, methodically, barely able to say a word.

Soon after there were the bouts of rage, when she would lash out at Holt for no reason, screaming and cursing, sometimes grabbing him by the wrist and shoving him against the wall. And there were the nights, the long and lonely nights, when his mother would spend hour after hour staring out that blackened window, waiting. For what? It was as if she blamed Holt for Ophelia's madness, blamed him for the darkness that hovered over their lives now that his sister was gone.

As Holt grew, turning seven and then eight and then nine, his mother spent more and more time in church, more time reading the words of the Bible, more time on her knees in prayer. She tried passing this religiosity on to him, and before Holt went to bed she would stand over him, watching closely as he prayed, making sure the words he mumbled were reverent and holy.

And on each Sunday, she would take him to Mineral Lake, near their house, and baptize him anew. "No sins," she would whisper. "None."

Despite her zealous religiosity, despite her bouts of depression, despite her frequent cruelties, for much of his childhood Holt wanted nothing more than to please his mother. He studied for hours on end to get perfect grades. He became a Boy Scout and then an Eagle Scout. He volunteered at the homeless shelter. And he made her cards, so many cards, filled with hearts and words of adoration.

But none of it worked. After Ophelia was taken away, he could never please his mother, could never gain her love, not completely. So, as Holt got older and entered high school, he pulled away from her. He got mixed up with some unruly people and took to staying out all night. He drank and fought and fucked. His grades began to suffer, but that didn't bother him. What was he going to do with an education, anyway? He got suspended twice and in trouble a lot more often than that.

But his mother didn't seem to care, not about him, not about anything. She was too far gone, in her own little world of melancholy and imaginary spirits. As soon as Holt turned seventeen, old enough to drop out of high school, he left that house, left Thompsonville. His mother had commanded him to stay, shouted that it was a mean old world filled with demons of the worst kind, but Holt ignored her. He wanted to hurt her, so he told her that he didn't believe in God, never had, and told her that he couldn't stand her voice, her smell, her touch. She cried, and that made him feel good. He knew he needed to find his own way, even if the demons joined him.

Over the next several years he bounced from town to town (Salida, Fort Worth, Tulsa, Fayetteville) and from job to job (welder, oil field worker, short order cook, mechanic, custodian). He made some friends, but none of the friendships lasted. When he was twenty-three he met a girl named Michelle, and she had the darkest brown eyes and the prettiest lilting laugh. They began spending time together. For some reason she loved him, and he tried to love her too. Her family was from Topeka, and she convinced him to move there. Her brother, Hal, worked as a paramedic for the fire department, and Holt liked the idea of fighting fires. He took some classes to become an EMT, and then Hal pulled some strings and got him hired. He liked the job. Good hours, good people, a sense of purpose. A way to provide salvation, if not to himself then at least to a stranger in need.

But things with Michelle didn't last. She wanted to get married, wanted to have a baby. Holt thought that maybe he would be a decent husband. But not a father. Never a father. And so he refused. "Is it because your own daddy left you?" Michelle asked. "Is that why?"

"That's not it," he said. "It's because I wouldn't be able to keep him safe. Not me. Somebody else maybe. But not me."

Michelle did her best to convince him otherwise. She told him that he was a good man. That he was a strong man. But he didn't believe her. The truth was that he was terrified. The truth was that he didn't trust himself. He couldn't bring a baby into this world. And all the convincing in the world wouldn't change his mind.

He never blamed her for leaving, and he never tried to win her back.

Holt hadn't planned on going back to Thompsonville for his mother's funeral. There was nobody he wanted to see and nobody he needed to comfort. But then he got to imagining the pitiful sight of his mother being lowered into the ground with only paid mourners and a scattering of acquaintances as witnesses, and he decided he would attend. A regression, perhaps. One last chance to please her. He called his shift chief and told him the situation, requested bereavement leave. The next morning, carrying a suitcase stuffed with a cheap suit, two changes of clothes, and those same worthless souvenirs he brought with him two decades earlier, he hopped into his car and drove west.

But when he drove, and the radio had faded away, and the highway stretched forever in front of him, he couldn't stop his mind from wandering, and the thoughts were dark ones. No matter how hard he tried to force them from his consciousness, they remained, burrowing into the tissue of his prefrontal cortex. He thought that maybe his mother had the right idea, eyes bulging, body dangling from a cottonwood tree.

Six hours of driving and eventually the golden-brown grass turned green, and the empty horizon gave way to distant purple mountain majesties. And soon the town of Thompsonville, partially framed by the abandoned sugar mill to the east and the still-operational turkey plant to the south. Holt drove down Highway 119, which eventually turned into 3rd Avenue, the main artery lined with car dealerships and fast-food restaurants and empty lots. And then a right on Main Street with its pawn shops and liquor stores and pay-by-the-hour motels.

He'd been gone forever, but everything looked the same. He didn't feel nostalgia so much as a longing for a life that never was, a life with a family of his own. He passed by some of the businesses from his youth: a grocery store (Sal's, where he used to buy baseball cards), a hardwood store (now called Lumber Jack's), and a restaurant (still called Lucille's). He passed the post office and the library and the police station. And then, a few blocks west on 5th Avenue, the old brick First Lutheran Church. How many *Praise Jesuses* had his mother hollered there, he wondered? How many tear-soaked eulogies had she witnessed? Another few blocks west was the old residential neighborhood. Many of the houses showed signs of a brighter past: Victorians and cottages that might have once been lovely, now faded and weary. Some of the houses had neatly trimmed lawns and flower gardens, maybe a wind chime dangling from the porch roof, while others weren't as well cared for.

The farther west he drove, the smaller and more rundown

the houses became. Near the westernmost edge of town was Baker Street, which was parallel to the Santa Fe railroad line. The houses on this block were bungalows and brick ranches, most of them caged in by metal fencing. There was something menacing and unsettling about these properties. Here, the children playing appeared dirty and wild. Here, the curtains were all closed and there were more weeds than flowers. Here, desperation lay heavy in the air.

One of the houses on this block was a midcentury brick ranch with a busted downspout fallen on a yellowed lawn. A pair of unpruned bushes reached to the bottom of filth-coated windows, and an American flag angled from the front. This was Holt's childhood home. He parked the car across the street, killed the engine, and stepped outside.

In a way, it didn't seem like he had ever been gone. Maybe it was because he always held so tightly to the misery of this place. Pulling up the collar of his jacket, Holt walked slowly around the perimeter of the house. The leaves were falling, and they crunched beneath his graveyard boots. In the backyard, there was the same old wooden table with the same old metal chairs. There was the same chain swing, now badly rusted, that his uncle Bobby had put up for him when he was a kid. He remembered sitting on that swing and having Bobby push him harder and harder, sending Holt flying toward the setting sun. Now the swing rocked slowly and sadly in the breeze. He sat down at the table and stared at the house, waiting for something—exactly what he couldn't say. A tremendous wave of sorrow washed over him. For the things his mother had left behind. For the things she'd never had.

After twenty minutes or more, he rose to his feet and returned to the front of the house. Joyce Brandt had left a key beneath the woven welcome mat. Holt unlocked the door and stepped inside.

CHAPTER 3

Holt half expected to find his mother sitting on the couch, maybe reading the Bible or knitting a scarf, her dress buttoned to her neck, her hair strangled tightly in a bun. Instead, all that was left inside the house were the material remnants of her existence: high-heeled shoes lined neatly by the door, a gray jacket tossed onto a chair, a magazine on the coffee table. The living room furniture was the same as when Holt had left so many years ago, although the dark leather of the couch was beginning to crack. He opened the blinds and could see dust motes spinning in the air.

For you were made from dust, and to dust you will return.

Holt walked through the living room and into the hallway. Photographs, now faded, still lined the walls, proof of happier times. Here they looked like every other family, grinning for the cameras. There were photographs of Holt as a young child, playing baseball, splashing in a water fountain. There were photographs of Ophelia as a teenager, and she was so pretty with her long blond hair and those dark brown eyes. Holt missed her, he missed her so much. But if he was honest about things, he never knew Ophelia all that well. His memories of his sister were vague and blurry, maybe only fantasies.

He studied one of the photographs more closely. She stood in the shadow of an oak tree, a half smile on her face, staring off into the distance. What had she been thinking then? Had the demons already started haunting her, the same demons that would eventually destroy his mother? And then a disconcerting thought. What if he too was fated for lunacy? After all, his mother had taken her own life. His sister had been locked away and medicated. Wasn't madness hereditary? He thought about the baby that he'd rescued from the fire. It should have caused him great satisfaction, but instead he kept imagining that there had been a mistake, that the baby had perished, that he had been carrying a tiny corpse across the burning floor and down the metal ladder.

He walked upstairs. His room, the room where he used to sleep, where he used to play, where he used to dream, had been converted into a storage room with boxes and books piled high. He stepped inside and stood there, hands buried in his pockets, and glanced around, trying to recall something, anything. With his eyes open, it was no good. But when he closed his eyes, he could remember.

He remembered himself as a small boy, huddled over his Star Wars figures—Han Solo and Luke Skywalker and Darth Vader and his prized Boba Fett—lining them up for battle, his imagination vast and uninhibited. He wondered if those action figures were boxed up somewhere, or if they'd been discarded. He remembered sitting at his cheap blue plywood desk, filling out worksheet after worksheet of multiplication facts. He remembered lying in bed, under the covers, listening to the Nuggets broadcast on his little black transistor radio. He'd gotten mad one night when the Nuggets lost and he'd thrown the radio against the wall, shattering it. After that, he didn't get to listen to as many Nuggets games. No more Alex English, no more Fat Lever. And what else did he remember? The yelling. The crying. The screaming. His own hands covering his ears.

He continued down the hallway to his sister's room. Even though she had been taken away when Holt was only five years old, all through his childhood the room had remained hers. The walls remained covered with her posters, and the dresser remained filled with her clothes. Each week, Holt's mother would come in and change the sheets on her four-poster bed. Holt had always known the room was off limits to him. Once, he recalled his mother saying, "Perhaps Ophelia will come home one day. It would be terribly sad for her if she returned and her bedroom was all gone. She might cry, don't you think?"

Even today, the room remained her shrine, essentially untouched from when she was young. When he stepped in, he immediately felt his breath sucked away. It was as if her ghost hovered in the space, watching him with melancholy and protectiveness. The floor was gray carpet, freshly vacuumed, and the wall was covered with posters of Joan Jett and the Clash and the Ramones. On her desk, there was a tape recorder and a Walkman and a telephone. On her bookshelf, dozens and dozens of mixed cassette tapes, the song tracks written in her messy handwriting. Mostly punk and new wave—none of that mid-80s MTV pop for her. There were also books like *The Stranger*, *Catcher in the Rye*, and *The Trial*. Lined next to the books were a handful of Ophelia's journals.

"Don't cry, Holt," she used to say. "Things are never as bad as they seem." Or maybe he'd only imagined her saying it.

Holt pulled out one of her journals and began flipping through the pages. It was filled with artwork (skulls and bleeding hearts) and poetry (about the same). The artwork was heavy-handed, but the verses of the poems moved Holt. He did his best to remember her voice and her laugh and her sighs. *My rib cage must be made of crushed glass / why else would my heart be bleeding so?* He closed the journal and returned it to the shelf.

And what else? Her bed was covered with a thick comforter, a multitude of pillows, and a well-worn teddy bear that she must have loved as a child, before Holt was born. Nothing punk about that, he thought. Inside her dresser were torn jeans, sweatshirts, concert T-shirts, and flannels. He pulled one of the flannels out, held it to his face, and breathed deeply. But as much as he wanted to, he couldn't smell her memory. He refolded the shirt and placed it in the drawer.

He could have spent more time rifling through drawers and reading Ophelia's journals, but it wasn't his sister's room that he was most curious about. After all, for more than three decades her diseased mind had been an unspoken warrant: that trying to understand her wouldn't do any good. She had too long ago disappeared into that forest of mirrors, and it was hopeless to chase after her. No, it was his mother's room, his mother's secrets, that he felt most anxious to ransack. Maybe he could find out, maybe he could understand, why a woman of God would give up all hope and choose to tie that noose against her soft skin.

Holt pushed open the door of his mother's room. He stood there for some time, heart quickening, hands trembling. A desk light was still on, creating strange shadows on the floor. He shoved his hands into his back pockets, his own temporary straitjacket. And then he stepped forward.

Inside her room, everything was neat and in order. This is what happens when you're planning on killing yourself, Holt thought. The bed was neatly made, just like in Ophelia's room. Several magazines, as well as a leather-bound Bible, were stacked tidily on the nightstand. On the bookshelf were dozens of children's books and nearly as many workbooks (cursive, multiplication, geography). Several religious and pastoral paintings hung from the wall, as well as a corkboard with a pair of drawings her students had made for her, quick and messy, probably done at the behest of a parent in order to get in Ms. Davidson's good graces.

Still, they must have meant something to her. "Thanks for being such a good teacher!" one of them said, with a drawing of a tall stick figure (Holt's mother) in a square dress holding the hand of a small stick figure (the student) also in a square dress. "Have a very merry Christmas, Ms. Davidson!" said the other, below which was a rudimentary drawing of a Christmas tree with a star on top, but no ornaments. Three decades of teaching, and that's what she had to show for it. Two drawings. To Holt, it was more pathetic than endearing.

The room smelled faintly of tobacco (Had she taken up smoking? Holt wondered.) and mothballs. At the foot of the bed, there was a wooden chest. He opened it, and inside were a dozen or more sweaters folded neatly. She was always cold, his mother, even in the summer months. When he would go running around outside with a T-shirt and shorts, she would be wearing slacks and a sweater. A problem with her circulation, she had told him.

He let the wooden cover of the box slam closed and then strode over to his mother's desk, where a single rose wilted in a narrow vase. He pulled out the chair and sat down. He rubbed his temples with his fingers. A few minutes passed, and then he pulled open one of the drawers, feeling a pang of guilt for rifling through his mother's personal belongings. The desk was filled with the nostalgia of the aged: postcards and letters and ticket stubs and faded photographs. Her own worthless souvenirs. Holt sat at the desk, flipping through those souvenirs, for a long time. He didn't know what to feel.

Outside, the sky darkened, and he could hear ghostly violin music playing somewhere. A cool breeze blew through the open window, and one of the blank postcards (*Greetings from Estes Park*) slipped off the desk and fluttered to the floor. He bent down to pick it up, and was about to return it to the drawer when something caught his attention. Beneath the desk, he noticed that a single floorboard was ajar, barely jutting above the floor.

He could have left it alone. It was an old house, after all. But he was curious. He got onto his hands and his knees and began pulling at the edge of the board. It didn't come up right away, but after straining for a while, the board did pop out, a single nail spinning on the floor next to him. Breathing deeply, he got down on his stomach and looked in the gap where the floorboard used to be.

And that's when he saw the revolver. And next to that, a box of some sort. His heart began to pound.

He tried reaching toward the gun, toward the box, but the gap in the boards was too narrow. He stuck his hand beneath another board and tried yanking it out too, but this one wouldn't budge. He needed a pry bar or hammer. He glanced around the room but didn't see anything that would help. Cursing under his breath, he rose to his feet and hurried through the hallway to the back door, which opened to the garage. His mother hadn't organized the garage the way she'd organized her room, and the overhead light was dim, so it took several minutes of searching before he found an old, rusted claw hammer resting on top of a blue metal tool box. He gripped the hammer, pushed back into the house, and returned to his mother's room. He got back on the ground and began yanking at the board. It didn't come out cleanly, and so he pounded it with the hammer, causing it to splinter.

Perspiration dripped down his temples, and his hands

ached, but eventually he was able to remove enough of the board to get at the revolver, get at the box. The gun was a small Smith & Wesson. He opened the chamber. Three bullets were inside. He placed the revolver on the ground next to him and picked up the box. It was made of cheap pasteboard and was about half the size of a shoebox. On the top was a drawing of a ballerina spinning through the sky, surrounded by purple stars and pink clouds. The sides were decorated with flowers and suns and ballet shoes.

Buried beneath the floor for who knows how long, the pasteboard box had begun to rot and the drawings had begun to fade. Holt sat cross-legged on the floor and with trembling hands snapped open the miniature metal latch. A tiny ballerina popped up from her springs, ready to dance, heels together, one arm above her head. Behind the ballerina was a narrow oval mirror, and in front of her was a small compartment covered with pink cloth. Holt wound the music box. He watched, wide-eyed, as the ballerina performed a jerky pirouette while Beethoven's "Für Elise" played, muted and warped. When the music slowed and the ballerina stopped, he rewound the box and watched the performance again, and another time still. He felt like crying.

He breathed deeply and stared at where the cloth flap concealed the compartment. Out of curiosity, he lifted it. He was surprised to see that underneath was an envelope, sealed but not stamped. Instead of an address, there were five words written in red ink that he recognized to be in his mother's handwriting:

Each little world must suffer.

"The hell?" Holt whispered.

He removed the envelope from the box and unsealed it. Inside the envelope was a letter, yellowed with age. As Holt read it, he was worried that it might crumble in his hands. It was written in thin blue ink and the handwriting was beautiful.

My love,

I'm not a poet, but I know these things to be true: a heart can only ache so much until it ruptures. Eyes can only cry so much until they're blinded. A soul can only long so much until it withers.

I wonder: Do you have any idea how much I want to tell the world about us, about how I feel about you? Any idea how much I want to stand on rooftops and shout at the top of my lungs? But I know that the world would not allow it. Because they wouldn't understand. Because they mistake love for sinfulness.

And so, I will wait in quiet. In the darkness of my room. But know that you are the first thing that I think of when I open my eyes in the morning. You are the last thing I think of when I close them at night. And you are all that I dream of as the sky stays dark. I know that your heart aches as much as mine. Just know that someday we'll be together. This I promise you. Someday I'll take you far from this pathetic little town, and we'll never look back.

I love you. I love you more than you know.

There was no signature.

Holt read the letter a few times, trying to figure out who could have written it, but he came up empty. He recalled a few men coming to the house when he was very young, but he couldn't remember their names or faces. And once his mother was under the spell of the Lord, he couldn't recall her going out on even a single date.

Was it possible that she had a secret love, someone who sent her love letters, someone who dreamed only of her?

Holt went to place the letter back in the envelope, deciding that maybe a secret love should remain just that. But as he reopened the envelope, he realized that there was something else inside: an old Polaroid photograph.

He removed the photograph and held it front of him. A gasp escaped from his mouth.

It was an image of a man, body angled grotesquely against a wall, mouth open, eyes bulging. Blood covered his shirt and the floor beneath.

Holt was pretty sure that he was dead.

That night, Holt decided to get drunk. It was the way he solved a lot of problems.

With all sorts of unpleasant thoughts banging around his skull, he got into his car and drove through the neighborhoods, so quiet and still, and down to Main Street. There was nobody downtown either, except for one man, already a bottle of whiskey ahead of Holt, staggering down the sidewalk and bouncing off storefronts. Holt drove south past the turkey plant, all windowless white concrete, and toward McCarthy's—a sad and surly bar where, when Holt was young, angry slaughterhouse workers were known to drink and fight. He parked next to a rusted blue Dodge Neon, its right side crushed, the headlight dangling from its wires like the ruptured eye of some wounded monster. The moon was hidden behind blackened clouds.

Inside the bar everything was quiet. There was no music, no customers, no bartender. Nothing. "Hello?" Holt called out. Nobody answered.

Holt sat down at the counter and stared at the row of whiskeys and tequilas and vodkas behind the bar. Maybe the bartender had stepped outside for a smoke. This is what the world will be like on its last day, he thought. Streets and parking lots empty, and Holt sitting by himself in some shithole bar.

He reached into his jacket pocket and took out the photograph, placed it on the counter, face down. In the upper right-hand corner, there was some faded ink that he hadn't noticed before. He picked it back up, holding the photograph closer so he could read in the dim light.

His last breath. 11/12/84.

"Fuck," Holt whispered. "Fuck."

He exhaled and flipped over the photograph. His chest tightened as he stared again at the grotesque image, trying to make sense of it. Was it fake? Just a costume, somebody having some fun a couple of weeks after Halloween? He laughed, but the laugh was forced and empty. He knew damn well it wasn't a costume. Those bulging eyes weren't prosthetics and that darkened blood wasn't canned. Why did his mother have this photograph of death hidden beneath the floorboards?

The only plausible answer to that question led to another Holt didn't want to ask. Was his mother capable of murdering somebody, whoever the somebody was? Holt wanted to believe that he was being ridiculous, but deep inside he knew that the line between sanity and madness was thin, and with the right circumstances we're all killers. He thought of Ophelia, poor Ophelia, being dragged away by those men, her fingernails scratching at the hardwood floor, her face twisted and grotesque.

And then another memory, from years later. His mother sitting at the kitchen table, fingers trembling around a glass filled too high with bourbon, her King James Bible fallen uselessly to the floor. Eyes bloodshot, body swaying, she turned toward Holt. "I just can't forget, Son. No matter how hard I try." Then:

"Maybe we'll be forgiven for the blood we spill. Otherwise . . . what will become of us all?"

Holt wanted a drink, but he was too exhausted to move and too honest to steal. So instead he just sat there, staring at the photograph, staring at death. As he continued gazing at the photograph, he became convinced that he'd seen the man before. But from where?

Holt sat at the bar for another forty-five minutes, just thinking. The bartender never came. Nobody did. Shortly before midnight, he rose from his stool and left. The night was cold, and he could see his breath swirling in the air. He didn't want to go back to his childhood house, not tonight. He didn't want to search for a hotel room either. Instead, he drove across town to Thompson Park, where, as a child, he used to hang on the monkey bars, and parked beneath a burned-out streetlight. Using his jacket as a blanket, he reclined the seat and closed his eyes. It didn't take long until he was asleep.

He didn't dream.

CHAPTER 4

Holt woke the next morning to the sun shining through his cracked windshield. He rubbed his eyes and stretched his body, a groan escaping from his lips. He hit the ignition, turned on the radio to old-time country, and stepped out of the car to piss. He grabbed his toothbrush from his bag and brushed his teeth without water and then combed his hair in the reflection of the car window. He felt as bad as he looked, and that was plenty bad.

An hour later, dressed in a too-tight suit, he parked across the street from First Lutheran Church. He felt that old, familiar repulsion, the one that came whenever he saw a cross or heard a hymn. After Ophelia had been taken away, his mother would take him to church every Sunday. He would sit in the pews as the pastor preached about God punishing the sinners and rewarding the saints, as if one could ever know the difference. And after the sermon, after the blood and body of Christ, straight to Mineral Lake for his weekly cleansing. And now here he was, back again, the prodigal fucking son, a week too late. He didn't want to get out of the car. Maybe he could just sit here until the funeral was over. Or maybe he could speed off and return to Mineral Lake, to baptize himself anew.

But, no. It was too late for all of that. He'd been spotted by at least a few of the mourners as they stood outside, waiting for the service to begin. He'd come this far. Heart drowning in misery, he took a deep breath, killed the engine, and pushed open the door.

A dozen or so people—all of them strangers to Holt—were milling about, heads bowed and hands buried in pockets. Holt wished he were anywhere but here. He didn't belong—in this town, in this church. He never had. It had been a mistake to come, and he could feel the old regrets and resentments bubbling beneath his skin. Still he walked toward the church, loose gravel crunching beneath his feet.

A man wearing a white robe and a gold stole, his cheaply dyed hair molded into an unmoving side part, greeted Holt at the door and shook his hand. His hands were soft, and Holt never trusted a man with soft hands.

"Holt," he said somberly. "All the blessings of Christ to you. I'm Pastor Boswell. All my sympathies are with you."

"Thanks."

"Your mother was a woman of God, and she will be missed by the community. Over the last several years, she was here every Sunday. Sometimes two services. Every day she prayed for the souls that were lost. But I think she prayed for you and your sister most of all."

The pastor smiled and touched Holt's shoulder with those soft hands. Holt felt the urge to shove the pastor against the wall, to tell him that he never wanted his mother's prayers, never wanted God's mercy. But instead he just nodded his head and thanked the pastor for the kind words.

"I'm just glad she's with Jesus," Holt said through clenched teeth.

The inside of the church looked the same as when he was a kid. The wooden pews. The stained glass windows. The oversized cross. And just like when he was a kid, his breath became shallow, and the sweat trickled down his temple.

A simple wooden casket was in the center of the nave, and he knew that inside the casket were the flesh and bones of his mother. The casket was closed, and he was thankful for that. He walked slowly down the middle aisle to the front of the pews. Organ music played from the balcony. A heavily perfumed and abundantly flabby woman appeared from nowhere and hugged him and told him how terribly, terribly sorry she was. Holt nodded his head and pursed his lips, said, "She was a good woman. She will be missed," and he sounded like he was talking about a distant acquaintance, not his own mother. Other strangers squeezed his shoulders and patted his back and said, "Bless you, bless you, bless you."

But also, he could have sworn that he heard people whispering about the cause of her death. Or maybe, he thought, he was only hearing things, whispers from his own unconscious.

Is it true? Did she hang herself from a cottonwood tree?

Some teenagers found the body. Such a gruesome sight. They must be traumatized. Those eyes bulging from her skull.

What demons must she have been facing?

I can hardly imagine.

He took a few deep breaths, trying to quiet his mind. But then, from the back of the pew, a baby started crying, and a vision came to him of the fire, of the baby huddled crying in the closet, of him grabbing the infant and holding him to his chest. But then he saw his mother, and she was also holding a baby, but this baby was quiet and still, and it was his mother who was crying, whispering. *It's not too late, Jesus. It's never too late.*

Holt rubbed his eyes, trying to wipe away the image.

Holt spotted Joyce Brandt standing in front of the casket, dabbing her eyes with a handkerchief. She was by herself, and Holt recalled hearing that her husband, Mike, the police lieutenant, had died a few years back. In any case, it had been a long time since Holt had seen Joyce, and he was taken aback by how old she looked. Her once curly blond hair now resembled a white dandelion, and her face was fleshy and creased by wrinkles.

He walked to where she stood and nodded his head. "Hi, Ms. Brandt."

"My goodness," she said, covering her mouth. "Holt Davidson. It has been a long time, hasn't it?"

"Yes, ma'am. More than a minute."

Joyce stood there for a while, just staring at Holt, and then the emotions overtook her, and she shook her head and began sobbing. He realized it was she who needed the comforting, so Holt pulled her toward him, and she buried her face in his shoulder.

"Oh, Holt," she said. "Why'd she have to go and do that?"

He thought of the words on the envelope, *Each little world must suffer*, and he pulled back from Joyce's embrace.

"I don't know," he said. "Maybe she was just in a bad place, maybe she got caught out in the rain. Maybe if it had been another night, things would have been different."

They stood in awkward silence. Then Joyce spoke again. "Listen to me. I know she didn't always show it, but your mother really did love you."

Holt felt his chest tighten. He stared at his shoes. One of the laces was untied. "You don't have to say that. Every mother-son relationship is complicated."

"Yes. That's probably true. But the way she treated you at times—well, it wasn't fair." Joyce paused. "Anyway. It looks like you're just about the only family that's here. No Uncle Bobby. I suppose he's too important to spare an afternoon for his sister. He did send me a speech for me to read. Haven't decided if I will."

Uncle Bobby had been the star of the family, the one who'd

hit it (kind of) big in New York. By playing a guitar, by singing some songs. He wore a porkpie hat. Ophelia had idealized him.

Ophelia.

"And what about my sister?" Holt said in a voice that didn't sound like his own. "How is she? I've called the home a few times but I haven't been able to—"

"She's about the same as she's always been. They take good care of her."

"I plan on seeing her while I'm here."

Joyce shook her head. "I don't think that's a good idea. She won't remember you. It wouldn't do any good."

"I didn't say it would do any good. But she is my sister."

"Yes. Do what you need to do, Holt. I'm just telling you . . ." Joyce trailed off.

Telling me what? Holt wondered, but he didn't have time to ask because a man he didn't recognize sidled up to him and introduced himself as Chuck.

"Your mother was a special woman," Chuck said. "The kindest woman I knew."

Holt thought of the photograph of the dead man. "Yes. She was kind to most everybody."

The funeral began, and it was about what Holt expected. The pastor praised Vivian Davidson as "a woman of God, a woman of faith." He said that she had finally been rewarded and that she was with her Lord. Some people were sobbing, and some of their sobs might even have been genuine, but Holt was having a hard time feeling much of anything. He didn't used to be this empty. He used to be able to cry, used to be able to love. When Michelle left on that cold January night, she had said, "You're a broken man." And he'd known she'd been right. But maybe not broken forever.

Joyce delivered the eulogy. It was long and rambling and

heartfelt. She talked about Vivian as a daughter, how she was the one who cared for Holt's grandfather when he suffered from Alzheimer's and, later, when his grandmother suffered from cancer. Joyce talked about Vivian as a teacher: how she was strict but loving, how she'd taught a thousand kids to read and, more importantly, how to think. She talked about her as a mother, how Vivian had given everything she had to Holt and Ophelia, despite the challenges that God, in His wisdom, had provided them. "But for me," she said, "I knew Vivian as a friend.

"I wish I could express how much she meant to me," she went on, "but I'm no poet. I can tell you that she would laugh with me when I was happy and cry with me when I was sad. When my own husband, Mike, passed away, it was she who came to my house and made me dinner every night that week. We drank wine and reminisced, and somehow it made things bearable. I'm going to miss her. I'm going to miss her so much."

Holt should have felt grateful. The eulogy was a reminder that his mother had been a kind person. But instead, he felt even more uncomfortable and agitated. Maybe it was because she hadn't directed this kindness at him for decades. Or maybe it was because of his own narcissism, the certainty that nobody would tell these types of stories at his funeral, if anybody showed up at all. He knew he was being pathetic, but he couldn't help himself.

Joyce wiped away her tears with the back of her hand and blew her nose into a tissue. "Vivian's brother, Bobby, couldn't be here today, but he wanted me to express how devastated he is. He wrote something and asked me to read it."

She unfolded a piece of paper and spread it on the lectern. She removed a pair of reading glasses from her purse and placed them on the tip of her nose.

"Vivian was my sister," she began to read. "Not only that, she was my best friend in the world. Not to say I was always the perfect brother. I tormented and tortured her as most big brothers do. Vivian, if you can hear me, I want you to know that I'm sorry. I'm sorry for when I used to pin you down and allow saliva to fall in a string from my mouth before sucking it back up. And I'm especially sorry for those rare occasions when the saliva got away from me and landed on your face. I wasn't a perfect brother. But as we got older, we became friends. And for that, I'm forever grateful. I'm grateful for those memories of jumping into piles of leaves and building snowmen and watching the sunset and chasing fireflies. I'm grateful for the girl you were and the woman you became. Vivian, losing you is like losing the sky. I'll miss you every day. I love you. I love you so much."

Joyce wiped away more tears and folded the letter. She wasn't the only one crying. She walked off the stage and handed the letter to Holt as she passed.

"He wanted you to have this," she said. Holt placed the letter in his jacket pocket.

By the time the service ended, Holt was feeling even more anxious than when he had arrived. And still there was the matter of the burial. Joyce kept glancing at him and must have been able to sense his discomfort. She leaned in and said, "You okay there, Holt? You don't look so good."

"I'm okay."

"Go to your mother's house. Get some rest. No sense in torturing yourself."

"I figured I should at least go to the burial. Considering I'm her son."

But Joyce just shook her head. "Mourn in your own way. Get away from death. I'll tell people you weren't feeling well. It's fine."

Holt thought for a moment. "Okay," he said. "Thank you."

"Listen to me, Holt. I know this is all tough. Take care of yourself. You need anything, I'll be around."

He rose to his feet. As he pushed his way through the mourners, he made eye contact with an old woman, a funeral hat on her head, a cane resting on her lap, and her lips pulled into a frown. He was sure that she was judging him, was sure that they all were judging him. And he didn't blame them.

CHAPTER 5

Holt needed to find out who the man in the photo was.

Over the next hour or two, he sat in his car scrolling through his iPhone, trying to find any articles about unsolved murders that took place in Thompsonville back in November of 1984, but he came up empty. He thought about going to the police, maybe lying that he had found the photo buried in the woods or inside a discarded Bible at the local landfill, but he quickly decided that was a lousy idea too. What if his mother had, in fact, been the murderer? Did he want her to be investigated, judged, and sentenced postmortem? He couldn't do that to her, even if she deserved it. Then he thought about coming clean with Joyce. Maybe she would know why his mother had the photograph or, at the very least, who the man in the photo was. But Joyce was a straight arrow. Hell, she'd been married to a damn police lieutenant. She'd demand they go to the authorities, and then he'd be in the same situation.

No, for the time being, he needed to figure things out on his own.

He decided to try the library, an old brick building on Collyer Street. He hadn't been inside since the third grade, maybe even before. He entered through the heavy wooden doors and stood in the entrance for a moment, hands buried in pockets.

Even after all of these years, the library felt familiar. Without really thinking, Holt wandered to the young adult section and began running his fingers along the spines until he located the collection of old Hardy Boys books, the same ones he used to read when he was a kid. He'd probably read every single one of those books when he was eight or nine, and probably hadn't read a novel since. He pulled a couple of the books from the shelf and stared at their lurid covers. *The Tower Treasure*: the boys hiding behind a tree while, off in the distance, a mysterious light shines from the top floor of a creepy tower. *While the Clock Ticked*: the boys bound and gagged while a devious man hides behind an old grandfather clock.

Gazing at those covers, flipping through the pages, Holt remembered the way he used to be. Full of innocence and wonder, dreaming of a world of mystery and danger. In those days, he'd wanted to be a detective, just like Joe and Frank Hardy. And if not that, the point guard for the Nuggets. He figured he could be whoever he wanted, could do whatever he wanted. What had happened to that boy, anyway? Had he died in his own skin? Holt's mortality suddenly felt very fragile.

Holt placed the books back on the shelf and wandered over to the help desk. He stood there for a minute, subtly clearing his throat, while an oversized woman with oversized hair and an oversized dress and oversized glasses typed on her computer and ignored him.

"Excuse me," he finally said.

"Give me a minute," she said. She didn't look up.

He waited two. Finally, she looked up without a trace of humor.

"What can I help you with?"

"I'm doing some research," he said. "About a relative of mine. He was killed. Murdered. Back in the '80s. I want to find out more information."

She removed her glasses and placed them on the counter. Then she smiled condescendingly. "And have you tried googling his name?"

"That's just it," he said. "I don't know his name. It's a long story. But I know when he was killed. At least I think I do. So if you have any old newspapers, I could—"

"We don't have original copies anymore. But we do have microfilm. All the way back to 1891. It's not indexed, but if you have the dates—"

"I do. November 12. 1984. Around that time. If you could just show me how to use the microfilm . . ."

The woman sighed because this was an unreasonable favor, but then she rose from her chair, came out from behind the counter, and told him to follow her. She walked with a slight limp.

"Not many people use the microfilm anymore," she said. "But it's not hard. I bet you could figure it out without me."

"I don't think so."

They walked in silence for a bit. Then the librarian turned to Holt and said, matter-of-factly, "You know, my grandfather was murdered. Back in 1953."

"Is that right?"

"Yes. And you know who did it?"

He shook his head. "I don't."

"My grandmother. Stabbed him with a kitchen knife. I guess she had her reasons."

And that was all she had to say about that.

They walked upstairs past the computers and book stacks, past the tables where students studied and homeless people slept, to the back wall of the library where there was an enormous metal cabinet labeled with various dates and local newspapers.

"So here they are," Holt said, nodding his head.

"Here they are."

The librarian opened up one of the drawers and pulled out a reel. She walked Holt over to the microfilm machine and showed him how to load it, how to move it forward and backward, how to zoom and focus.

"See?" she said. "Easy."

"I'm sure I would have fucked it up without you."

The librarian smiled. "Good luck," she said. "I hope you find what you're looking for."

"Thanks. So do I."

Holt returned to the metal cabinet, sliding his finger along the drawers until he finally found the date was looking for: November 1984. He pulled out a half dozen reels and walked them back to the machine. He took a deep breath and rolled up the sleeves on his flannel. Then he got to searching.

He scrolled through newspaper after newspaper, day after day. November 12, 13, 14. Stories about the election and a woman who collected teapots and the Lakers beating the Nuggets. November 15, 16, 17. A man who found a dinosaur bone in his backyard and Kathryn D. Sullivan performing a spacewalk and a teenager killed by a drunk driver. And then, November 18, six days after the date on the photograph, he came to a front-page article with the headline "Local Man Murdered in His Home." As soon as Holt saw the photograph on the cover, a mugshot, he knew it was the dead man.

The man's face was expressionless and his eyes were empty. Holt removed the photograph from his jacket pocket and compared it to the newspaper image. Yes, it was the same man. There was no question at all.

He zoomed in on the article and read slowly, pointer finger tracing the words on the screen, lips moving silently.

> A Thompsonville man was found dead in his home yesterday, the result of gunshot wounds. The body of Ruben Ray, 32, was discovered by Janet Dovoavich, the owner of the house located north of Highway 66 near Liberty Hall.
>
> "As soon as I opened the door, I could smell the stench," Ms. Dovoavich said. "And then when I entered the kitchen, I saw him lying there, covered in blood. It was a shock. He always seemed to be a friendly enough fellow. Never bothered no one."
>
> Ray was shot several times in the chest and stomach. His body was not discovered for several days. Owing to the isolated area of the house, there weren't any reports of gunshots that night.
>
> Police lieutenant Mike Brandt says that there are no suspects, but there are several persons of interest. "As is always the case in a homicide, having members of the public come forward with any piece of information, no matter how seemingly insignificant, will be crucial to a successful investigation."
>
> The Thompsonville police department has created an anonymous hotline at 1-800-352-9876. Lieutenant Brandt can also be reached directly at 303-357-7621.

"Mike Brandt," Holt whispered: Joyce's dead husband. And then, "Ruben Ray."

He squeezed his eyes shut. And now he started to remember, although the memories were hazy. One of these memories: a man who must have been Ruben Ray standing in the living room and handing Holt a present wrapped in shiny blue paper. And inside, the prized Boba Fett. "I hope you like it, son. Your mother told me you liked Star Wars." Another one: Ruben pressing his mother against the wall, kissing her too hard and too long. "She's a pretty woman, son, don't you think?" And a final one: the man's contorted face pressed against a darkened window, his lips mouthing the words "Let me in. You hear me, you little son of a bitch? Let. Me. In."

Yes, he remembered Ruben Ray after choosing, for such a long time, to forget.

Holt stared at the photograph and reread the article, trying to glean any useful information, trying to make sense of things. . . . *the house located north of Highway 66 near Liberty Hall.* And then the description of Ruben, from the landlady: *He always seemed to be a friendly enough fellow.* But wasn't that always the case? Friendly. Quiet. Kept to himself. What's clear, Holt decided, is that people never really know their neighbors. Never really know their parents, either.

And finally, this line: *Lieutenant Mike Brandt says that there are no suspects, but there are several persons of interest.* Was Vivian Davidson one of those persons? Had she been the one who pulled the trigger?

And, if so, why?

He thought of Ophelia, thought of the night she had been taken away. Was it possible that her descent into the valley of madness had something to do with Ruben Ray and his violent death? After all, those men took her, what, less than a year later? Holt felt an overwhelming sadness and sense of regret. He'd never gone down that valley and tried to rescue her. Not when he was a child, not when he was an adult.

He rose to his feet and stuck the photograph in his back pocket.

"Each little world must suffer," he whispered. But, he thought, maybe not forever.

PART II

1984

CHAPTER 6

The name should have tipped Vivian off. Fred Tapioca. No joke. Just like the pudding. And when she first saw him, honest to God, her first thought was that his face looked just like his name. All wet and pasty and lumpy. He also had an obvious bald spot, which he tried to conceal by combing the back of his vanilla hair up and over the crown of his head. As if he was fooling anybody. Actually, he looked a little like a poor man's version of Willard Scott. Not that Vivian had a problem with Willard Scott—she really liked his work on *The Today Show*, especially when he wished sweet old ladies a happy birthday.

It didn't matter that Fred had a good job at the bank, didn't matter that he owned a nice house on Pratt Street, didn't matter that he had brought her flowers (lilies, her favorite). It wasn't going to work out. This, Vivian knew right away. He was boring as hell, for one thing. Narcissistic, too. And she didn't even like pudding.

They sat at a small table at McCarthy's, not exactly a classy joint, what with the Iron Maiden playing on the jukebox, the skinheads gathered at the counter, and the bikers milling around the pool table. Everything smelled like beer, vomit, and sin. Not to say Fred needed to treat her like Princess Diana or anything, but maybe he could have taken her to a place with a door on the bathroom stall. Fred spent most of the evening doing his best to sell himself. He talked about how he'd just been named assistant manager at the biggest bank in town, how he drove a brand-new Porsche 911, how he worked out at the gym every single day, and how many women were very, very interested in him.

He didn't ask any questions about Vivian, of course, because why would he care? Not that she was all that eager to talk about herself. Not with him, anyway. The only question he asked of her—and he asked this many times—was if she wanted another drink. He must have been impatient that she was sipping her glass of wine so slowly while he had finished, what, four gin and tonics? How would he ever get her to bed, how would he ever get her on her knees, if she wasn't good and drunk? And he was probably right about that. She needed another fifteen drinks at least to consider kissing those lips, which looked like sausages with the casings still on.

"Come on, now," he said. "Drink up. You sure you only want red wine? How about a shot of tequila? No need to be a cheap date."

A smile and a shake of the head. "I'm fine, thanks. I'm not much of a drinker." Which wasn't always true, of course.

She wanted to leave, she wanted so badly to leave, so every minute or so she would look over his shoulder at the door or glance at her watch, hoping he would notice, get frustrated, and give up. But, no, he just kept talking and drinking, and now she felt like he was staring at her a bit more aggressively, eyes drifting to her chest, a smarmy half grin on his face.

She couldn't help but feel angry as hell at Sue, the other kindergarten teacher, for setting her up with ol' Pudding Face. "You'll like him," she'd said. "He's a super nice guy. And he's got money." She hadn't mentioned his looks, of course.

It was nearing ten o'clock, and even though her children

were probably fine (Ophelia in her room listening to the Clash, Holt sitting on the couch watching *Knight Rider*), she decided to use them as an excuse to leave.

"I hate to do this, but I really should be going," she said. "See, my son is only five years old, and he gets very anxious at night. He'll be wondering where I am."

But Pudding Face just laughed. "Oh, relax. He'll be fine. The neighbors can always help if something comes up. Let's have another drink, shall we? Or maybe two. Or three."

Vivian forced a smile. "I don't think so. It's been fun, but I really should go."

She reached into her purse, making a halfhearted effort to help pay for the drinks. Fred shook his head and smiled. "No need for that," he said.

"Well, thank you."

And that should have been that. But things were never simple for Vivian. When she got up to leave, Fred startled her by grabbing her wrist. He squeezed tightly, forcing her back to her seat.

"C'mon now," he said. "No need to rush off. I think you're a beautiful woman."

"Thanks. Can you please let go of my wrist?"

But he didn't. "The night's still young," he said.

"I need to go."

And now he leaned toward her, breath stinking from gin, and whispered, "I don't think you're being fair to me." Vivian met his glance and saw cruelty in his eyes. "I don't like having my time wasted."

Even though there were dozens of people in the bar, Vivian suddenly felt scared and alone. What if he tried hurting her? Would anybody intervene? What if he tried dragging her from the bar, raping her in his Porsche? Still, she tried holding it together, tried remaining calm.

"Let go of my wrist," she said in a measured voice. "I'd like to leave."

This whole time, Vivian hadn't noticed the burly, tatted-up man shooting pool on the other side of the bar. She hadn't noticed how he kept glancing up from his game, how he kept gripping his pool stick a little bit tighter.

Vivian again tried rising to her feet, but Fred wouldn't let go. With a violent jerk, he pulled her chair toward him, her mouth inches from his. His other hand maneuvered beneath her skirt, fingers pressing against the inside of her thigh. It took Vivian a moment to realize what was happening, and when she did realize, she reached back with her free hand and slapped him across the face. She didn't get a clean shot, though, and ended up scratching him with her nail, drawing blood. That set him off. He spat in her face, calling her a bitch and then a cunt.

What happened next, happened quickly. The tattooed man strode from across the room and stood behind the banker. Without pause, he wrapped one arm around Fred's neck, the other still holding his cue stick. He yanked hard, causing Fred to release his grip on Vivian and topple to the ground. With animalistic rage, the man pounced on Fred and pressed the cue stick hard against his throat. Vivian took a few steps back, her hand covering her mouth. The other people in the bar just spun around in their seats or turned their heads but otherwise didn't move, not wanting to get involved in another man's conflict.

The tattooed man pushed down on the cue stick harder and harder, his biceps bulging beneath his white T-shirt, and Vivian was sure he was going to kill her date. Fred kicked his legs, and his pudding face turned red and then purple.

"Stop!" Vivian shouted, but the tattooed man didn't, not right away. Fred's eyes bulged before rolling into the back of his head. He stopped kicking, and Vivian thought he was dead.

Another few seconds and the man released the pressure and got to his feet. Expressionless, he stood over Fred, who began moaning and groaning and coughing. The banker tried getting to his knees and then his feet, but the man wasn't having it. He swung the cue stick hard, hitting Fred in the side of the head, causing him to crumple back to the floor.

Snarling, the man dropped the stick and glanced up at Vivian. Their eyes met. He reached into his pocket and pulled out a five-dollar bill. With a nod of the head, he stuck it on the table and said, "For your drink." Then he stepped over the banker and walked toward the door, his boots echoing on the linoleum.

It only took that one moment for her to fall madly in love with him.

How long did she wait? Twenty seconds? Only ten? Her mind was made up, and she followed after him, ignoring the skinheads who whistled and clapped as she passed by them. Once outside, Vivian spotted the man walking north on Main Street, a full moon balancing on top of the turkey plant. She called after him, saying, "Hey! Wait up! Hey!" but he kept walking, head down, hands buried in pockets.

It wasn't until he reached the top of the hill, at 3rd Avenue, that he finally stopped and turned around. Vivian jogged, holding her dress down against the breeze. It was strange that she didn't feel anxious approaching this brutish-looking fellow who'd just nearly killed a banker with a pool stick.

He nodded at her. "What do you want from me?"

Despite his bulging biceps, despite all the tattoos, despite the scar on his weathered face, Vivian was sure she glimpsed kindness in his eyes.

She cleared her throat and pulled a strand of hair behind her ear. "I don't want anything from you. I just want to know why you did that back there."

"Did what?"

A pause. "Protected me."

He shook his head. "I wasn't protecting you. I don't know you. I just thought that guy was an asshole. I don't like assholes."

"What's your name?"

"Why does it matter?"

"It doesn't, I guess. I'd just like to know."

"Ruben."

"Ruben. I like that. I'm Vivian. It's nice to meet you."

For just a moment, his face seemed to relax. "Yeah. Nice to meet you, too."

"So," she said. "How about grabbing a drink?"

He stared at her for a long moment, measuring her up. "I don't think that would be a good idea. I've got to get up in just a few hours. And, besides, there's no other bar around here."

"Who said we had to go to a bar?"

He smiled, just barely, and shook his head. "Lady, you sure you want to do this?"

She didn't answer him. Instead, she leaned forward and kissed him on the lips. And even though he didn't kiss her back, for that single moment, she was sure they were going to live happily ever after.

She'd read those kinds of stories before.

CHAPTER 7

Over the next several weeks, Vivian and Ruben spent a lot of time together. They drank at McCarthy's. They ate at Mike O'Shays. They bowled at Centennial Lanes. And they had sex at his place, a rundown farmhouse out by Liberty Grange.

She didn't tell him, but he was only the third guy she'd ever slept with. There was her ex-husband, of course. And before him was Russ Howell, in the backseat of his Dodge when he was drunk as hell and she wasn't, an experience so short and depressing that she really couldn't remember anything but the Dodge: a blue 1973 Monaco with an electric clock, armrests, and fake-wood door trim. How she'd loved that car.

When it came to sex, Ruben was all business all the time. No conversation. No smiles. Just get in, get the job done, and call it good. Not that she was complaining. He never got rough with her, never hit her, never called her a disgusting whore.

That's as much as a girl can ask for, isn't it?

Sometimes when they were done, they did talk, although it was Vivian who did most of the talking. She didn't tell him any secrets or anything, but she did tell him about her job, teaching kindergarten at Central Elementary, and how she would have liked to say she loved it, that she loved kids, but that she didn't like to lie. She told him about her ex-husband and how he had left her when she was pregnant with her second child, run off with some waitress from Greeley. She'd only kept his last name out of convenience. She told him about her children: Holt, who had just turned five and was the sweetest boy in the world, and Ophelia, who was fifteen years old and who would have been beautiful if she wasn't always frowning. And she told him about her faith, a faith that wasn't as strong as she would have liked. Every Sunday, she and the kids went to church, and every night, they said their prayers, but she couldn't help doubting, and that made her feel ashamed.

And even though he was usually quiet, Vivian did learn a thing or two about Ruben. She learned how he was from Plano, Texas, originally. How his father had been a minor league pitcher in the Rangers organization, although Ruben hadn't met him more than a handful of times, the last time being twelve years ago. His mother, meanwhile, was a common drunk, so he didn't have much to say about her. She ended up dying from cirrhosis of the liver when he was only eighteen. Yeah, he admitted, life had been tough for him, and he'd made some mistakes along the way. He'd been in jail on three separate occasions: once for driving with a suspended license, once for his third DUI, and once for something else, he wouldn't tell her what. He served three years in prison for that and swore that he would never go back.

"I'm a changed man," he said, seeming to overlook the fight he'd gotten in at McCarthy's. "I stay out of trouble. I work hard."

And work hard he did—slitting throats and draining blood at the turkey plant. But none of that bothered Vivian. Not the time in prison. Not the work at the slaughterhouse. And not the empty look in his eyes. She was just happy that somebody had protected her. And that somebody was holding her.

Something else he told her. He had a daughter, only a year older than Holt. Her name was Rose, and he kept a creased and faded picture of her in his wallet. In the picture, she was just a toddler, and that's because he hadn't seen her since he went to prison. He'd been trying to gain custody, but judges didn't have any use for ex-cons, and Rose's mother, who was just a kid herself, wouldn't let her see her father, not even for an hour.

"You bitter about it?" Vivian asked one night, stroking his chest.

"Damn straight," Ruben said. "You don't think I've thought about finding where she lives and stealing my girl away? A woman like her shouldn't have my daughter. A woman like her would be better off dying every single day of her life."

And it was those moments when he talked about his ex, his left eye twitching in rage, that Vivian got anxious and worried that maybe he was as cruel as the rest of them.

Even as Ruben and Vivian got more serious, she hesitated to tell Ophelia and Holt about him. She'd gone out with a few other guys in the past, and things never went that well. The kids acted suspicious and surly, both of them. She could only imagine how they'd act when they met Ruben, who wasn't exactly clean-cut. After all, in recent months Ophelia had been moody and miserable, locking herself in her room for hours at a time to listen to her punk music, and even Holt had begun acting out, throwing explosive temper tantrums, sometimes tearing the living room completely apart, couch pillows scattered and chairs toppled.

Not that Ruben was all that anxious to meet them, anyway. "Never been all that comfortable around kids," he said with a growl. "And they've never been all that comfortable around me."

But Ruben and Vivian were spending an awful lot of time together, and it was inevitable that the kids would find out about her new man one way or another. And eventually, they did. It was early August, evening time, when unbeknownst to Vivian, Ophelia stood at the living room window while she and Ruben were going at it hot and heavy in his car. Ophelia must have been watching the whole time.

When Vivian got inside, Ophelia flashed a knowing smile. "So Mom? Who was that?"

"A friend," Vivian said, blushing.

"A friend. Right. Well, just make sure your friend wears a rubber."

And so the secret was out. Vivian decided it would make sense to have him over. Ruben wasn't thrilled, but she was tired of sneaking around like a thief in the night.

The night of the dinner, Vivian reminded her children over and over again how important it was to be polite to Ruben and make a good first impression. How they shouldn't speak unless they were spoken to. How they needed to ask to be excused before they could leave the table. Rules that normally weren't in place.

Vivian didn't usually spend that much time getting ready, but tonight she did, locking herself in the bathroom to feather her hair, hoping that she'd somehow look like a brunette Heather Locklear. She forced Holt to take a bath and wash his hair, which usually didn't happen more than once a week. She requested that Ophelia wear nice clothes, maybe a dress, but that request was rejected in favor of her usual punk T-shirt and torn jeans. Vivian didn't have the energy to fight her on this.

Ruben was supposed to arrive at six, but he pulled up ten minutes early and stayed in his truck. Holt and Ophelia watched from the living room as he smoked one cigarette and then another.

"Aren't cigarettes bad?" Holt asked his mother.

"A lot of things are bad."

"I guess all the respectable men are taken," Ophelia muttered.

As soon as Ruben stepped out of his truck, flicking the cigarette butt on the pavement, Holt and Ophelia screamed in unison and scattered to their rooms.

"Now, you get back here, kids!" Vivian shouted. "What did I talk to you about?"

But their doors had slammed shut. Vivian smiled anxiously and shook her head. She quickly ducked into the bathroom to check her hair and her makeup. While she was there, she undid an extra button on her blouse.

Ruben rapped on the door, three quick knocks, and Vivian hurried to open it.

She had to admit he'd done his best to look presentable. His hair was combed off his forehead, he was cleanly shaven, and he wore a sports coat—old and ratty, but a sports coat nonetheless. In each hand he held a gift, hastily wrapped.

"You brought presents?" Vivian said.

"I did. For your kids."

"You didn't have to do that." She leaned in and they kissed.

Eventually, the kids reappeared, Holt peering cautiously around the corner and Ophelia standing pigeon-toed in the hallway. Vivian waved them in.

"Holt. Ophelia. I'd like you to meet my friend, Ruben. Ruben, these are my children."

They all smiled awkwardly and then shook hands. Holt asked if the presents were for them.

"Yes, sir," Ruben said. He handed Holt and Ophelia each a gift, and Holt quickly ripped open the wrapping paper. Inside were a pack of Topps baseball cards and a Boba Fett Star Wars figure. Holt was thrilled, but forgot to say thank you. Vivian pinched him on the neck so that he remembered.

"Glad you like them," Ruben said.

Ophelia opened hers, and there was a red gel necklace and matching hoop earrings.

"They're great, except my ears aren't pierced," she said.

Vivian's face reddened. "Ophelia—"

"Oh, it's no problem," Ruben said. "I can return them."

"No need to do that," Vivian said. "This will give us an excuse to finally get her ears pierced, won't it? About time she became a lady."

Vivian made lasagna for dinner. It was one of the only fancy meals she knew how to make. Before they ate, she forced everyone to hold hands while she recited a long and rambling version of grace, giving thanks to the Son, the Father, the Holy Spirit, President Reagan, and anybody else she could think of. She explained how blessed they were to have food on the table and Ruben, her tattooed ex-con, in the chair. When she finally finished, they all mumbled amens and then passed around the lasagna and bread and salad.

While they ate, Vivian proudly told her kids the story of how Ruben had beat up Fred "Pudding Face" Tapioca. She added some superfluous and erroneous details about how he'd forced Fred to get on his knees and apologize, forced him to kiss Vivian's feet. Holt and Olivia didn't seem all that impressed, and Ruben, for his part, remained stony-faced throughout her retelling, his gaze drifting to Ophelia and then back to his plate.

"Ruben also has a daughter," Vivian said at some point. "But she lives in another town. Her name is Rose, and she's your age, Holt. Maybe someday she'll join us for dinner, right, Ruben?"

"Maybe." He shrugged. "Her mother is a bitch."

Ophelia snorted, and Holt covered his mouth with his hand.

For the rest of dinner, Ruben shoveled down portion after portion, drank beer after beer. Holt was in his own world, sitting at the corner of the table, playing with Boba Fett and making explosion sounds with his mouth. Ophelia barely touched her food and barely spoke, responding in one-word answers and refusing to make eye contact with Ruben.

"What grade did you say you were in?" he asked.

"Tenth."

"You got a favorite subject?"

"Nope."

Eventually, dinner ended. Holt disappeared to his room to continue Boba Fett's battle. Ophelia helped her mother clear the dishes. Ruben remained at the table, hands folded, staring straight ahead.

Once in the kitchen, Ophelia pulled Vivian aside and said, "I don't like him."

"Stop it," Vivian said. "You just met him. He's a good man."

"There's just something about him. He'll break your heart or worse."

"Oh, come on now, sweetheart. I'm not saying you have to call him Daddy or anything. But just give him a chance. Will you do that much for me?"

Ophelia sighed and rolled her eyes, but eventually she said she would give him a chance. Just as long as Vivian promised that she and Ruben would never be alone together.

"Ophelia, you're being ridiculous."

"He's been watching me funny," she said. "From the moment he got here. Looking me up and down."

"Now you just stop that," Vivian said. "You're imagining things."

"It's not my imagination, and I can't help how I feel."

She'd barely finished speaking when Ruben appeared, and it was unclear if he'd heard any snippets of their conversation. He looked at Vivian and then back at Ophelia, and his gaze rested on her for a moment too long. This time Vivian noticed.

"Need any help loading the dishwasher?" he asked.

Vivian shook her head. "No. We've got it. You go sit down and make yourself comfortable. We'll have dessert up shortly."

"That's sounds fine," he said. He winked at Vivian. "I see the cherry pie over there on the counter. How'd you know it was my favorite?"

Vivian wiped her hands on a dishtowel and forced a smile. "I don't know. I suppose I just guessed right about you."

"Yes, ma'am. I suppose you did. I'll go sit down then. My mouth's watering a little bit."

He returned to the kitchen and, once he was gone, Ophelia looked at her mom and raised her eyebrows. Vivian shook her head and mouthed, "Stop it."

Ophelia giggled. "I'll serve the pie." And then, in a mocking voice, "It's his favorite."

CHAPTER 8

It wasn't until another month had passed that Ruben started treating Vivian poorly. In fact, in the weeks following the dinner he was a perfect gentleman (for the most part), even taking her out to a fancy dinner at the Empire Grill and bringing her flowers not once, not twice, but three different times.

But then something changed. Maybe it was because Vivian hadn't invited him to her house again, or maybe it was because she wasn't interested in having sex three times a day any longer, or maybe it was because she kept pressing him to give her details about his prison stint. After all, she had still never learned what exactly he did to earn three years behind bars. Whatever the reason or reasons, he turned mean.

It started with him telling her to rest her mouth, how he was tired of listening to her prattle on about things he didn't care about. Instead of telling him to go to hell, she apologized, promised to do better, and hated herself that she couldn't stand up to him.

But that wasn't all. Soon he got to talking about her weight, something that she had always been a little self-conscious about. "All I'm saying is that you could afford to lose a few," he said.

"Otherwise you'll end up looking like that sweat-hog waitress at Gil's Café. You don't want that, do you?" No, she didn't. So maybe she began starving herself a bit. She lost four pounds, although he didn't seem to notice.

All of this made her think of her ex-husband, and how he used to berate her, how the verbal abuse eventually turned to something worse—

Things with Ruben got really bad over her lipstick. It had been a thing with him, ever since they started dating. He wanted her to wear lipstick when they went out. Not just any lipstick. Bright red lipstick. "Like a whore," he said, grinning. And at first, she had thought it was funny and kind of kinky, and so she agreed.

Until one night she forgot.

They were going out for dinner and drinks, and Ruben was waiting outside her house in his car. Vivian was doing her best to get dinner prepared for Ophelia and Holt while simultaneously trying to get beautified for the date. She wore a blue dress, the one that pushed her breasts up toward her chin, and her continuous feathering was getting her closer and closer to achieving that Heather Locklear hair. While Holt ran through the house, arms extended, wearing only his Superman Underoos, she rushed to the bathroom to put on makeup (rouge and concealer, eyeliner and mascara), but then she heard Ruben's car honking. He didn't like to be kept waiting.

"Fuck me," she said under her breath, and left the bathroom, a tube of red lipstick forgotten on the sink.

The timer on the stove buzzed, and the boiling water for the mac and cheese was overflowing, so she cursed some more, dumped the noodles into a strainer, and added the milk and butter and powdered cheese and mixed it until it wasn't chunky. Ruben honked the horn again, and she served the mac and cheese into two plastic bowls and also scooped out some applesauce. She went into Superman's room, where Holt was now fighting an alien from Mars, and kissed him on the cheek. And then into Ophelia's room where she made her promise that she wouldn't invite any friends over, especially boys, and she reminded her to take good care of Holt and make sure that he was in bed by nine thirty, lights out.

A deep exhale, and Vivian put on her jacket, patted down her hair, and stepped outside. Red purse pressed against her hip, she strode down the pathway to where Ruben's car idled. She sat down in the passenger's side seat and slammed the door shut.

Ruben didn't look up. He finished his cigarette and flicked it out the window. "What took you?"

Vivian pulled her hair out of her eyes. "Just trying to get dinner ready for the kids. It's not so easy."

Ruben grunted and then jerked the car into drive. The radio was off, and Vivian noticed the quiet.

"Ophelia," he said after a few minutes. "She's old enough to make dinner."

"I guess she is. But I guess I still consider her my little girl."

Ruben shook his head, placed another cigarette between his lips. "She's not your little girl anymore."

"No. Maybe it's just that I wish she still was."

A pause. And then: "Has she had sex yet?"

It was a strange question to ask. Inappropriate. But, still, Vivian answered. She always had a hard time pushing back against him. "No," she lied. "I don't think so."

Ruben chuckled, sucked down more smoke. "I bet you ten bucks she has."

"Yeah, well. I'd rather not talk about my daughter's sex life."

"That's fine," he said. "But you should be more aware.

Otherwise, the next thing you know she'll become pregnant. I've seen it happen. And then what? Her life is fucking ruined. Yours, too. Like I said, she's not your little girl anymore."

Vivian didn't respond. She stared out the window. She hadn't noticed that they were going in the wrong direction. The opposite way of downtown.

"Where are we going?" she said.

"Somewhere private," he said.

"You don't want to eat first?"

He didn't answer. He pulled the car off the road. They were in the middle of nowhere, only a transmission tower looming overhead like some apocalyptic monster.

"You forgot to wear lipstick," he said, and now his voice was serious.

She laughed, trying to play it off. "Yeah, sorry about that. Like I said, I was rushing all over the place. I was going to put it on but then—"

"Do you have some in your purse?"

"I . . . I don't remember."

"Check. You look better with lipstick. Younger."

It was a cruel thing to say, and Vivian should have told him to knock it off. But she didn't. Instead, she began rifling through her purse. Receipts, a vanity case, earrings, tampons, but no lipstick. "No," she said. "It must be at the house."

"That's too bad," he said. "I figure I take you out, spend my hard-earned money on you, the least you could do is look decent. Take some fucking pride in your appearance." A pause. A long one. "Maybe there should be some punishment."

Again, Vivian laughed. She hated herself for laughing. "Punishment?"

"That's right. You hate giving blow jobs. I've learned that much about you. So maybe that's what you should do."

"Ruben—"

"Or would you prefer letting me fuck you up the ass?"

"Stop it. I think that maybe you're angry about something at work and—"

Ruben laughed, and it was a cruel laugh. "Something at work? What the fuck would you know about my work? Huh? What the fuck would you know about it?"

"I know that it's hard. Killing animals. Being covered with blood."

"You don't know shit, Vivian. You don't know shit."

And now Vivian knew things were bad. She didn't know why she always ended up with creeps, always ended up with abusers. Maybe she just liked it better when the pain came.

"I'd like you to take me home now," she said in the calmest voice she could muster.

But Ruben just stared out the windshield, his hands gripping the steering wheel.

"Please," she said again, "take me home."

He shook his head. "Suck my dick."

Outside, the sky was black as pitch. There were no stars. There was no moon. Her kids were home alone. She was a terrible mom. A terrible person. She tried opening the door. He reached across her and shut it. He was going to rape her, she was sure of it. She had friends who had been raped. Like Joyce Brandt, her college boyfriend had raped her. And Susan—her uncle had been the one. And now she was going to get raped. She squeezed her eyes shut, waited for his next move of violence.

Instead, he twisted the key and the engine roared to a start.

"Fuck it," he said. "Let's go to dinner."

And that's what they did.

Vivian was too afraid to break up with Ruben in person. She was too afraid to break up with him over the phone. But she knew she couldn't see him anymore. Not after what happened in the car.

She went to her friend Joyce's house and confided in her. Joyce always seemed to know what to do in these situations. She wasn't a mess like Vivian. She had a good marriage, drama free. Her husband, Mike, was a solid man, had worked his way up from a lowly officer all the way to lieutenant of the police department. He was ethical and fair—even the criminals he'd busted for assault or possession would tell you that.

And something else. Back in high school, Mike had kissed Vivian. Back in high school, Mike had told her that he loved her. Vivian had never told Joyce about any of this.

"What were you thinking getting involved with him in the first place?" Joyce asked in between bites of Bundt cake. "He's an ex-felon. And you still don't know what he did."

"I don't know, Joyce. I'm an idiot."

"He could have murdered someone. Did you ever think about that? Slit some beautiful girl's throat? Some girl that looked just like you. Maybe that's his MO, you know? Meeting recently divorced women, desperate for love—"

"I'm not desperate for love."

"—and then slitting their throats. Burying them beneath the basement or something."

Vivian worked on cutting another piece of cake for herself. Every once in a while, you just had to eat cake. "You think that's what he was in for, huh?"

"Could be. Why not?"

"Because I don't think they release murderers after a few years."

"Sure they do. Our governor is soft on crime. Haven't you seen the commercials?"

"Anyway," Vivian said, "if he is in the business of slitting throats, I probably shouldn't break up with him. At least not to his face."

Joyce thought for a moment. "No. Probably not. Of course, I could go with you. It would be hard for him to slit two throats at once. I mean, while he's slitting your throat, I could come up from behind him and hit him with a frying pan or something."

"A frying pan?"

"I'm not going to shoot him, if that's what you're asking."

"No, it's not."

"Although, maybe Mike would." And now she called out for her husband. "Mike, come here!"

A few moments later, he stepped into the kitchen, holding a hammer in one hand and a beer in the other. Mike was tall, handsome, good. Vivian was glad that Joyce had found him. And maybe a little miserable that she'd let him go.

He looked at Vivian and nodded his head, and she wondered if maybe, just maybe, he felt the same way. Then she felt ashamed for thinking those thoughts.

"How are you, Vivian?" he said.

"I'm okay."

"No, she's not," Joyce said. "She's dating a psychopath."

"Is that right?"

"He served time. But Vivian doesn't know what for."

"Well, I could certainly find out, if you'd like me to."

Vivian shook her head. "Don't worry about it. I'm sure it's nothing."

"She's sure it's nothing," Joyce said. "I'm convinced he's a murderer. Or maybe just a rapist. Anyway, Mike, what do you think about paying him a visit and shooting the son of a bitch in the forehead?"

"Well, sure," Mike said. "Let me just finish nailing the

floorboards and then I'll take care of killing him. Because that's what we do. Serve and protect."

"But first," Joyce said, "you should have a piece of cake. It's delicious. Extra butter."

"That sounds more my style."

Mike sat down at the table, and Joyce served him a thick slice of cake. While he ate, he glanced up at Vivian. There was something in his eyes that meant something, but she didn't really know what. She looked away, dabbed the corners of her mouth with a napkin.

"So this guy," Mike said, "who may or may not be a murderer. He get rough with you?"

Vivian shook her head. "No. Not yet."

"Not yet?"

"That is, he's been acting strange. Aggressive. Making me nervous. Last night, I thought he was going to get violent. The way he was talking to me. The way he was looking at me with those dead fish eyes. He didn't. But next time . . ."

Mike nodded his head slowly. He took another bite of cake and then pushed away his plate. "You think he's home right now?"

"I don't know. I mean, he should be. He usually gets home from work about five. He'll drink a six-pack from five to seven. Then eat dinner."

Mike rose to his feet. "Okay, then. Give me his address."

"You gonna kill him?" Joyce asked.

"Not tonight. But I'll have a talk with him. Let him know that Vivian is no longer interested."

Vivian was going to protest, tell him that it wasn't necessary, but the only thing she said was his address. "9316 County Line Road 5."

Mike grabbed his jacket from the back of a chair and put it on. Then he nodded at Vivian.

"He's a tough guy with the ladies. Doubt he'll be so tough with me. I'll even leave my badge here."

And he left.

Over the next hour, Vivian and Joyce talked about anything and everything—jobs, *The Cosby Show*, cold weather, Michael Jackson, body fat, "Where's the beef?"—everything, that is, but Ruben. Eventually, they switched from coffee to wine. The sun fell below the horizon, and the sky darkened. Vivian called her children on the telephone and said that she would be home soon, and that Ophelia could make a couple of TV dinners, Salisbury steak and Yankee pot roast. Ophelia responded by saying it sure would be nice if her mom cooked every now and again. Vivian told her to be thankful for what she had and hung up the phone.

Seven o'clock, and still Mike hadn't come home, and now both Joyce and Vivian were getting worried. Joyce was pacing around the kitchen, washing dishes that had already been washed.

Finally, just before seven thirty, the door opened, and Joyce dropped her towel and Vivian finished her glass of wine. Mike entered the kitchen, his face was serious, and his hair was a mess.

"Mike!" Joyce called out. "Are you okay?"

He nodded his head. "Yes. I'm fine."

"So? Did you find him? Did you talk to him?"

Mike went into the refrigerator and grabbed a beer. He cracked it open and leaned against the counter. "Yeah," he said. "I found him."

"And?"

He took a long swallow of beer and then glanced at Vivian for a little bit too long. "We had a nice little talk. Came to an understanding. He won't be bothering you no more."

Vivian touched her hand to her chest. "Thank you, Mike. You didn't have to do that."

"By the way, I checked on a few things. Not a murderer, but he's got a past. Assaulted another man. Tore his ear clean off."

Vivian shivered. "Nice."

"You can do better," he said. "But you knew that."

"We all knew that!" Joyce said.

Mike glanced at his wife and then back at Vivian.

"Listen to me. He bothers you again, you let me know. And in the meantime, it's probably a good idea for you to make sure you can protect yourself."

He reached into his pocket and took out a little .38 Special revolver and placed it on the counter.

Vivian shook her head. "I don't need that, Mike."

"I'm sure you won't. But with a fellow like Ruben around, I just figured . . . well, only take it if you want to. Only if you feel comfortable."

For a few moments, Vivian remained where she was. Mike and Joyce watched her, waiting. She squeezed her eyes shut and visualized Ruben and his dead fish eyes, and her skin began to itch and she wanted to scream. She opened her eyes and took a deep breath. Then she took a few steps over to the counter. She grabbed the gun and held it in her hand.

It felt cold and heavy and terrible.

CHAPTER 9

A week passed. Two. There was no word from Ruben, but still, Vivian couldn't relax. At night, when the pipes creaked and groaned, she would convince herself that Ruben was inside the house. Wide-eyed, she would sit up in bed and stare at the door, waiting for it to open, waiting for Ruben to enter and pin her down and rape and beat her.

Sometimes when her imagination got the better of her, she would reach beneath her mattress and take out the pistol Mike had given her, and she would point it at the door—waiting, waiting. She wondered if she would actually be able to use it. Even if Ruben did enter, even if he did try to rape her, could she pull the trigger? If she was being honest with herself, the gun didn't make her feel safer. It just made her think of suffering, of Hell, more often.

It was on one of these fearsome nights, near midnight, when the phone rang. She knew it was Ruben. She sat in bed staring at the phone on her nightstand. It kept ringing, five times, ten times. She knew she shouldn't answer, but it kept ringing. Soon Ophelia and Holt would wake.

She picked up the receiver and didn't say a word. She heard breathing on the other end. And then—

"Hello? Vivian, is that you?"

It wasn't Ruben. It was another voice she recognized: her brother, Bobby. She sighed in relief. It had been a long time since she'd spoken to him. A year, maybe more.

"Bobby? Is that you?"

"Damn right, it's me. How you doing, sis?"

"Good. I'm fine. Are you okay? Why are you calling so late? It's nearly midnight."

"Midnight? Oh, shit. I must have got my time zones messed up. I'm sorry. Did I wake you?"

"No. I'm awake. It's fine. It's good that you called."

Bobby Hartwick was Vivian's older brother, the creative one. Art, poetry, music—she had to admit, he really was brilliant. Whenever she would take the kids out east to her parents' farmhouse, the same house where Vivian and Bobby grew up, Ophelia and Holt would marvel at their uncle's artwork scattered across the walls and stored in shelves. Bold and colorful, the paintings suggested a freedom of soul Vivian most certainly didn't have. But it wasn't art that was Bobby's passion, it was music. And so, when he was eighteen years old he had packed up a bag and his guitar and headed east. Chicago, St. Louis, and finally New York City. He ended up playing lead guitar for a bunch of different punk and blues outfits, including Clyde and the Wannabees, who had one minor hit in '76. Bobby had joined them after the hit had faded into obscurity.

"Everything good with you?" he said. "Got any new suckers in your life?"

"Ah, shit, Bobby. There was this guy. He started getting controlling. A real asshole. So I broke it off."

"Jesus, sis. What is it with you and these shit-stains? Don't you know you deserve better?"

"You're one to talk. Seems that you've dated your share of basket cases."

"But they're always hot."

"Right. Hot basket cases."

"It's what works for me."

It had always been that way. Bobby always got the prettiest girls. Meanwhile, Vivian got the dirtbag boys. Life wasn't all that fair.

"So are you going to be on MTV soon?"

Bobby laughed. "I don't think so. You see the types of bands they're playing on MTV? I'm too ugly. That's the problem. I can play licks like Eddie Van Halen but I look like fucking Ric Ocasek."

"Stop making excuses. The Cars are on MTV."

"That's true. And he's dating that supermodel."

"See?"

"You're right. There's hope for me yet."

Vivian laughed. She loved hearing his voice. She only wished he called more often, only wished he was a bit more involved in her kids' lives. But then, he was a musician. What did she expect?

"But the music is going well?"

"Yeah, yeah. I've hooked up with a few fellows who used to play backup for Warren Zevon."

"Warren who?"

"The guy who sang 'Werewolves of London.'"

"Oh, yeah. I know him."

"Anyway. We started a little band. Call ourselves the Crying Bastards. Play a sort of rockabilly-punk hybrid. Playing wherever they'll take us. Which is why I'm calling."

"You coming out this way?"

"I am. Got a gig next Saturday at Herman's Hideaway in Denver. Wondering if you could put me and the boys up for a few days."

It had been several years since Vivian and the kids had last seen him. He'd come through town after finishing a tour and slept in the living room for a week. Holt had just been a baby, Ophelia still a little kid. Bobby had spoiled the kids rotten and cooked every meal. He fixed a leaking faucet, cut down a dead tree, and hung up a swing set. He told stories and sang songs. The kids wanted him to stay forever.

But as much as Vivian loved him, and as much joy as she felt in seeing her kids happy in his presence, she had begun to experience some of those old resentments from childhood. Doesn't every younger sister have resentments? He'd been the gifted one. He'd been the one with big dreams. And she'd been the ordinary girl with the ordinary face, the kind of face that people forgot three minutes after meeting her. She had been glad when he left. But she never would have admitted that to anybody.

"You and the boys? We've got a small house. How many are we talking about?"

"Twelve. Plus a couple backup singers."

"You're kidding me, right?"

Bobby laughed. "I am. Come on, sis. You're still gullible. There's three of us. Drummer, bassist, and me. And they can stay in a motel because they're animals. It'll just be me."

"Ah, better. I think we can find the space for one, even a weirdo like you. Actually, it'll be great to see you. The kids will be thrilled. Especially Ophelia. She looks up to you for some reason. And she's really getting into music. The Ramones. The Clash. Punk stuff. She'll show you her cassette collection."

"Good taste."

"I guess. I prefer Billy Joel. Hall & Oates. But it's fine."

"Well, you've always been the Uptown Girl."

"Saturday, you said?"

"That's when the gig is. We should arrive sometime Friday. Cool if I call you from the road?"

"Yeah, that's fine."

"Okay. I'll be seeing you soon. And, sis?"

"Yeah?"

"Stop dating shit-stains, okay?"

"I'll try my best, Bobby."

As soon as Vivian hung up the phone, there was a knocking on the bedroom door, and once again the fear returned. Which was stupid, because if Ruben was planning to sneak into her house and rape and kill her, he probably wouldn't knock on her bedroom door. It was only Ophelia, standing in the hallway, grinning and jumping up and down.

"Uncle Bobby's coming to town?"

"Were you eavesdropping?"

Ophelia laughed. "How long is he staying?"

"Just for a few days, I think."

Ophelia jumped into bed with her mother, and Vivian realized how much she missed those days when the two of them could snuggle.

"Is he playing a show here?"

"He is."

"Can I see him play?"

"I'm afraid not, sweetie. He'll be playing in a bar. Eighteen and older."

"I can pass for eighteen."

"Maybe so, but they'll check your driver's license. And that'll say you're fifteen."

"I'll figure out a way to get in."

"I'm sure you will."

Ophelia didn't move from the bed, and Vivian didn't ask her to leave. Soon Ophelia had fallen asleep. A little later, Holt appeared in the bedroom, rubbing his eyes and sucking his thumb. He'd had a nightmare about being trapped in a room full of rabid squirrels, so he slept in her bed, too. That night, Vivian held both of her children tight and listened to Ophelia breathing, listened to Holt mumble in his sleep.

It was terrifying loving two people as much as she loved them.

CHAPTER 10

It seemed like it had been forever and a day since Ophelia had something to look forward to.

Most of the time, it was just the constant drone of teenage life. She hadn't been on a vacation since her family drove west to Lake Tahoe more than two years ago, and there were no plans to leave town in the near or distant future. Christmas was months away and her birthday farther still. Considering nobody had asked her to homecoming (surprise, surprise), she didn't even have a stupid dance to look forward to. And she certainly didn't look forward to the daily torture of school.

Not that she was one to moan and bitch, but things had been pretty miserable over the last few months. Make that the last few years.

So when she found out that Uncle Bobby was coming into town, Ophelia couldn't help but feel a bit giddy, a bit free. The last time he'd come to town had been wonderful, some of the best days of her life. Now whenever she felt sad or lonely, which was often, she would close her eyes and transport herself back those days with Uncle Bobby.

Before that, she felt like she barely knew him. But they

connected over massive portions of pasta, overflowing root beer floats, and bags of jelly beans. It was embarrassing for her to admit this now, but when he'd first arrived she wore ridiculous cowl-neck sweaters and Cinderella pajamas. She listened to Christopher Cross and Air Supply. Uncle Bobby wasn't having any of that. He exposed her to a bunch of punk music, and he took her clothes shopping. By the time he left, just a couple of weeks later, she was decked out in torn jeans and a leather rocker jacket. She wasn't a little girl anymore. She was a flat-out badass.

Had he indoctrinated her? Damn straight, and she was glad he had. But it wasn't just about the style and music. She felt like he understood her in a way that her mother didn't. She couldn't really explain it.

After he left town, they stayed in touch by writing letters. Well, that wasn't entirely true. It was mainly Ophelia writing him letters and waiting in vain for a response. Occasionally, he would write her back, although the letters weren't all that heart-felt: *Make sure you take good care of that kid brother of yours . . . I hope you're working hard in school . . . You ever listened to the Misfits? I bet you'd dig them.*

And so now that she knew Bobby was coming to town and staying with them, she couldn't think of much else. During class, instead of listening to the teacher, she would sketch pictures of him and his guitar. At home, she spent hour after hour writing song lyrics. Maybe, she figured, Bobby would like some of them and add some music and then perform her new song at the gig. "Here's one my niece wrote called 'The Love You Destroyed.'" (Overwhelming applause.) And even if he didn't like the lyrics, she had a bunch of good song titles: "And Then the Fire," "Only the Wicked Survive," "Tomorrow's Sins," "Love's Grave." They could collaborate like Elton John and Bernie Taupin or Johnny Rotten and Sid Vicious.

A girl could dream, right?

She could tell that her mother was excited as well. Instead of being agitated and moody like she usually was, she was in a cheerful mood, preparing after-school snacks of cookies and milk, whistling happy tunes, and making everything in the house look just right. In fact, by the time Thursday rolled around, all the laundry was put away (for the first time in forever), the bathrooms were spotless (also for the first time in forever), and Holt and his mom had created a big "Welcome Back" sign and hung it across the kitchen wall, above the stove.

Meanwhile, Ophelia fretted about what clothes to wear when he arrived, and she seriously considered getting her hair cut, maybe going short, but ultimately decided against it because of the high risk (the last time she went super short, she ended up looking like a wigged-out Peter Pan). Instead, she settled for buying a Misfits T-shirt and painting her fingernails and toenails black. If nothing else, that would prove to Bobby that she wasn't so prissy. It would prove to Bobby that she had a touch of darkness in her soul, and maybe that would impress him.

The week moved slowly, so damn slowly, but finally Ophelia made it to Friday. Despite the excitement of knowing that Bobby would arrive that evening, it was a typical school day for her (angst, misery, depression). Ophelia never did all that well in school, and she didn't like being there. She spent most of her lunchtimes smoking cigarettes in the girls' bathroom and most of her class time writing disturbing poetry in her notebook (*The blood from your eyes, the skin from your cheek / the melody from your bones, you'll suffer till you reek*).

It was evident that none of her teachers liked her all that much either, but it was Mrs. Parker, her French teacher, who really had it out for her, and she could never figure out why. Maybe it was the way she dressed: aside from her uncle's influence, she also imitated the style of the British punks she'd seen now and then in battered copies of *NME*, the magazine that her on-again, off-again friend Emily had stolen from her glue-sniffing brother. Or maybe it was because she was god-awful at French: no matter how hard she tried, no matter how many hours she practiced phrases, she could only manage to respond with a pathetic "*Je ne sais pas*" whenever Mrs. Parker called on her. Or maybe it was because Mrs. Parker had found out that Ophelia had once given Parker's son, an acne-covered boy named Paul, a hand job at the Twin Peaks movie theater. He'd cum in the popcorn, which was a big waste of four dollars and fifty cents.

So every day at one forty-five, 8th block, time for Mrs. Parker's French class, Ophelia's stomach would ache. She would feel light-headed and wish that she was anywhere but that goddamn classroom, covered with stupid posters of ridiculous-looking French people with their fucktard berets and loaves of bread and pencil-thin mustaches. She'd sit in the back corner of the room and stare at her drawings and poems, careful to avoid any eye contact with her teacher. Mrs. Parker would stand in the front of the class and speak in a series of nonsensical sounds, and the rest of them seemed to get it. They would dutifully write things down in French and laugh at Mrs. Parker's French jokes and answer in French when she called on them. Then Mrs. Parker would walk slowly down the aisle toward where Ophelia sat, and she just wanted to die.

"Mademoiselle Ophelia," she would say. "*Quelle heure est-il?*"

And Ophelia would only shake her head and whisper, "*Je ne sais pas*," and the class would laugh, and that was how everybody had their fun in that school.

But on this particular day, Ophelia decided that her teacher and classmates would have to have fun at the expense of somebody else. On this particular day, while everybody else rushed to their 8th-block class, Ophelia made a beeline from her locker to the back door of the school. She pushed open the door and stepped outside, and it was a beautiful autumn day, and Uncle Bobby was coming in a few hours, and he would show her how to play the guitar and take her for ice cream and sneak her into his show, and maybe she'd never go back to that stupid French class ever again.

Feeling strangely empowered, she walked down Hover Street toward 3rd Avenue. A few blocks west of the train tracks, and not far from her house, there was an industrial area filled with storage lots and a car junkyard, and just past the junkyard there was a small lake called Mineral Lake, surrounded by old cottonwoods. This was where Ophelia liked to come when she wanted to get away from the world. She would sit at the water's edge and put on her Walkman and listen to her music.

Usually, nobody else was here. She felt like it was her own personal lake. But things had been different this past summer. That's when Holt and her mother, but not Ophelia, had been baptized in this very water.

It still seemed odd to Ophelia that it had happened at all. Over the past year, her mom had been taking them to church more and more frequently. Not every week, but at least once a month. "I just think it's a good thing for all of us to get to know Jesus a little bit better," she'd said, but Ophelia felt like she was trying to convince herself as much as them. During the service, Holt would curl up on the bench and sleep, Ophelia would use a pen to draw intricate designs on her wrist, and Ophelia's mom would pretend to listen to the sermon.

One Sunday, a member of the congregation, an old skinny fellow named Ed Hawkey, got to talking with Ophelia's mom, asking about her and her kids' relationships with Jesus. He asked her whether Ophelia and Holt had ever been baptized. Her mom admitted that they hadn't been, admitted that she herself hadn't been baptized either. That was the opening Ed needed. He told her about an old-fashioned baptism that he and his wife were going to perform the following weekend. Full submersion into the lake, just like John the Baptist used to preach about. Ed told her mom that she should come. He told her that she should bring the kids. He told her that they couldn't be saved unless they were baptized, and what a better time than now?

Ophelia's mother hemmed and hawed and tried making excuses, but Ed could sniff salvation, and he wouldn't let it go. Ultimately, she agreed.

Once they got home, Ophelia freaked out a little bit. She told her mom that the day she would let some Jesus freaks submerge her in some filthy lake was the day she would vote for Reagan's reelection. Ophelia's mother tried convincing her, smiling and telling her that it would be fun, that it was no big deal, but Ophelia refused.

"Fine," Ophelia's mother finally said. "Holt and I will get saved then. By ourselves."

And so on that hot summer's day, Holt and his mother got dressed in their swimming suits and walked through the neighborhoods and then past the storage lots and car junkyard toward Mineral Lake for their holy submersion. Ed had promised that there would be plenty of people getting baptized, but when they arrived they realized it was only them, and that Ed and his wife would be performing the baptism. Ophelia watched from the shore as they walked her mother and brother into the water, Ed holding Ophelia's mother's hand, and Ed's wife holding Holt in her arms. They submerged her mother first, holding her below the water for several seconds, before pulling her back up.

"Just as Christ was raised from the dead by the glory of the Father, so we too might walk in newness of life," Ed and his wife intoned in unison. "I now baptize you in the name of the Father, the Son, and the Holy Spirit, for the forgiveness of your sins, and the gift of the Holy Spirit."

Then it was Holt's turn, and again they held him below water. But it seemed like they held him down longer, and when he came above water he was crying, and their words were drowned out completely.

Now, as she walked along the shore, Ophelia was glad that she hadn't been pushed underwater that day. If she went to Hell, at least Sid Vicious would be there to keep her company.

She sat down with her back against a tree and gazed at the lake, and despite the beer can, plastic bag, and dead bird floating near the shore, Ophelia felt happy, or as happy as a fifteen-year-old girl in Thompsonville, Colorado, could feel. She reached into her jacket pocket and pulled out a packet of cigarettes. She stuck one in her mouth and lit it. For a moment she felt as cool as Patti Smith, but then she started coughing and hacking, and she knew that she was a phony just like everybody else. She stayed beneath that tree for an hour at least, hacking her way through another three cigarettes, turning up the collar of her jacket when the clouds darkened and the wind blew. She listened to more Sex Pistols on her Walkman, and, when that cassette was done, she removed it and put in one from the Dead Kennedys, *Fresh Fruit for Rotting Vegetables*. And then she snuck in Air Supply's *Greatest Hits*, just for old times' sake. Hey, she wasn't perfect.

Ophelia crushed out her last cigarette against her boot. There was flash of dry lightning and then a distant rumble of thunder. And then, something else.

From behind her, Ophelia thought she heard the sound of leaves crunching. Was it the breeze? A squirrel? Then she had the paranoid thought that somebody was moving slowly toward her, eyes gazing at the back of her head. She didn't turn around, not right away. Instead, she remained still, staring at the shimmering lake. For the next few minutes, it was silent again, except for the occasional growl of thunder. She breathed more freely and her body relaxed.

But then she heard the sound again.

She turned around slowly. Standing behind her not more than five yards away was the man that her mother had brought home to dinner not that long ago. Ruben Ray.

He wore a Carhartt jacket and a red hunter's hat. His hands were buried in his pockets, and he was just standing there, staring straight at her. Had he followed her from school? How long had he been watching her?

Ophelia didn't know what to do. "Hello," she said. Her voice was high-pitched like a child's.

Ruben nodded. "I was just out walking. Trying to get some fresh air. And I saw you there."

It was strange the way he spoke, and Ophelia was sure he was lying. None of this felt right. "I come here sometimes to listen to music."

"Sure. But shouldn't you be home? Won't your mom be waiting for you?"

It was a creepy thing to say. Ophelia rose to her feet. She felt light-headed. She should have walked away then, maybe run, but she didn't. Instead she stood there, still as an idol, facing Ruben. He was a bad person. She'd known that the whole time.

He took a step forward, and then another one. "Ophelia," he said. "It's an unusual name."

"Not that unusual, I don't think."

"Funny thing is, I used to know another girl named Ophelia. She was a mean one. Stole my car once. I didn't get it back for nearly a week. You're not like her, though. Prettier, for one thing."

Ophelia's heart was racing. She tried speaking, but no words came out.

"I don't think you like me," Ruben said. "And I'm not sure why."

"That's not true."

"I'm a nice guy, when you get to know me."

"I'm sure that—"

"Did your mother tell you about the things I did?"

Ophelia's eyes darted around like fish in a bowl. Planning her escape, if need be.

"Well? Did she?"

Ophelia shook her head.

"That's good," he said. "The past shouldn't be weaponized. Not that I'm ashamed. I was young and angry. Couldn't control myself. I paid the price and then some."

Ophelia: "I'm sorry to hear that."

He smiled, but there was no humor there. "But you don't have to be frightened of me. I promise you. I'm a changed man. I would never do anything to hurt you, Holt, or your mother."

"I should go home."

"Sure. That's probably a good idea. But you shouldn't walk by yourself. Too dangerous. I'll give you a ride."

"No. I can walk."

"You don't trust me? Your mother talking shit about me?"

"It's not that. I just like the fresh air, that's all."

His expression turned dark. His arms hung limply at his side, and his shoulders heaved up and down. Ophelia knew something was going to happen, but she was paralyzed.

Five seconds, ten.

He darted quickly toward her, reaching out for her arm. She screamed and stumbled backward, falling onto her side. She tried scrambling to her feet, but his hand gripped her ankle.

She went in full panic mode, kicking and flailing and screaming. She must have somehow made contact with his groin because she heard him grunt, and then his grip released. Adrenaline flowing, she got to her feet and started running, and it was like somebody else was controlling her body. She'd never run so fast, but still she heard his footsteps behind her, heard his voice calling her name.

She kept waiting for him to catch up to her, to grab her and force her into the water, a baptism before death. But eventually his footsteps and voice faded away, and when she finally got the courage to stop and turn around, he was gone, vanished into the swaying cottonwoods.

By the time Ophelia arrived home, the sky had turned gray and the wind was swirling around, causing a copy of that day's newspaper to cower against a metal fence. But when she pushed open her front door, she was greeted by the sound of music and laughter.

Her mother and Holt were in the living room dancing wildly in front of the fireplace, and Uncle Bobby, *her* Uncle Bobby, was standing on the coffee table, guitar strap slung around his neck, boot banging the rhythm, fingers strumming the chords. His lip was yanked upward by an invisible fishhook, and he was crooning through a rockabilly version of "Hound Dog."

Ophelia watched him, and for a moment, just a moment, everything was okay.

But when Uncle Billy saw Ophelia—her hair a mess, her eyes bloodshot—his boot stopped banging, and his fingers stopped strumming. He stepped down from the coffee table and slung the guitar off to the side.

"Hey, hey, Ophelia? You all right there, kid? What happened?"

And now her mother and Holt turned around, and they both stared at Ophelia and their smiles vanished. Ophelia covered her face with her hands and then she rushed toward her uncle.

"It's okay," he whispered. "I'm here."

He pulled her to his chest. She had missed him so much, and pretty soon she was shaking and crying in his arms, and she couldn't stop, not now, not ever.

PART III

2018

CHAPTER 11

The night of the funeral, Holt slept at his mother's house, in her bed. He could smell her memory and hear the echoes of her voice. His sleep was fitful, interspersed with anxious dreams, dreams that his teeth were shattering, turning to powder, likely a result of him clenching his jaws. When he woke, his head ached, and he remained in bed for another hour, staring at the death photo and reading the love letter over and over and over again.

. . . a heart can only ache so much until it ruptures . . .

. . . Someday I'll take you far from this pathetic little town . . .

. . . I love you more than you know.

And then back to his obsessive thoughts, back to Ruben Ray. Was he the one who wrote the letter? Was his mother the one who'd killed him? Maybe she was, he thought, maybe she had stood before him on that cold night and raised that revolver and squeezed the trigger and then watched as he slid down the wall, leaving a stain of blood behind—

But why?

He needed to get outside of his own head. Fortunately, Joyce Brandt had invited him to her house for coffee and cake, calling the house after the funeral the night before. She knew that he was alone and told him that she was worried that he might get depressed and start drinking. She might have been right. Holt agreed to come as long as nobody else was there. He couldn't bear the idea of listening to condolence after condolence from people he didn't know or remember, couldn't bear the idea of them asking where he'd been all these years.

He showered, shaved, and dressed. He left the love letter on her desk, but he stuck the photograph in his shirt pocket.

Safe keepings.

She lived on Collyer Street, a few blocks east of Main, in a pretty red brick Victorian. A Colorado state flag hung from the house, swaying in the breeze. He remembered her telling him once that she'd lived in that same house for almost her entire life. It had been her childhood home, and just two years after graduating from high school her father had died of a stroke and then her mother had died of a broken heart. Joyce moved back into the house more out of pragmatism than nostalgia. She eventually met and married Mike. Now that she'd outlasted him, Holt supposed there was nowhere else for her to go.

Holt parked out front, one tire on the sidewalk, and stayed in his car for a few minutes, listening to a Tom Petty song and watching the leaves from a giant maple flutter to the ground. The song ended (*the waiting is the hardest part*) and he killed the engine. He glanced at his reflection in the rearview mirror—not great—and stepped outside. The wind was blowing cold, and he pulled up the collar on his jacket and made his way to the front porch where the screen door was creaking open and shut.

He rapped on the front door a single time. Joyce answered right away, as if she'd been standing there all morning, just waiting for him. She smiled, but it was a sad smile, and that's all he'd seen lately.

"Hi, Joyce," he said. "Thanks for having me over. I really appreciate it. You didn't need to, you know?"

She pursed her lips. "Oh, stop it. Your mother would have wanted me to. She would have scratched my eyes out if I didn't. How was your night last night? Were you able to sleep, at least a little bit? I couldn't. I miss her so much, already. I miss her and Mike, both. It's kind of a lonely world, when you really get down to it. Anyway, come on in. The Bundt cake is ready. My special recipe."

Holt followed her inside. The place was exactly how he remembered it from his childhood. The floor was hardwood with a large red-and-yellow oriental rug, perfectly centered. The walls were covered with a blue floral wallpaper that must have been forty years old at least. People find their style and stick with it, Holt figured. There was a couch and a loveseat and a coffee table. Against one of the walls were glass shelves lined with various knickknacks: china teacups, peacock pendants, ceramic Easter eggs, pig saltshakers, quill pens. On another wall was a portrait of Joyce and Mike when they were young and happy. He was dressed in an ill-fitting suit; she in a blue dress. It was a reminder to Holt that she was once pretty, that Mike was once alive. There were no pictures of children because they'd never had any.

Joyce noticed Holt staring at the portrait. She stood next to him, crossed her arms, and stared at it as well. "He's been gone for eight years now," she said. "I can hardly believe it. I still talk to him every day. When I wake up in the morning, when I go to sleep at night. If somebody were to sneak inside and watch me, they'd think I was crazy. And maybe I am. They tell you it gets easier, but for me, it never really has. I miss him as much today as I did the day he died."

"And how'd he die?" Holt asked, and right away he regretted the crudeness of the question.

She breathed deeply and looked away. "Complications of pneumonia," she said. "Lungs filled with fluid. He couldn't breathe. It's like he drowned on his own bed. An awful way to go."

Holt thought of the woman in the fire. Thought of his mother hanging from a noose. There were a lot of different ways to die, and none of them good.

"I'm sorry. I shouldn't have asked."

"It's fine. We all die. Don't believe the movies: there's never been a happy ending. Not once in the history of the world."

She paused for a moment.

"I should tell you something else about Mike. Something you probably don't know. Maybe now's not the right time."

"It's fine."

"Mike—he loved your mother."

Holt didn't know how to respond. "I didn't know they were close."

"Yeah, well. These things happen. They slept together once. Maybe twice. What are you going to do? I still remember when he told me. It was shortly after you'd left home. So maybe twenty years ago? We were sitting in the kitchen, eating cereal. It came out of nowhere, really. He had to get it off his chest, I guess. I never held it against him. Never held it against your mother, either. After all, it didn't mean that I loved either of them any less. I always thought your mother was beautiful, but she never thought so. And so she settled. She could have been happy, I think. Under the right circumstances. In any case, I think Mike loved her until the day he died."

A thought hit him. The letter to his mother. Was it possible that Mike Brandt had written it? Was it possible that she'd held onto it for all those years? The thought made him happy for some reason.

He kept it to himself.

They walked into the kitchen. More floral wallpaper, this time light pink. There was an old refrigerator and an old dishwasher. There was a round table covered by a white doily tablecloth. Holt sat down, crossing his legs and then quickly uncrossing them. Joyce's house felt suddenly oppressive. Maybe it was because everything was from the past, and that's not where he felt comfortable. Death didn't scare him as much as remembrance.

Joyce stood at the kitchen counter and cut the Bundt cake. She placed ridiculously large slices on both plates and brought them to the table.

"This was Mike's very favorite kind of cake," she said. "The key is the butter. Twice as much as the recipe calls for. You see why I'm no longer a size two?" She laughed. "And how do you take your coffee?"

"Black is fine," he said.

"Oh, good. I don't have any cream."

She poured the coffee and sat down at the table, a streak of sunlight spreading across her lap. Holt took a bite of the cake, and his arteries would be good and clogged by the time he finished it. He washed it down with a gulp of coffee and wiped his mouth with the back of his hand.

"I got to tell you," he said. "I feel guilty I didn't go to the burial. I should have. I know that."

Joyce shook her head. "You didn't miss anything, sweetie. Ashes to ashes, dust to dust. Nothing new under the sun. And your mother doesn't care, not anymore."

"No. I guess she doesn't."

Holt ate more cake, even though he didn't particularly like it. He thought of the photo that was in his shirt pocket.

"Why do you think she did it?" When he spoke, his voice

sounded like that of a stranger, low and ragged. "Why do you think she hung herself?"

Joyce shook her head. "I wish I knew. There was no note, you know, so it's hard to know for certain."

"And she wasn't sick? Nothing that would have caused her to—"

"No. I mean, as you know, she was never a cheerful woman. Not after Ophelia was taken away. Not after you left home. But she got by. I never would have thought it would come to this. She must have had demons that I didn't know about." She studied him. "That you didn't know about either."

Holt rubbed his eyes and sighed. "Yeah, I guess that must be it. Demons."

They sat in silence for a minute. There was nothing to be gained by delving into the past, only misery. But he was compulsive and couldn't help himself. More questions. Maybe Joyce could answer them. Maybe.

"Ruben Ray," he said.

Joyce's head jerked upward. "Excuse me?"

"What do you know about a man named Ruben Ray?"

Her expression turned dark, her eyes narrowed beneath hooded lids. She didn't say anything, not right away. Instead, she got up from her chair and walked over to the kitchen sink. For a long moment, she just stood there. Then she turned on the water and began washing dishes that were probably already clean, drying dishes that were probably already dry. Her back was to Holt, and when she spoke again, her voice was hushed, and he had to strain to hear her.

"Where did you hear about him? About Ruben Ray?"

"From a friend," he lied. "Tell me what you know about him."

"I know that he was nobody important. Frankly, that's all there is *to* know."

"Is that right?"

"That's right."

Holt slapped the table, a mild show of force. "No. I don't think so. Be straight with me, Joyce. You owe me that much. What was my mother's connection to him?"

She turned around slowly, wiping her hands on the front of her apron. "I wouldn't hardly call it a connection."

"Then what?"

"Oh, darling, you know how it is. After your father left, your mother dated a few people. Ruben was one of them."

"How long did they date?"

Joyce shrugged. "Not long. A few months, tops. Like I said, he was just a guy. Nothing special. You don't remember him? Tattoos up and down his arms?"

Holt shrugged. "A little bit. But the memories are blurry. I was young."

Joyce returned to the kitchen table and sat down. As she scooped up the last piece of cake with her fork, Holt noticed that her hand was trembling. "It's just interesting that you should bring him up. I haven't thought of him in a while."

Holt stared at her without blinking. And now he asked the question he already knew the answer to.

"And so what happened to him? What happened to Ruben Ray?"

For a moment, she froze. Then she sighed through her nose and shook her head.

"What happened to him? He died. Somebody shot him. In that old farmhouse out by Liberty Hall." A long pause. "The same place your mother hung herself."

Holt's jaw tightened. His skin felt suddenly cold. "So then maybe he was a little important to her, don't you think?"

"I don't know what to think."

"And did they ever find the guy who did it?"

A quick shake of her head. "No, they never did. You know how it is. A fellow like him probably had a lot of enemies. So it could have been anybody."

Holt looked at his hands, which had clenched into light fists. He reached into his shirt pocket and pulled out the photograph. "The other night," he said, "I spent some time searching through the house, through Ophelia's room, through Mom's room. I found an envelope. And this photograph was inside. I think my mother took it."

He slid the photograph across the table. For several moments, Joyce was still. Then she picked up the photograph. One second, two, and her expression changed from bewilderment to horror.

"Oh, my God," she said. "What . . . who . . .?"

"A dead man. Ruben Ray."

"And . . . and it was in your mother's room?"

"It was."

"I don't understand. Why—"

"Maybe it was a souvenir. A reminder."

"A reminder of what?"

"Of the night she killed him."

He hadn't planned on doing this. Hadn't planned on telling Joyce this. But here he was, doing just that.

She was silent for a moment. Then, "I'm not sure how to respond, Holt. Do you really think your mother was capable of something like that?"

He shrugged his shoulders. "We're all capable of something like that."

"Your mother was kind. Your mother was good."

"Sometimes she was. But I was around her when she got mad, too. When she slapped me hard. When she pushed me to the ground. So yes, I think she was capable."

Joyce shook her head and pursed her lips. "Whatever suspicions you have, whatever agony you're dealing with, you shouldn't stain your mother's memory."

"I'm not staining anything. I just need the truth. Maybe I've been avoiding it for most of my life. No more. I don't think you've told me everything. Tell me what you know."

And now Holt noticed that Joyce was breathing heavily, her shoulders heaving up and down. She rose from her seat and walked across the kitchen floor. With her trembling hands barely under control, she opened up the cabinet and took out a bottle of bourbon, half finished. She returned to the table and dumped some into her coffee. She motioned to Holt's coffee, and he nodded his head. She gave him a couple of fingers worth, at least.

Joyce took a sip of the bourbon-coffee and shivered from the shock. "Okay," she said. "I'll tell you what I know. I owe you that much."

Holt nodded his head, barely. He gazed at Joyce, waiting for her to speak. And then she did.

CHAPTER 12

"The first thing you need to know is that Ruben Ray was a bad person. An abusive person."

"He beat up my mom?"

"He might have."

"What else?"

"He spent time in prison."

"For what?"

"Assault. Mike managed to get the police report from Texas. The details were pretty heinous. Tore this fellow's ear completely off. Sentenced to five years but only served three. Good behavior. Whatever the hell that means."

"Why'd my mom like him then?"

She shook her head. "I don't know if I can answer that question. I mean, he was decent looking, I guess. Well built. Those are superficial things, I know. Maybe most importantly, he stood up for her one time when another man was mean. Not many people stood up for your mom."

Joyce closed her eyes and shook her head. Her eyelids became moist and tears began streaking down her cheeks. Holt moved his chair and placed his hand on her shoulder.

"It's okay," he said. "Whatever you need to tell me, it's okay. I know the world is a mean old place. I don't judge people for trying to defend against it."

Joyce wiped away the tears with a napkin and blew her nose. She breathed slowly, trying to calm herself down. Then she continued.

"Mike. He was worried about your mother. He thought Ruben might hurt her. And so he gave her a gun."

"Did my mother know how to use it?"

Joyce laughed through her tears. "Yeah, she knew. Remember, she grew up on a farm. Used to shoot beer bottles. Used to shoot rabbits. I think she even won some marksmanship contest."

"I never knew that."

"Your mother was humble."

"She was."

Joyce took another big swallow of the bourbon-laced coffee. "I can't tell you anything for sure. Understand that. But I'm telling you what I know. It was late November, 1984. I remember that the rain was falling, soaking the fallen leaves. I was home, sitting on a couch, watching TV. Mike was gone for the evening."

Holt felt anxious, his stomach tightening. "Okay," was all he said.

"It must have been near ten o'clock, when I heard a pounding on the door. The knocks were quick, panicked. My first thought was that something had happened to Mike. Ever since we'd been married, I'd had the fear that he would die at the hands of some lunatic. I worried that another police officer was going to be standing there with his hat in his hand, forced to tell me the bad news.

"But, no. It wasn't a police officer. It was your mother. I remember she was wearing a white dress, and her hair was a damp mess from the rain. She was crying and shaking. I opened the door and let her in. She just stood there, and I'd never seen her so distraught. I asked her what was wrong, asked her why she was crying, but she wouldn't speak. Not for a long time. I got her dried off with a towel, wiped away her tears, gave her dry clothes to wear. We sat down in the living room. And that's when she said Ruben's name. Said that he was a monster. Said that he didn't deserve to live. I didn't know what to think. Not then . . ."

"And that was the night—"

"Yes. That was the night that he was shot. That was the night that he was murdered."

"And at that moment? Were you suspicious? Did you think she had killed him?"

Joyce shook her head. "I don't know, Holt. We have a way of rationalizing. It's what keeps us sane, I guess. I didn't find out about his death until a week or so later. Your mom wasn't the one who told me. Mike did. And then I thought about it for a while, but I convinced myself otherwise."

"And my mother never admitted anything to you?"

"No. Never. And here's the thing. Mike protected her. I discovered that later on. Made sure the investigation went in a different direction. Made sure certain evidence never saw the light of day. Made sure they left Vivian alone."

Holt's head was spinning. "You're saying that Mike sabotaged the investigation?"

"I don't look at it that way. Sometimes justice isn't so clear. Like I told you before: Mike loved your mother. And the way he figured things, Ruben Ray didn't have any business living. No business at all. Besides, what good would it have done to have your mother locked up? She did what she had to do. She destroyed that which had robbed her. Can you blame her? Can you blame my husband for protecting her?"

Holt shook his head. He didn't know. He didn't know anything.

Joyce had said all she was going to say. They sat there in silence for a while. And then Holt thought of the letter again.

"I've got an odd request," he said.

"What's that?"

"Do you have any old documents that Mike wrote on? So I can see his handwriting?"

"His handwriting? But why—"

"It's probably nothing. Really. But I just want to make sure."

Joyce nodded her head. "Yes. Of course. I've got some things saved. In my lockbox. If you'll only give me a few minutes."

"Thank you, Joyce. And I'm sorry."

Joyce rose to her feet and left the kitchen. She was gone for several minutes. Holt remained at the table, staring straight ahead.

She returned with some documents and a stack of greeting cards.

"He wasn't a romantic," Joyce said. "But he always gave me a card for my birthday. For Valentine's Day. For our anniversary."

She handed Holt a few of them, and he opened the first one, an anniversary card. On the front were pink roses and typically cheesy Hallmark sentiments (*For my wife: love of my life; beauty of my world; friend of my heart.*) Inside the card, Mike had written a short inscription: *Joyce. You mean the world to me. And then some. Happy anniversary. Love, Mike.*

Holt studied the handwriting. He'd left the love letter at the house. He tried to remember what those letters and words looked like, but it was hard to recall.

"Mind if I take a couple of these cards? I'll bring them back."

"Of course. They're just silly old cards. But I'm still not sure what—"

"When I found the photograph, I also found a love letter. To my mother. I wasn't sure who wrote it."

"And now you think it might have been Mike?"

"I don't know what it would mean other than—"

"Like I told you. He loved her until the day he died. It's possible he wrote her a letter. Love is a funny thing, don't you think?"

After that, both of them drank more whiskey-coffee. Eventually Joyce refilled both of their mugs, no coffee this time. They were both quiet, and Holt could hear the rain softly pelting the windowpanes. A few minutes passed before Holt spoke again.

"What you said. About her destroying that which had robbed her. What did you mean by that?"

"Holt, I—"

"Why'd she kill him? What did he do to her? What had he stolen from her?"

Joyce placed her wrinkled hand inside of his. "Oh, darling. I don't know exactly. Really, I don't. I would tell you if I did."

"Tell me what you know. You said you would."

"I want to. It's just that I don't know much. What I do know—that is, what I think—is that it had something to do with your sister. With Ophelia."

Holt felt a stab of pain in his chest.

"Ophelia? What about her?"

"Vivian would never tell me. Neither would Mike. Just hints. Words unsaid."

"What kind of hints?" Holt's voice was calm, but he felt that familiar dread.

"Oh, Holt. I wish I could tell you more. But I don't know. Really, I don't." She looked at him, and her eyes were bloodshot. "I want you to listen to me. Whatever happened is already done. It's the past. I think you need to let this go. We just buried your mother yesterday. There's no sense in digging deeper than we already have."

Holt rose to his feet. "No. I'm sorry. I need to know. I don't know if it will do me any good, but I need to know. I'm going to pay my sister a visit, talk to her. I don't want to hurt anybody. Not Ophelia. Not my mom. Not you. But I need to find the truth, the whole truth. You can understand that, can't you?"

She nodded her head. "Yes. I can understand that."

"Thanks for the cake. And thanks for being my mom's friend through all these years. Even if she and your husband—"

"She was a good woman. You need to know that. And you're a good man."

At this, Holt felt a stab of pain. But still he nodded his head. "I'll keep these greeting cards safe. I promise."

He walked out of the kitchen, through the living room, and out the front door. He got in his car and hit the engine. A song by Bruce Springsteen was playing, and it had been a long time since Holt cried, and over the next five or ten minutes, he sure made up for it.

A short time later, Holt sat at his mother's desk. On the left side of the desk was the love letter. On the right side were Mike's greeting cards. He'd been staring at them for a long time, comparing them. The handwriting wasn't that far off, he supposed. But it wasn't that close either. The more he analyzed, the more he was certain. Mike Brandt hadn't written the love letter.

In a way, Holt felt disappointed. It would have been nice if Mike had been the one who had written the letter. It would have been nice if he'd been the one who'd killed Ruben Ray.

But he hadn't killed Ruben Ray.

His mother had.

CHAPTER 13

Holt didn't know exactly what he was expecting, but it was something else, something a bit more institutional. The Balsam Halfway House was a nondescript trilevel home located in a rundown 1960s suburban neighborhood filled with other nondescript trilevel homes. He'd called Balsam two hours earlier, and an affable-sounding man named Dr. Tom had said that certainly Ophelia was free to receive visitors, but he would have to check with her first to make sure she was of the right mind. Five minutes later, the doctor called back and said that Ophelia had smiled and nodded when he mentioned Holt's name.

"Ophelia looks forward to seeing you, Holt."

For nearly two years following Ophelia's hospitalization, Holt's mother had frequently taken him to visit her, and the experiences were nearly always traumatic. His mother would remind him that Ophelia wasn't well, wasn't well at all. He had to speak in a very quiet voice and couldn't make any sudden movements around her. It was very important, his mother told him, that he didn't do or say anything to make Ophelia upset. When Holt would enter the hospital room and see a girl that barely resembled the Ophelia he knew (her face now pallid and gaunt, her frame skeletal), he would just stand there with his hands buried in his pockets and stare at his feet, not saying a word. His mother would talk to Ophelia, discussing trivialities such as the weather or celebrity gossip, trying to maintain as much normalcy as possible, but Ophelia wouldn't respond. She just sat in her chair, staring at the empty wall.

And so on those visits, Vivian would sometimes turn to prayer, getting on her bruised knees, placing her hand on Ophelia's knee, and squeezing her eyes shut. Sometimes she would ask Holt to join her. It didn't take long before Ophelia would become frustrated, shouting and cursing and flailing about.

After too many of these chaotic prayer sessions, Holt's mother decided it would be best if he didn't accompany her, and so he didn't. And though for many years after this his mother continued to visit Ophelia, the visits eventually became less and less frequent. At one point, when Holt was about fourteen, he overheard his mother telling somebody over the phone that Ophelia was going to be released from the hospital and was going to come back home. But within a week, those plans had been scrapped, and it was clear that her psychosis was a lifetime curse.

As Holt grew from a boy to a man, he thought about his sister less and less frequently, and when he did think of her, the memories were hazy and jumbled. On those rare occasions when he would speak to his mother after he left Thompsonville, she almost never mentioned Ophelia. It was as if she were trying to forget she had ever existed. He guessed in some ways she'd succeeded. Sometimes, however, Ophelia would still appear in his dreams, not as the skeletal girl from the psychiatric hospital, but as his beautiful older sister from his childhood home. In those dreams, she would smile and laugh and hold his hand, but when he woke up, she was always gone, and he would feel a profound sadness, as if he had lost her all over again.

On one occasion, Holt saw her when he was awake. He and his unit had been called to put out a house fire in the Baker neighborhood, and as he was hosing down the burning structure, he gazed at the upstairs window and, through the flames and smoke, saw Ophelia—beautiful Ophelia—pressing her hand against the window. He called out her name once, twice, but she was gone, dissolved into smoke. It had been his imagination, of course, his own fears manifesting themselves.

And now he was going to see her again, and this time for real. Holt parked on the street, one tire on the sidewalk. Several other vehicles, all of them old and rundown, were parked haphazardly in the driveway. In the front yard was a badminton set, an old Huffy bicycle, and a half-buried rake. Holt killed the engine, but still he sat there, hands gripping the steering wheel, knuckles whitening. Finally, he took some deep breaths and stepped outside.

An old woman sat on the front stoop wearing overalls, her bare legs crossed at the ankles. Her head was bald in patches, and an unlit cigarette dangled from her mouth. On her lap was a Disney coloring book, open to a crudely-colored picture of Snow White. Holt approached the woman and forced a smile.

"Hi. I'm looking for Dr. Tom. Is he here?"

The woman scowled. When she spoke, the cigarette bounced up and down in her mouth. She was missing several teeth. "You're a stranger. I shouldn't talk to strangers."

"Fair enough. But I'm not really a stranger. My name is Holt. I'm Ophelia's brother."

A raise of the eyebrow. "Ophelia never mentioned she had a brother. Are you lying?"

"No, ma'am. I haven't seen her in a long time. But she is my sister."

"Why haven't you seen her?"

Holt hesitated before saying, “Lots of reasons.”

At that, the woman reached into the front pocket of her overalls and pulled out another cigarette. “You want one of these?” she said.

“No, thanks. I’m trying to cut down.”

“If you don’t light them, they’re not bad for you. That’s the way it is with everything.”

“I never thought of it that way. Yeah, in that case, I’ll take one.”

The old woman handed Holt the cigarette, and he stuck it in his mouth.

“Thanks. This is much better than the way I usually do it. Healthier.”

“No nicotine,” she said. Then, “Ophelia is one of the few people I can stand here. She doesn’t talk hardly at all. That’s why I can stand her. The rest never shut up. Especially Paul. He talks all day about interest rates. Makes me want to strangle him. That’s why I’m outside smoking my cigarette. Dr. Tom told me I should get some fresh air. Paul kept talking about interest rates. How they’re bound to go up soon. Think I care, motherfucker?”

“I don’t think you do.”

“Fuck no. And what about you? Have you refinanced?”

“No. Not one time.”

“Then don’t talk to Paul. You’ll regret it.”

The front door opened, and a young man appeared. He was dressed in jeans and a button-down shirt and had a fauxhawk. He smiled and stuck out his hand.

“You must be Holt?”

“Yes.”

“I’m Dr. Tom. We talked on the phone. I see that you’ve met Doris.”

“Yes,” Holt said. “She gave me this cigarette.” He stuck it behind his ear.

Dr. Tom laughed. "Nicotine-free if you don't light them. Why don't you come inside? I think Ophelia is excited to see you. She's had a good few weeks. Relaxed."

Dr. Tom walked through the door and Holt followed. Inside the house, two young, bearded men, one skinny and one fat, sat at a long wooden table huddled over a desktop computer. They both looked up when Holt entered.

Dr. Tom addressed them. "Hi, guys. This is Holt. Holt is Ophelia's brother. Say 'Nice to meet you, Holt.'"

Both of the men said, "Nice to meet you, Holt." Then, the fat one said, "Ophelia doesn't like visitors."

"Oh, that's not true," Dr. Tom said. "She's just very particular about who she speaks to." And now Dr. Tom pointed to the computer. "They're working on a newsletter. Michael is a very fine writer. And Dan is strong visually. They make a good pair."

The skinny one, most likely Michael, said, "I want to title this month's letter 'Welcome to Hell House,' but I know Dr. Tom will say no. He wants it to be more generic."

"Not generic," Dr. Tom said. "Appropriate."

"Whatever."

"Now, if you'll excuse us, we'll go find Ophelia. Is she in her room?"

"Don't know. She's been spending most of the morning pushing that damn shopping cart around."

"We'll find her," Dr. Tom said.

Dr. Tom and Holt walked through the kitchen, where several patients were sitting at a table eating peanut butter and jelly sandwiches, and down a long hallway lined with doors on both sides. Dr. Tom seemed to never stop smiling, which made Holt nervous.

"What you should know is that Ophelia is making great strides," Dr. Tom said. "When she first came here, she was pretty helpless, having spent so many years institutionalized. Unnecessarily, in my opinion."

"Unnecessarily?"

"Maybe I'm biased, but I feel that they rely too much on medication in those places. Not enough therapy. Not enough socialization."

"But now?"

"She's been with us for close to three years. She does her own cooking. Her own laundry. She's fairly self-sufficient, which is no small feat. True, she does still have difficulty leaving the house. It makes her anxious. But she'll get there eventually. Our purpose is to empower our tenants to be more independent. More confident."

Tenants, thought Holt. Not patients. Tenants.

"That young man said that she pushes a shopping cart. What's that all about?"

Dr. Tom's smile widened. "Oh, that. Funny story. Last year, we went for a group outing to the grocery store. You know, encouraging them to pick their own food and pay for it. Independence. When we were finished, Ophelia wouldn't let go of the god-darn shopping cart. None of us could figure out what had gotten into her. I tried reasoning with her, letting her know that the cart didn't belong to her, but she was stubborn. She refused to let it go. Eventually, one of the managers approached. He told us that Ophelia could keep the cart. That it was a gift from the supermarket. I think he just wanted us to leave without creating more of a scene. In any case, Ophelia was thrilled. For the next week or so, she pushed that shopping cart wherever she went, even if she was going to the bathroom."

"Okay. Any idea why?"

Dr. Tom shook his head. "There's not always a reason for these things. Just weird hang-ups and attachments. We all have them. Maybe hers are a bit more prominent. Eventually, she stopped pushing the shopping cart all of the time, but to this day, whenever she gets anxious, she begins pushing."

"I guess today's an anxious day, huh?"

"Just relax, Holt. It'll be fine."

They reached the end of the hallway and came to a door that was closed. Taped above the handle, in scribbled red Sharpie, was a sign that read, *Private Property. Stay Out!*

"This is Ophelia's room?" Holt asked.

"It is. Most of our tenants—we've got nine in all—share a bedroom, but Ophelia lives by herself. You see, she doesn't always play well with others."

"What's that supposed to mean?"

"As I said, she's making strides. But there are still the occasional bursts of violence. Rare, but they happen. It's better that she has her space." Dr. Tom slapped Holt's back. "And on that note, are you ready?"

He wasn't ready, of course he wasn't, but still he said, "Yes."

Dr. Tom knocked on the door a few times and then backed away.

"Ophelia?" he called. "I've got that visitor I talked to you about. I've got your brother, Holt. Can you open the door?"

There was no response. Dr. Tom waited twenty seconds or so and then knocked again.

"Ophelia? Please open the door."

Another minute passed. Holt was ready to call the whole thing off. It had been stupid for him to come here in the first place. He would leave and never come back. After all, he didn't know her anymore, not really. She was a stranger to him. Nobody could blame him. But then he heard hurried footsteps on the floor and saw the door creak open. Then more hurried footsteps away.

Dr. Tom put up his hand, indicating for Holt to wait. Finally, after a long pause, he nodded at Holt, and they entered.

The room was simple—a neatly made bed with pink pillows and a comforter with pictures of horses on it. Cotton curtains hung over metal bars. In the corner of the room, a small bookshelf, empty, and in front of it, the Safeway shopping cart. And there was Ophelia, sitting at a metal desk, her back to the men.

Her hair was long and beginning to gray. Was that possible? Was she really that old? Time is cruel, Holt thought, time and trauma doubly so. Her back was hunched, and she was scribbling furiously in some kind of a makeshift journal, really nothing more than a bunch of sheets of lined paper stapled together. Was she writing poems, or songs, like when she was a kid? Or darker tales, tales of lunacy?

Dr. Tom spoke. "Ophelia? Can you stop writing for a moment? Can you say hi to your brother? He came a long way to see you."

Ophelia didn't respond. Instead, she continued writing feverishly, pencil scraping against paper, grunts escaping from her mouth. Dr. Tom and Holt stood just inside the doorway, waiting. Eventually, her back straightened. She carefully placed the pencil down on the desk, next to the notebook. Her shoulders heaved up and down, and she raised her right hand slowly.

No words, but an indication of greeting.

Dr. Tom nodded his head. "Okay," he said. "I'm going to leave. I'm going to give you two some time to get caught up. It's been a long time. So much has happened. To both of you. If you need anything, I'll be in the kitchen, helping with lunch preparation."

Dr. Tom left the room, closing the door softly behind him. Holt felt his throat constrict. He couldn't believe he was here, standing in this room, staring at the back of his sister's head.

And then he remembered Joyce's words about the killing, and he shivered.

It had something to do with your sister.

"Ophelia," Holt said. "It's me, Holt. Your little brother. Do you remember me? It's been a long time."

Ophelia didn't answer, but her hand twitched into action. Once again, she began writing, this time for another two or three minutes, although the effort was less frantic. When she was finished, she again placed her pencil neatly next to the notebook. And then she spoke.

"I'm writing about my childhood," she said. Holt was surprised at how clear and articulate she sounded, surprised that she sounded exactly the same as before, when she was still a young woman. "It was such a long time ago," she continued. "But I remember it all. Every second. Don't let Dr. Tom tell you otherwise. I remember it all."

"Yes," Holt said, taking a step forward. "I'm sure you do."

Ophelia turned around slowly, and for the first time Holt got a look her face. It was full of pain and misery and trauma. She was fifty but looked at least ten years older than that. It was hard to reconcile that the girl's voice he knew so well came from this woman's mouth, hard to reconcile that this was really his sister. Her lips spread slowly into a grin, but there was no joy in it.

"In particular," she said, "I'm writing about you."

Holt felt a coldness rise up inside of him. "Me?"

"Yes. About the things you did."

She wasn't well. He had to remember this. "I don't know what things you mean."

That grin again. "You wouldn't."

After all these years. Still not well. He asked: "Can I read it?"

She shook her head quickly. "That would be a bad idea. The words would hurt your feelings."

"I don't mind having my feelings hurt. Honestly, I don't."

"I'm sorry, no. Some of what I write is mean. Unnecessarily so. Remember the lake by our house? Mineral Lake?"

"I do."

"It's a pretty lake. Deep and blue. But if you get too close, searching for answers you already know, you might drown yourself in it."

Holt laughed. Not because her statement was funny, but because he wasn't sure where it came from.

"Okay," he said. "I won't read it if you think it's a bad idea."

"A bad idea. A very bad idea."

Holt took a few more steps forward until he was standing directly in front of her. He took a deep breath.

"Listen. There is something you should know. Whatever you think of me, I want you to know this. I've always missed you. Always wondered about you. Is it okay for me to say that?"

Ophelia wouldn't make eye contact with him. She stared at his shoes, stained with dried mud. When she spoke again, her voice was softer. "It's okay. I might have missed you too. Whatever became of you? Through all these years?"

Holt shrugged. "I don't know. I moved away from Thompsonville. I became a firefighter."

"A firefighter?"

"That's right."

"Helping people? Or burning them?"

"Helping them."

"And did you get married? Have kids?"

Holt shook his head. "No. I never did."

"Why not? Why didn't you have kids?"

He thought of the baby in the fire. Heard the sound of him crying. He gritted his teeth.

"I don't know. It wasn't in the cards, I guess."

And now Ophelia did look at him, her brown eyes still lovely. "You used to visit me. A long time ago. Why did you stop?"

It was a hard question. One he didn't know how to answer. "I don't know. Maybe because I was a coward."

She shook her head. "A coward?"

"Yeah. You know, when you first went away, I was young. Just a kid. Mom used to take me to see you. But it was hard for me seeing you struggle. So I stopped. And once I stopped, it became harder and harder to start again. Does that make sense? If I'm being honest, Ophelia, I guess I abandoned you. Just like everybody. For that, I'm sorry. For everything. I'm so sorry."

Ophelia squeezed her eyes shut, and Holt worried that she would start crying. But after a few moments she opened them, and there were no tears.

"Mom's dead, huh?"

Holt nodded his head. "Yes. She is. That's why I'm in town. I came back for her funeral. Funerals are terrible. There's nothing you can do with dead people. Nothing you can tell them."

"Dr. Tom was the one who told me. He tried to be gentle. He said, 'There's something you need to know.' But I already knew. I've always had that power. I don't know how she died, though. Dr. Tom wouldn't tell me. I hope it wasn't painful. She didn't deserve a painful death."

"No," Holt said. "It wasn't painful. She died peacefully. In her sleep."

Some lies were good. Some lies were compassionate.

Ophelia's face relaxed, and he saw a glimpse of the girl he remembered. "That's good," she said. "In her sleep. I hope she was having a good dream."

And that's when Holt should have embraced his sister. That's when he should have stroked her cheek with the back of his fingers, should have promised never to abandon her again. But he didn't. He couldn't help himself, he needed to know.

"Tell me about Ruben Ray," he said. "Tell me what he did to you."

At the mention of Ruben's name, Ophelia's face contorted into a silent shriek, her carotid artery visibly pulsing. Holt looked into her eyes, and he saw a flake of madness. He figured it was there for good.

"What—What did you say?"

"I want to know about Ruben Ray. I want to know what he did to you."

The flake of madness was growing. She stood up from her chair. She began chewing on the webbing of her skin, between her thumb and forefinger. Then she laughed without smiling.

"Ruben Ray? Ruben Ray was a cockroach."

"What did he do?"

"He was in the wrong place at the wrong time. And he got crushed. You want me to cry for him? Is that what you want? Huh? Cause I won't do it."

"No. I don't want you to cry for him. But I need to know the truth. Before the funeral, I spent some time in our house. I found a photograph in Mom's room, of this Ruben fellow. He was bloody and dead. I talked to Mom's friend, Joyce. Remember her? Sure, you do. She admitted some things, about how her husband, Mike, loved Mom. And about how Mike gave Mom a gun to protect herself. And how Mom might have shot Ruben a few times right in his home.

"I pressed her on it. Wanted to know why. I figured it was because Ruben was abusive to Mom. That's what I figured. But Joyce said that wasn't the case. Joyce said it was because of what Ruben had done to you. That's why I need to know. What did Ruben do to you?"

Ophelia yanked at her hair and spat on the ground. "Ruben didn't do shit to me."

"I don't believe that, Ophelia. Tell me the truth. Please."

"He was set up. Fucking cockroach. You think I cared that he was shot? You think that?"

"What do you mean he was set up?"

Again, that frightening laugh. "Why the fuck would I tell you? You're a goddamn liar. A phony. How do I even know you're my brother?"

"Oh, come on, Ophelia."

"You could be playing tricks on me. One of Dr. Tom's plans. He drugs my scrambled eggs. That's why I don't eat them."

"What do you mean he was set up?"

"Figure it out, little brother. Go see the doctor."

"What doctor? Dr. Tom?"

"Not Dr. Tom. Dr. Yamamoto."

"Dr. Yamamoto? Who is he? Why should I talk to him? What does he have to do with this?"

"He's a corroborating witness. Go talk to him. I'm not the liar. You're the liar. Mom's the liar. She said I was crazy. I wasn't crazy. She betrayed me in the worst way. When I said she didn't deserve a painful death, I was lying. I hope she suffers in Hell for eternity. That's what I hope. For eternity . . ."

"Ophelia. Please. Just let me—"

But that was all she would say. She pushed past her brother, her eyes even crazier than before, and grabbed the handle of her shopping cart. Moments later, she was out the door. As Ophelia walked down the hall, Holt could hear the sound of the shopping cart spinning down the hallway, one of the wheels jammed and dragging along the hardwood.

Holt remained just inside the doorway, his shoulders heaving up and down. From behind him, he heard a voice.

"And how was your conversation with Ophelia?"

Holt spun around. It was Dr. Tom. Smiling as always.

"She left," Holt said. "She got angry at me."

In his right hand, Dr. Tom held a badminton racket. Holt wondered if he was even a real doctor.

"Don't blame yourself," Dr. Tom said. "She's a tricky one. It's all about building trust. Maybe the next time you see her, she'll be more open."

"Maybe. I don't think so. You ever heard of a Dr. Yamamoto?"

"Yamamoto? I don't think so—"

"Could be a made-up name. Could be."

Dr. Tom shrugged. "Your sister. She's getting better. But she's still not well."

"No," Holt said. "I don't think she is. In any case, I thank you for letting me come here. I thank you for letting me see Ophelia."

"Of course. But would you like to—"

Before Dr. Tom could finish speaking, Holt pushed past him and into the hallway. He hurried through the house and shouldered open the front door. Doris, the woman with the cigarettes and the Disney coloring book, was still on the front porch. When she saw Holt, she handed him another cigarette. He stuck it in his mouth.

"Ophelia is the only one I can stand," she said. "But I didn't know she had a brother. You learn something new every day."

Holt nodded his head. "Take good care of her, Doris. Promise me?"

Doris chewed on her own cigarette. "Yes, mister. I promise. She's the only one I can stand."

CHAPTER 14

Holt was surprised to find that Dr. Yamamoto was a real person, and that he was still practicing. He was also surprised to find that he wasn't a psychiatrist or a medical doctor. He was a dentist.

Holt hated dentists.

Holt tried calling his office to see if he could talk with him, but Dr. Yamamoto's secretary said he wasn't available, that he had a full schedule. Holt decided to take a different route.

The dental office was located on Francis Street in a generic strip mall just to the west of the high school, sandwiched between a hair salon called "Chez Curls" and a shoe store called "Heart and Soles." It was called "Happy Smiles," and on the sign there was a drawing of a giant disembodied smile.

The inside of the office was sterile, furnished only with two couches, two chairs, and two paintings, both pastoral landscapes. A gray-haired woman sat behind a wooden desk, her hands folded in her lap. When she saw Holt, she smiled the requisite smile that all secretaries must learn in secretary school.

"Welcome to Happy Smiles," she said, with maybe a trace of irony. "How can I help you?"

It was time for Holt's performance. He'd been in a play

once, back when he was in fourth grade, although it had been a non-speaking role: Townsperson #4. Now Holt pointed vaguely at his mouth, grimacing in pretend pain.

"I was hoping I could see Dr. Yamamoto."

"Mm-hmm. And are you a patient of his?"

"No, ma'am. That's just it. I'm actually from out of town." And then a dramatic pause. "I'm here for my mother's funeral."

At first, the secretary looked at him with suspicion, but then her expression became less severe. "Oh, my. I'm so sorry to hear that. My deepest condolences."

"Thank you. Anyway, it's just been over the last day or so that I started having sharp pain in one of my teeth. I was hoping I could get some relief. See, I'm working on getting the estate straightened out, so I probably won't be able to go home for a couple of weeks. One of my mother's friends recommended Dr. Yamamoto, so here I am."

The woman placed a pair of reading glasses on her face and slid her chair toward her computer. "I understand," she said. "We wouldn't want you in pain. Especially considering everything else you're dealing with. Let me see what I can find."

For a few minutes, the secretary tapped away on her computer, while Holt leaned against the desk. Then her eyebrows raised.

"I could move some things around and get you in tomorrow afternoon. Twelve thirty. Can you manage until then?"

Another grimace. Not Oscar material, but it was the best he could do. "Yeah," he said. "Tomorrow will work. Thanks so much."

"It's my pleasure. Now if you could fill out this form, Mr.—?"

"Davidson."

"Mr. Davidson. And do you have dental insurance?"

He shook his head. "No. I haven't been to the dentist in a while. I brush my teeth, though. Floss occasionally."

A smile. "Just fill out that form, and I'll get you in the computer."

Holt sat down on the couch and begin jotting in his information. A minute or two later, the phone rang, and the secretary had an abbreviated conversation. She hung up the phone and cleared her throat.

"Mr. Davidson? I do believe your mother is looking down on you right now."

"Yeah? Why do you say that?"

"That was Dr. Yamamoto's four thirty. She had to cancel. Her daughter is sick. We can get that tooth taken care of, right now."

Maybe she was looking down on him. Probably not. Holt smiled and thanked the secretary. Hopefully he was cavity free.

Ten minutes later, Dr. Yamamoto appeared. He was Asian, in his fifties, with iron-gray hair parted neatly to one side. When he smiled, Holt noticed that his teeth were a bit crooked and yellow, and that was disconcerting. "I understand you've got some tooth pain."

"I do."

"Come on back. We'll get you taken care of."

Holt lay down on the dentist's chair, and Dr. Yamamoto hovered over him, a surgical mask now covering his mouth and nose, and Holt couldn't help but think of the torture scene from *Marathon Man*. Dr. Yamamoto adjusted the overhead light, momentarily blinding Holt. Then he sat down in his chair and hovered over him.

"Where does it hurt?" he asked.

Holt pointed to his back molar on the lower side. "Just a dull ache," he said.

Dr. Yamamoto grabbed a mouth mirror and sickle probe from the metal table. He began poking and prodding inside Holt's mouth, and Holt could hear him breathing out of his nose.

"Well, I don't see any cavities. You say the pain is in this back molar?"

Holt nodded. "Could just be gum pain. Sensitivity. Maybe that's what it is."

"Let's go ahead and take some X-rays. Just in case."

Dr. Yamamoto dropped a lead vest on Holt's chest and had him bite down on dental film. Holt needed to ask about what Ophelia said, about him being a corroborating witness, but he couldn't open his mouth. Dr. Yamamoto told him to hold still and adjusted the camera so it was pressing against his jaw. He went across the room and clicked the camera. Then he returned to the chair and pulled the bitewing from Holt's mouth.

A quick opportunity to speak. "You know, my older sister used to be your patient, I believe."

"Is that right?" But he didn't sound all that interested. "Here, open your mouth. Good. Now bite down."

Holt did as he was told, and once again Dr. Yamamoto snapped the X-ray and removed the bitewing.

"Some time ago. Must have just been when you were starting."

Dr. Yamamoto peered at the images on his computer, touching the screen with his finger. "And what was your sister's name?"

"Ophelia. Ophelia Davidson."

"Hmm. Okay, open up one last time. Good. And bite down."

One last click of the camera. Dr. Yamamoto removed the latest bitewing and disposed of it. He lifted the heavy apron from Holt's chest and hung it on the wall.

Holt cleared his throat. "Anyway. I only bring her up because she seemed to have some pretty vivid memories of you."

Dr. Yamamoto returned to his computer monitor and studied the latest image of Holt's teeth. Without looking up, he said, "Is that right?"

"It is."

"Well, everybody remembers their dentists. Because we cause discomfort. And people remember discomfort."

"And do you remember her?"

"Ophelia, you said?"

"That's right."

"Doesn't ring a bell. But then, I've seen lots of patients. And even more teeth. Your X-rays look clean. Not sure where the pain is coming from."

"Like I said, maybe I've just got sensitive gums."

"Could be. Or maybe you just wanted someone to talk to. Anyway, let me get your teeth cleaned. You've got some plaque built up."

As Dr. Yamamoto fumbled for his mirror and scaler, Holt said, "My sister mentioned something else that was kind of interesting. She said that you were a corroborating witness. Do you know what she might be talking about?"

The dentist stuck the scaler in his mouth. Holt thought again of *Marathon Man*. Is it safe?

"A corroborating witness? To what?"

But Holt couldn't answer because Dr. Yamamoto was scraping his teeth and poking at his gums. When he pulled the instrument out to wipe it off, Holt said, "I don't know. That's what I'm trying to figure out."

"Well, I'm sorry that I don't remember her. As I said, a lot of patients."

For the next ten minutes, Dr. Yamamoto scraped and poked, rinsed and polished. Then he raised Holt to a sitting position and removed the surgical mask from his face.

"You said she was my patient, right? Got an idea of what year this was now?"

Holt rinsed the blood from his mouth and shrugged. "I'm

not entirely positive. But I believe sometime around 1984."

Dr. Yamamoto peeled off his gloves and rinsed his hands in the sink. "Well," he said, "I guess that makes sense why I don't remember her."

"Why's that?"

"Because I didn't become a dentist until 1994."

"And you weren't a medical doctor before that?"

Dr. Yamamoto shook his head. "No. But my father was."

And now Holt felt like an idiot. He was talking to the wrong doctor.

"Your father. Of course. Shit. He practiced here in town?"

"He did."

Holt felt a sense of unease, shards of memories visible from the corner of his eye.

"And your father. Is he still alive? Is he still in town? Could I talk to him?"

The dentist's face became strained, his cheeks reddening, and Holt worried that he'd become too aggressive in his questioning.

"I'm not sure that would be a good idea."

"Why not?"

"He's not well."

"I'm sorry. It's just—"

"What you should know is that he was a good man. A good father."

Past tense. *Was.*

"What kind of a doctor was he?"

Dr. Yamamoto paused for a long moment before answering. "An obstetrician. He delivered babies."

Holt felt his chest tighten. "Delivered babies?"

"Yes. For more than a decade. He loved his job."

And now Holt thought of his sister—so young and innocent—and his eyes rolled back in his head. Then he thought of the baby in the fire, heard the awful crying. The baby's mother had died, smoke overwhelming her lungs. But the baby had survived. He'd saved him. He'd saved him—

"A corroborating witness," Holt mumbled.

"I can't speak to that," Dr. Yamamoto said. "Unfortunately, my father ran into some legal troubles. He had his license removed by the state . . ."

Holt wasn't sure he'd heard correctly. "I'm sorry? He had his license removed? Why?"

"I don't want to get into it. Not now. But I'll tell you this, it damn near destroyed him."

"Then what—"

"My father wasn't allowed to deliver babies anymore. But he didn't leave the field entirely. He took on a different role."

"What role?"

"The kind that got the religious-right nuts up in arms back in the '80s."

"I don't understand."

And now Dr. Yamamoto leaned in and spoke in a voice barely louder than a whisper. "He became an abortionist."

"An abortionist? So he—"

"Know that he wasn't being cynical. He truly believed he was making the world a better place. And maybe he was."

Holt's head was spinning. "What year was this? What year did he have his license removed? When did he start aborting instead of delivering?"

Dr. Yamamoto shrugged. "I couldn't tell you exactly. 1983? 1984? It was such a long time ago. I was just a kid. Anyway, now he lives by himself. In the Countryside Village mobile park. I suppose you could talk to him, but—"

And now Holt felt the urge to get the hell out of there. With great effort, he managed to pull himself from the chair and get to his feet. He felt unsteady. He turned toward the doctor and, in a weak voice, said, "I'd like to thank you. You've been very helpful."

"I'm glad. I hope you figure things out. Work on brushing more aggressively on your gums. And keep flossing."

"Yes. I will . . ."

As Holt walked out of the office, past the smiling secretary, he thought of his sister and what she'd said: *It's a pretty lake. Deep and blue. But if you get too close, searching for answers you already know, you might drown yourself in it.*

PART IV

1984

CHAPTER 15

"You've got to tell me this, Ophelia. When the hell did you get all grown up?"

It was Saturday morning; Vivian was at the grocery store getting food for the week and Holt was playing at his friend Graham's house. Bobby had woken up late, Ophelia even later.

"I'm not that old," she said.

Bobby was sitting on the couch, Ophelia was standing in the doorway. He wore blue jeans and a white T-shirt. Tilted on his head was a porkpie hat like the ones that the jazz musicians from the '40s and '50s used to wear. His black guitar case, covered with bumper stickers with names of obscure bands, lay next to the couch. His guitar rested on his lap.

"Yeah, I guess. But the last time I saw you, you were just a kid." He flashed a sideways grin. "And now . . . like I said, you're all grown up."

This was the first time they'd been alone together since he'd arrived in town the night before. That night, she hadn't told Uncle Bobby or her mother what had happened with Ruben Ray down at Mineral Lake. She hadn't told them about all the strange things he'd said or how he'd tried grabbing her. She hadn't told them about how she'd fallen to the ground and then run away while Ruben's voice echoed through the skeleton trees. Instead, she'd told them that she'd been scared by a loose dog, that's why she was so panicked. She wasn't exactly sure why she'd lied. Maybe it was because she was embarrassed. Maybe it was because she didn't want her mother making a big deal out of it. Or maybe it was because she didn't want Bobby thinking she was still a helpless little girl, running from the big bad wolf.

And now there was so much that Ophelia wanted to ask Bobby. About his music, about his band, about New York. But she didn't know where to start.

"You got any new songs?"

She winced. The way Ophelia asked the question, all high-pitched and overly-eager, she didn't think she sounded grown up at all.

"Well, yeah," he said. "Now that you mention it, I do. It's called 'Stand by You.' But the title is too close to that Ben E. King song, damn it. I've been working on it for some time, but I can't get it quite right. Something's wrong. The lyrics? The melody? I don't know. Want to hear it?"

She smiled and said, "Yes. I'd love that."

Better. Deeper voice, less eager.

Uncle Bobby nodded at her. "Have a seat. I'll give it a try. No making fun, though. That would crush me personally and professionally."

Ophelia laughed. She sat down on the couch next to him. He closed his eyes and took a deep breath and then started playing. She watched as his long, slender fingers bent and stretched along the strings, moved up and down the fret board. The guitar playing was lovely, haunting, an expression of the solitude Ophelia almost always felt.

She was transfixed. In a soft growl, Bobby began singing, and Ophelia had to strain to hear the lyrics.

When the world is mean
And you think you're through
When the tears keep falling
I will stand by you

He sang the rest of the song and strummed a few more minor chords, and then the house was silent. Bobby looked up and, perhaps seeing Ophelia's longing expression, grinned that half grin.

"It's shitty, isn't it?"

Ophelia quickly shook her head. "No," she said. "I love it. It's beautiful. And the lyrics—they're beautiful, too."

"Yeah. Maybe. Just something that's been spinning in my head for a bit. Like I said, I can't get it quite right. But maybe one day." He nodded at her. "You ever played a guitar before?"

Ophelia shook her head. "I'd like to. But I don't have the patience to go to lessons. Mom made me do piano lessons when I was young. I hated it. I couldn't read music."

"Well, that's the good thing about guitar. You don't really need to know how to read music. There have been plenty of bands who wrote some great tunes playing just three or four chords."

"I heard that, I think."

"It's true. You know the song 'Sweet Home Alabama'?"

"Sure I do. Lynyrd Skynyrd."

"Three chords. G, C, D. And 'Bad Moon Rising' by Creedence Clearwater? D, G, A. 'Wild Thing.' 'Ring of Fire.' Any motherfucker can play the guitar. Pardon my French."

"Any motherfucker except for me. I'm too uncoordinated."

"I don't believe it. Do me a favor. Hold my guitar."

He placed the guitar in her hands and she took it, looking at him with uncertainty.

"You can strum with your fingers or with a pick. Depends on the situation. It's easier with a pick, though." He handed her the pick. "Okay. Now use your pick to go up and down on the strings."

Ophelia strummed a few times.

"See? Nothing to it. All right. Now I'll teach you how to play a chord. C chord. Just need to put three fingers in position."

Bobby placed his hand, thick and calloused, on Ophelia's little hand and maneuvered her fingers into the proper position.

"When you play this chord, you just want to strum on the top five strings. You can go down and then up and then down again."

Face scrunched in concentration, Ophelia played the chord. Soon her face relaxed, and her mouth curled into a smile.

"How do I sound?" she asked.

"Like a fucking badass," Bobby said. "I'm telling you. It won't be long before you're crushing it on stage. You on guitar. Some laid-back dude on bass. Bassists are always the coolest motherfuckers. And then some maniac on drums. Like Animal from the Muppets. You'll be all set. Playing songs. Smashing guitars. I can picture it now."

And Ophelia could picture it, too. She kept playing that C chord, and it sounded good. And in that moment, right then, she was happy. As happy as she could ever remember being.

For the next hour or so, before Vivian and Holt came home, Bobby and Ophelia just talked. He told her about his adventures in New York City, about the music scene, about some of the stars he'd played with. His band had opened for Elvis Costello and the Attractions, and he'd gotten to jam with Billy Idol and the Stray Cats.

"Oh my God," Ophelia said. "Billy Idol? Are you kidding me?"

"No, missy. I kid you not. He came into CBGB while we were performing a set. He jumped on stage, and we tossed him a guitar. Dude doesn't usually front, but he can play. And a hell of a nice guy too. You ever come to New York, you can meet him."

"You've got his phone number or something?"

Bobby smiled, and Ophelia noticed his canines, long and jagged. "Something like that."

And then Bobby wanted to hear about Ophelia, about her school, about her friends, about boys. And, so, Ophelia talked, and it felt good telling somebody about her world, somebody who wasn't judgmental, somebody who could help her laugh at the absurdity of it all.

"For the most part," she said, "my teachers are real losers. They don't teach me a thing—only to hate school. Ms. Colette, my art teacher, is okay, but the rest of them are kind of pathetic, you know? They think they're molding our brains or something. They're not."

Bobby said, "Yeah, what's that Springsteen line from his new album? *We learned more from a three-minute record than we ever learned in school.* Some truth to that."

"Totally. And as far as my friends are concerned—well, I don't have too many of them. I used to hang out with Emily and Rosie, but they're both very dramatic, and I don't have time for that."

"Dramatic? What do you mean by that?"

"Every time somebody says something to them or about them, no matter how unimportant, they freak the fuck out. Like if a boy said 'Excuse me,' in the hall, they'd be standing in front of their locker, fanning themselves, convinced that he was madly in love with one of them. Or if they saw a couple of girls whispering while making eye contact with them, they'd be ready to punch the bitches in the throats. You know what I'm saying?"

Bobby sort of chuckled. Ophelia liked the way he laughed. Her father had never laughed. Not even when he took her to see *Smokey and the Bandit* or *Animal House*.

"Yeah. I know exactly what you're saying. But that's just the way high school kids are. Believe it or not, it doesn't seem that long ago for me. I can relate to some of the things you're saying. We had different styles then—don't get me started on bell bottoms—but the problems were the same."

Ophelia sighed and pulled her hair behind her ear. "And then there's the boys."

"Uh-oh," Bobby said, grinning. "Here we go."

"What do you mean by that?"

"I mean that boys—at least when they're in high school—are goddamn idiots. Complete waste of space. Plants should go on strike to prevent them from getting the necessary oxygen."

"Well, they're not that bad."

"Sure they are. And I'll bet a half dozen at least have their hearts set on you."

"That's not true."

"No?"

"No. In fact, they don't like me at all."

"I don't believe it."

"It's true!"

"Just because you don't know about those who like you doesn't mean they don't like you."

Ophelia rolled her eyes. "Oh, please."

Bobby punched Ophelia on the shoulder playfully. "And do you like any of them?"

Ophelia paused, a sure tell, and she knew it. She hoped she wasn't blushing. "Maybe one."

"Okay. What's his name? Doug? Matt? Biff?"

"His name is Ryan."

"Ryan. That's a nice name. My drummer's name is Ryan, although he goes by Howitzer."

"Howitzer?"

"It's a long story. Not for innocent ears."

"I'm not so innocent."

"Tell me about Ryan. He on the football team or something?"

Ophelia shook her head no. "He's in theater."

"Theater? I thought that's where the geeks hung out. At least that's the way it was when I was in high school."

"It still is," she said. "He is a bit of a geek."

"Okay—"

"But he still doesn't know that I exist. I plan out my passing periods so that I can see him, maybe bump into him in the hallways. Once he smiled at me. Or at least I convinced myself he was smiling at me. He was probably smiling at another girl. He's so beautiful."

"I'll bet he is."

"I go to his plays. Lots of times he's the lead. He's got a deep voice. He's funny. I think you'd like him, Bobby."

Bobby removed his porkpie hat, pulled back his hair with his hand, and then placed the hat back on his head. "You've got to let him know you exist. Go talk to him. You don't have to tell him you love him or anything. Just tell him you saw his play. Tell him you thought he was really good. Boys like to be flattered. Trust me on that."

"I don't know," Ophelia said. "I'd be too scared. I'd get flustered, say something stupid."

"And guys like that, too. You can't go wrong."

There was a long pause. Ophelia looked at Bobby and then looked away. Then she looked back again.

"Does it get better?" she asked in a small voice.

"What? High school?"

"No. Not high school. Life."

Bobby placed his hand on hers. "Yes," he said. "It gets better. It gets much better."

CHAPTER 16

Originally, the plan had been for Bobby to stay a single night. He had the show in Denver on Saturday, and then he and the band were supposed to hit the road again. But the next day, after doses of begging from each member of the Davidson family (but mostly from Ophelia), he gave in and agreed to stay on for a few more days.

"Hell, I don't have anywhere I really have to be for a while," he said. "Got a gig in Portland in a couple of weeks. The boys can go ahead. I can always buy a cheap red-eye or something. Be good to spend some more time with my family. Something I haven't done enough of."

And so it was settled, and Vivian thought Ophelia would burst from excitement. Ophelia always talked about how much she hated her father, and, honestly, Vivian didn't do much to discourage that talk, but now she could tell that Ophelia missed having a man in the house. And not just any man. Uncle Bobby. While he was there, Vivian thought that Ophelia seemed a little less sorrowful, a little less moody, a little less lonely.

As for Vivian, she also liked having Bobby around—if for no other reason than he could spend some quality time with

Holt and, especially, Ophelia. Over the last year or so, it had become harder and harder for Vivian to connect with her daughter. Whenever she tried making conversation, it was like talking to a wall. Ophelia wouldn't tell her anything, not about school, not about friends. Certainly not about boys.

But Ophelia would listen to Bobby. His word was gospel, whether talking music or movies or books or style. In Ophelia's eyes, Bobby could do no wrong. Vivian decided not to pop her daughter's balloon and tell her about the other Bobby, the one who could be narcissistic and arrogant and cruel. Not that she wasn't tempted to. Sometimes she hated how Bobby seemed to revel in the adulation, seemed to encourage it with his wolfish smile. But she resisted.

A few days turned into one week. One week turned into two. Two weeks turned into three. The Portland gig, he said, had been called off.

And then he'd been there for a full month, and eventually Vivian's gratefulness for having Bobby in the house turned to annoyance. Whereas the last time he'd stayed he'd gone out of his way to help around the house, this time he seemed more content to have his sister do all the work. It was Vivian who did all the cooking, Vivian who did all the dishes, Vivian who did all the cleaning. Bobby, meanwhile, did all the laughing and had all the fun.

Maybe she was being petty, but one time she called him on it. After slaving over a dinner of meat loaf and carrots and potatoes and then sitting in silence as he told story after story after story, she began to get agitated. She went to the kitchen and began cleaning up everybody's dishes, and she could hear him telling the kids another wild and maybe fictional story, this one about when the drummer in his band ate bad sushi before a show and ended up vomiting all over the drum kit, midsong. The kids thought this was hilarious, especially Holt who laughed and laughed and asked for more details. And so she peeked her head back in the dining room.

"You've got a million great stories, Bobby. So damn entertaining. Too bad they don't help pay the mortgage or buy the groceries or clean up after you."

Bobby's eyes opened wide, and he looked at Holt and then Ophelia and then Vivian. Then he began to laugh. That was the thing about her brother. He never lost his cool, never lost his sense of humor, and that could be frustrating.

"Damn, Vivian!" he said. "You saying I'm a freeloader?"

"Kind of."

Bobby's grin faded away. Ophelia looked down at her feet and began chewing on her nails.

"Yeah, sis," Bobby recovered. "Come to think about it, you're probably right. Actually, I know that you're right. And I'm going to make it up to you. Now you sit your butt down, and I'll take care of the dishes. Make sure they're extra clean even. And after that, I'll fold the laundry."

Vivian sighed and placed her hands on her hips.

"No," she said. "I'm sorry. I just—"

He rose to his feet. "No, no. I'm glad you called me on it, sis. I've got to earn my keep with more than music and entertainment!"

In the intervening weeks, Vivian had almost forgotten completely about Ruben Ray. After all, ever since Mike had paid him a visit the month before and threatened to tear him a new asshole or three, Ruben had left her alone. When Vivian did think of Ruben Ray, it was always in terms of regret. Why the hell had she hooked up with a guy like that anyway? An ex-con? Someone who was so controlling, so dangerous? She'd read somewhere that guys like him would never stop being obsessive, they would just shift their obsession to a new subject. She was thankful that he was out of her life, thankful that he'd moved on to another victim. But she should have known better, that it wouldn't be so simple.

It started with the phone calls. At first, maybe every few days. When she'd pick up the receiver and say, "Hello?" there would be no answer, only the sound of soft breathing and stubble scratching on the receiver. "Who is this?" she'd say, and then the line would click dead.

It happened to the kids, as well. At first Vivian didn't think anything of it. Wrong number, she figured, or maybe it was one of Ophelia's classmates wanting to hear her voice, too timid to ask her out. But when the frequency increased—once a day, twice a day, three times—she began suspecting that the calls weren't so innocent. She considered changing her phone number but eventually decided against it. She wouldn't let that son of a bitch scare her. She was too tough for that.

But self-talk only goes so far. One evening, while she was in the kitchen boiling water for pasta, the phone rang. Somehow, just from the echo of the ring, she knew it was Ruben Ray. With that familiar sense of dread, she walked into the living room and picked up the receiver, placed it to her ear.

This time, she didn't say a word. She could hear breathing, and still she didn't speak. Finally, after ten or more seconds, there was a voice on the other end. It was him.

"Hi, Vivian," he said.

She remained quiet.

"Hi, Vivian," he said again.

No response.

"Okay. So that's the way it's going to be. Fine. Do you think you're better than me?"

She shook her head but didn't speak.

"You know what I'm going to do?" he said. "I'm going to make you learn about pain. You and your family."

Vivian squeezed her eyes shut, her lower lip trembling. But still she didn't make a sound.

"Don't believe me?" he said. "Stupid fucking bitch. Stupid fucking slut."

And then he hung up.

For a minute or more, Vivian remained where she was, the receiver still pressed to her ear. Then she placed it back on the cradle. She walked slowly to the kitchen and returned to the stove. She tore open a package of spaghetti and dumped it in the boiling water, and she could feel the tears welling in her eyes. She held them back for a minute, but that was the best she could do. Soon she was sobbing, and she worried that she'd never be able to stop.

Holt, sweet Holt, had been in his room playing with his Star Wars figures, and he must have heard his mother crying or, at the very least, sensed it. Now he stood in the doorway of the kitchen, gripping Darth Vader in one hand and Luke Skywalker in the other.

"Mommy?" he said. "Are you okay?"

She didn't turn around because she didn't want him to see the tears. She didn't want him to see that she was weak.

"Yes," she said in a voice barely louder than a whisper. "I'm okay."

The phone rang again, and Vivian jumped. Deep breath. One ring, two rings, three.

He wouldn't stop. He'd never stop.

"Should I get it?" Holt asked.

Four rings, five rings. Six.

"No," Vivian said. "Let it ring. I don't want to talk to him. Not anymore. Help me stir the sauce."

She handed Holt a wooden spoon, and he stood on a stool and stirred the pasta sauce, and still the phone rang and rang and rang.

Vivian kept the gun, the one that Mike Brandt had given her, beneath her mattress. It was a lousy place, she knew it was a lousy place, but she couldn't think of anywhere better, at least nowhere where she'd have quick access to it. She should have gotten a gun safe, maybe, but she didn't think she'd be holding on to the gun for that long, and it would have been a waste of money, especially on a teacher's salary. Besides, she was responsible enough to keep the bullets away from the gun. She kept them buried, beneath papers and jewelry and knickknacks in her nightstand drawer.

Growing up, she'd been the one who'd been comfortable around guns, not Bobby. They made him nervous. "Don't like death all that much," he would say. "Don't like guns." So when she was thirteen or fourteen and was outside target practicing with her Chipmunk .22, Bobby would usually remain in his room painting or singing or playing the guitar.

"What're you going to do if some maniac breaks into our house when Mom and Dad are gone?" Vivian had asked her older brother.

He had just grinned. "I'll be hiding behind you, sis. 'Cause I know you'll shoot the fucker dead."

Of course, nobody ever did break into their house when they were children, and Bobby never did have to hide behind his diminutive sister. But now as an adult, as a mother, Vivian found herself reaching beneath that mattress and pulling out that little pistol. She would lie on her bed, touch the cold metal to her cheek, and picture placing it against Ruben Ray's temple. Then, she would imagine squeezing the trigger, imagine the earsplitting explosion, imagine the blood, the skull, the brains.

Her thoughts were becoming more and more morbid, and somehow she knew that someday she would have to use that gun.

It was a Tuesday, a week after Ruben's phone call, and Vivian had parent-teacher conferences that night—hour after hour of trying to convince parents that their precious children weren't so precious. She didn't get home until after eight. Exhausted and longing for a wineglass full of vodka, she pulled into the driveway and turned off the engine. She looked up at her house and noticed that all of the lights were turned off, all except Ophelia's bedroom. A warm breeze was blowing, and she could smell the hog shit from the animal factories out east. She got out of her car and walked toward the front door, her shadow from the streetlight spreading across the neatly trimmed lawn. Her high heels echoed on the wooden porch.

She tried opening the door, but it was locked. She reached into her purse and fumbled for a minute until she found the key. Then she pushed open the door.

It took a moment until her eyes adjusted, and then she saw Holt. He was standing in the middle of the living room in the dark, wearing only his Superman Underoos. His little chest was heaving in and out, and in his right hand he gripped a kitchen knife, the blade glinting from the streetlights.

Vivian stood there for a moment, her mind trying to catch up to the moment. Somehow, she managed to remain calm.

"Holt?" she said. "What's happened? Why do you have that knife?"

He didn't answer; instead, he just stood there, rocking back and forth like some punching doll. Vivian moved toward him and tried removing the knife from his hand, but he was gripping it too tightly.

"Sweetie. It's okay. You need to let go of the knife. Mommy is here now."

Holt's eyes focused and met hers. His mouth opened, but no words came out. A few more moments of silence, and his grip loosened and the knife clattered to the ground. Vivian exhaled audibly and took her son by the hand and walked him to the couch. As they sat down, she noticed that his hands were trembling.

"Okay," she said. "It's okay."

He began to sob, his chest inflating and deflating in spasms.

"What happened, Holt? Talk to Mommy. Where's Ophelia? Where's Bobby?"

He didn't answer. Not right away. Just sobs and gasps. But eventually the tears stopped and he wiped his cheeks with the back of his hand. He pulled away from her grip and straightened his back.

"There was a man," he said, and each word was a strain.

"A man?"

"He was in the backyard. I saw him hiding in the garden. And then he was on the porch. And then I saw him in the window. He started pounding on the glass. I got scared. I hid. And then I got the knife. In case he attacked me. I'm sorry, Mommy."

She smiled and stroked his hair. She needed to remain calm. No matter what, she needed to remain calm.

"That's good, darling. You did the right thing. Now tell me. Who was this man? What did he look like?"

But she knew. She already knew. Holt began crying again, his sobs sounding like mournful wails.

"What did he look like?" she said again.

Holt turned to look at his mother, his lower lip trembling. "He . . . he looked like your friend."

"My friend?"

"The one you had for dinner."

Vivian felt a sharp pain in her side, as if somebody had jabbed her with a nail.

"Ruben," she said. "It was Ruben."

Holt nodded his head. "He was trying to get in the house. He scared me."

"But it's okay now," she said. "He's not going to hurt you. I think he just wanted to see Mommy. But Mommy wasn't home. I should have been home. I won't do that again. I'm sorry he scared you. He doesn't want to hurt you."

"Does he want to hurt you, Mommy?"

She laughed even though she could feel her eyes welling up with tears, even though she felt scared, like she was a child too.

"No, Holt. He doesn't want to hurt Mommy. He just wanted to talk to me. He thought that I would be home. He shouldn't have scared you. That was wrong."

"Do you have a knife, Mommy?"

"A knife?"

"In case he comes in the house."

She shook her head and forced a smiled. "No," she said. "I have something better. I have a gun."

She shouldn't have said it.

"A gun? You have a gun?"

"Yes. I borrowed one. I won't have to use it, I don't think. But I have it. Just in case."

"Are you going to kill him, Mommy? Are you going to kill your friend?"

Vivian's tears were coming. She wasn't going to be able to stop them. "No. I'm not going to kill my friend."

"That's good. I don't want you to go to jail."

Vivian smoothed down Holt's hair. "When he came, did you tell your sister? Did you tell your Uncle Bobby?"

He shook his head. "No."

"Why not?"

"Because they were busy."

"Busy? What do you mean busy?"

"They were in her room. Busy."

Vivian's terror transformed into something like fury. She thought of Holt, her sweet Holt, terrified by a ghost in the night while his big sister and his bigger uncle ignored him.

"They should have helped you," she said. "You wait here. I'm going to talk to them. I'm going to find out why they didn't help you."

She rose to her feet.

"No, Mommy. Don't leave me here. The man might come back."

"I just want to talk to Ophelia. I want to talk to Uncle Bobby."

And so she marched through the living room toward the hallway, toward Ophelia's room. Holt followed right behind her.

"Ophelia!" she called out as she walked. "Bobby!"

No answer. She stood in front of her daughter's door and could hear music playing, Led Zeppelin maybe. She pounded on the door once, twice, and then tried opening it. It was locked.

"Ophelia! Open the door."

"They told me to go away," Holt said. "They were busy."

"Open the goddamn door!"

The music turned off. From behind the door, Ophelia spoke. "Jesus, Mom. Wait a second, will you?"

The door opened. Ophelia stood there in shorts and a cut-off shirt. Uncle Bobby was sitting on a chair, porkpie hat resting on the back of his head, guitar in his lap.

"Welcome home, sis," he said.

"Why is your door locked?"

Ophelia rolled her eyes. "Because we wanted privacy. Bobby was teaching me chords, and Holt kept interrupting us."

Vivian shifted her glance from Ophelia to Bobby, and she wanted to scream. She didn't know why she was so angry.

"Really? That's why her door is locked? Because you're teaching her chords? Or are you teaching her how to smoke pot?"

Bobby laughed. "Oh, come on, Vivian. Just take it easy. I haven't smoked pot since I was in college. Not my thing."

Vivian slapped at the wall. She knew she looked ridiculous, but she was livid.

"In the meantime," she said, "while you guys were practicing chords, Holt was scared out of his mind."

"I'm sorry," Bobby said, "but—"

"In the meantime, Ruben Ray was skulking around the house."

"Ruben Ray?" Ophelia asked. "You mean your creepy boyfriend?"

"He's not my boyfriend. Not anymore."

From behind Vivian, Holt spoke. "He didn't want to hurt me, I don't think. He wants to hurt Mom. But don't worry. She's got a gun. Just in case."

Bobby removed his guitar from his lap and placed it on the floor next to him. He lifted his hat and pulled back his hair with his hand and then flashed a grin.

"Okay. Okay, let's all take a deep breath," he said. "I think everybody is a little emotional here."

Emotional. Damn right, Vivian was emotional.

"Oh, stop with the deep breathing, Bobby. You're supposed to be the adult here. I left you with two kids, and one of them spent the evening wandering through the house, all by himself, carrying a knife, worrying that my crazy ex would attack him."

"I never said I would be a babysitter."

"I didn't ask you to be a fucking babysitter!"

Bobby rose to his feet. He walked across the room, until he was standing directly in front of his sister.

"You want me to apologize? I apologize. I didn't know Holt was so scared. I thought he was just making stuff up. I was wrong."

Now he turned toward Holt.

"Listen to me, buddy. Don't worry about that creep, Ruben. Even if you did see him, he's a coward. He won't hurt you. I promise that. I'm sorry you were scared tonight. That won't happen again."

"Promise?" Holt said.

Bobby crossed his heart. "Absolutely."

And so Bobby had defused the situation. Vivian sighed deeply and nodded her head.

"Okay," she said. "Why don't we forget all about this? Why don't we all start winding down and get ready for bed?"

"That sounds good," Bobby said. "A good night's sleep will fix things."

That night, Vivian slept fitfully. She dreamed of Ruben, and in her dreams, he was standing on the sidewalk outside the house, his face obscured by the shadows. She stood at the window, watching him watching her, and the gun was in her hand, but she knew that she'd never use it, that she was a coward, and eventually he'd find a way inside, eventually he'd squeeze her soft neck until she breathed no more.

At two in the morning, she threw the covers off of her and stumbled to her feet. She went to the bathroom and peed without sitting on the cold toilet seat, and then she went into Holt's room to check on him. He looked so innocent and beautiful, and she wouldn't let Ruben hurt him, not ever.

She walked through the living room, where Bobby was sleeping on the couch and snoring loudly, into the kitchen. She turned on the light, opened the refrigerator, and pulled out the carton of milk. She poured a large glass and drank it quickly, some of the milk dribbling onto her chin. She wiped her face clean with the back of her hand and put the milk back in the refrigerator.

She yawned and then reached to turn out the lights. She glanced out the window at the darkness. And that's when she screamed.

Standing inches away from the glass was a man, his eyes bloodshot, his teeth bared. Ruben Ray.

CHAPTER 17

Hearing the scream, Bobby came rushing into the kitchen, wearing only his boxer shorts and an A-frame T-shirt.

"Vivian! What is it?"

With one hand, she pointed toward the window. Her other hand covered her mouth, as if she could manually prevent herself from screaming again.

"What?" Bobby asked. "Is somebody out there?"

Vivian's hand slid away from her mouth and rested at her throat. "It's him."

"Who? Ruben? The guy Holt was talking about?"

She nodded her head yes.

By this time, the kids had both staggered from their rooms, Holt's eyes wide with terror and Ophelia nervously biting her lower lip. Holt grabbed his mother's leg and began whimpering. Ophelia stood in the corner, not saying a word.

"It's the bad man," Holt said. "Isn't it?"

"Yes," Vivian said. "It's the bad man."

Bobby said, "Are you sure? Are you sure you saw him outside? I mean it's dark and—"

"Yes, Bobby. I'm sure."

Bobby pulled back his unruly hair with his hand. Then he turned toward Ophelia.

"Ophelia, I need you to pick up the phone and call 911. Tell them there's a man on our property. Tell them that it's your mom's old boyfriend."

"911? Wouldn't it make more sense to—"

"Do as I say. I'll go outside and find him."

"No," Vivian said. "Not you. I'll get my gun. I know how to use it. You don't."

"Don't be stupid," Bobby said. "That's a bad idea. You go out there with a gun and something bad is bound to happen."

But now it seemed to Vivian that Bobby was the one who was panicking, that she was the one who was calm. So while Ophelia called the cops ("Yes, I think it might be an emergency"), Vivian pushed past Bobby, walked into her bedroom, and knelt by her bed. With a quick whispered prayer, she reached under her mattress and located the little pistol, the one that Mike Brandt had given her. Then she opened up her nightstand drawer and removed a box of cartridges. With surprisingly steady hands, she loaded the pistol and then returned to the kitchen where Bobby, Ophelia, and Holt were huddled against the back wall.

"The police are on their way," Ophelia said.

"Did you ask for Lieutenant Brandt?" Vivian asked.

"No. I didn't think of that. Should I have?"

"It doesn't matter."

"Mommy?" Holt said. "Is he going to hurt you?"

"No, darling. He's not going to hurt me. He's not going to hurt anybody."

And with that Vivian walked out of the kitchen and toward the front door.

Ruben was somewhere in the darkness. For several long moments, she stood there on the porch, courage dwindling. She glanced up and down the street for a sign of Ruben's truck but didn't see anything. Doubt started creeping in. Maybe she hadn't really seen Ruben. Maybe, after Holt's stories, it had just been her imagination. A trick of the brain.

But, no. He'd been out there. He had scared Holt. He had scared her. She raised the pistol in the air.

"You out there, Ruben? I know you are. You best get off of my property. You hear me? The cops are on their way."

There was no response, only the sound of the wind rustling the branches. Then, a few moments later, the distant sound of sirens. Vivian walked down the porch stairs and onto her lawn. Leaves crunched beneath her feet.

"You out there, Ruben?" she said again, but this time her voice was softer and more timid.

She knew it was stupid to be out here, just like Bobby had said. She knew she should just wait for the police to arrive. Nothing good could come from this. And yet she felt the urge to confront him, as a way to confront her fears. Too often she had played the victim, let herself be subjugated by abusive men. Her ex-husband. Fred Tapioca. Ruben.

Those days were gone. She didn't have time for fear. Not anymore.

She walked deliberately around the perimeter of the house, stepping over some of Holt's toy guns and stuffed animals, and a bed of weeds where flowers had once grown. In the backyard, the metal swing set was trembling in the breeze. She stopped and looked around. The sirens were getting louder. Ruben was gone. She would go back inside and wait for the police like she should have from the beginning.

But she was just turning around to walk toward the house when she was sure she saw a movement behind the old poplar tree.

Was it Ruben? She froze. And now she raised her gun.

For a long time, she stared at the tree, waiting for the figure to reemerge. The moon slipped behind the clouds and everything was dark. She didn't move. After a while, she noticed that she'd stopped breathing and forced herself to exhale.

"I know you're there," she said in a voice so quiet that he probably wouldn't have heard it even if he was standing next to her. "Stay away from my family. You hear?"

But there was no answer and no movement.

By now all of her courage had disappeared, so she made her way back to the front yard, up the stairs, and into the house where Bobby, Ophelia, and Holt were all huddled on the couch, waiting.

"So?" Bobby asked.

Vivian shook her head. "I didn't see him. He must have already gone."

A few minutes later, Vivian could see the red and blue flashing of police lights through the curtains. There was the sound of slamming doors and footsteps on the pavement. And then there was a knock at the door.

Vivian opened the door, behind which stood two police officers, one tall and thin with a wispy mustache, the other stockier, black hair slicked straight back.

"Evening, ma'am," the thin cop said. "We received a call about an intruder. Are you Ophelia Davidson?"

Vivian nodded toward her daughter. "That's her right there. She's the one who called."

"Did the intruder enter the house?"

"No. He was outside. On our property. Staring in windows. He scared my son. And then he scared me. Lieutenant Brandt knows about him. Maybe if we call him—"

"Lieutenant Brandt is on another call. The intruder. Do you know him?"

"I do. He's my ex-boyfriend."

Voices crackled from a two-way radio. The thin officer nodded at his partner.

"We'll take a look around the property. Do you have any dogs outside?"

"We don't."

The officers walked around the property, just like Vivian had done, and just like Vivian they returned shaking their heads.

"Didn't see anybody," said the thin officer. "Maybe the sirens scared him off. Anyway, we can sit patrol for a while, if it'll make you feel better."

But Vivian only shook her head. "No. He was just trying to scare us. I guess he succeeded."

There really wasn't much else the police officers could do, they explained. They weren't going to arrest him, not for skulking around her property. She could always try to get a restraining order placed against him.

"Sometimes that works," said the officer with slicked-back hair. "But other times it just pisses them off more."

And that was that. The police officers left. It was nearly three in the morning, and Holt was all wound up. He asked if he could sleep with his mommy.

"Just for tonight. Please?"

Vivian was too exhausted to fight him. And besides, it would feel good to have somebody close, even if that somebody was even more vulnerable than she was.

But Holt wasn't the only one who was anxious.

"What about me?" Ophelia said. "I don't want to be alone. He could come back. He's crazy."

"He's not going to come back," Vivian said. "Not tonight."

"How do you know, Mom? You don't know that."

"I just don't think that—"

"I'll stay with Ophelia," Bobby said. "Sleep on the floor."

Vivian rubbed her eyes and nodded her head. "Fine. I'll get you the sleeping bag."

And so nobody would be alone. Not tonight.

CHAPTER 18

During the days that followed, there were no more strange phone calls, no more unwanted appearances at the house. Nobody spoke about Ruben Ray, and that was probably for the best.

Meanwhile, Vivian didn't say a word to Bobby about what she was feeling about him. Truth be told, she thought that he had acted like a goddamn coward staying inside, protected by walls and windows, while she had gritted her teeth and gone into the dark of night all alone to confront her tormentor. Sure, he had made a halfhearted plea to assist, but a real man wouldn't have asked. A real man would have taken action. A real man would have tried protecting her.

And come to think of it, Bobby had *never* protected her, not really. Not now, not ever. Like when she'd been fourteen—younger than Ophelia!—and the boys in her school started spreading rumors that she had done it with Erik Schmidt and all of his friends. "Five guys at once!" they'd said. It had been the worst day of her life up until that point. She'd never even kissed a boy. She didn't dare tell her parents about the rumor, but she did tell her Bobby. Instead of being furious, instead of finding the boys who had started the rumor and beating the shit out them, Bobby simply asked Vivian if she had really done the things they said. If she had fucked five boys at once?! Even when she denied it, he didn't believe her. He told her that if she didn't want people talking about her that way, she needed to stop acting like a slut.

No, Bobby had never protected her.

Maybe it was because Bobby sensed Vivian's resentment building that he soon announced he was leaving town.

They were sitting at the dinner table, the silence between them magnified by the sounds of forks and knives scraping on the plates, when Uncle Bobby cleared his throat and spoke.

"Listen up, folks. I want to let you guys know that I've appreciated the hospitality, but I'm going to be moving on."

"Moving on?" Vivian said, doing her best to sound disappointed, but secretly relieved.

Bobby stuck a piece of steak in his mouth and chewed for a few moments before nodding his head. "I've been in your space for long enough. It's not fair to any of you."

"We'll be sorry to see you go," Vivian said.

Bobby nodded his head and smiled. "Maybe the kids will be," he said.

She dabbed at the corner of her mouth with her napkin. "I'll be sorry, too."

"Anyway. The boys lined up a few shows in the Berkeley area. So that's where I'll be heading. Got a plane ticket already. Red-eye leaving tomorrow night."

Holt said, "We'll miss you so much, Uncle Bobby," but Ophelia didn't say a word. She pushed her plate away and sat there staring straight ahead. Vivian could tell she was upset.

"I'll make sure I come back soon," he said. "Whenever there's another break from touring. Or whenever I've got a show lined up in Denver."

"You're welcome anytime, Bobby. You know that."

He nodded at Ophelia. "Maybe your mom will let you come and visit me one of these years. Once I get back to New York, I mean. I'll show you around. Take you to CBGB or the Bottom Line. You'd love it. Just keep practicing that guitar and one day you'll play there."

Ophelia looked up at him with her big brown eyes and then shook her head mournfully. She dropped her silverware on the plate and rose to her feet. Then she rushed away from the table and toward her room, and the whole way down the hallway she was crying.

She slammed her door shut, and for a few moments Vivian and Bobby looked at each other. Bobby cut off another piece of meat and stuck it into his mouth.

"I guess she wants me to stay," he said. "She'll forget about me by Friday."

"You should talk to her," Vivian said. "And, trust me, she won't forget about you. She didn't forget about you all those years you were gone. She certainly won't forget about you now."

"Yeah, maybe not. I'll talk to her. But first, I want to eat dessert."

"Of course you do," Vivian said.

A few minutes later, Holt helped his mother clear the table and load the dishwasher. Vivian brought out a plateful of brownies.

"Could use some coffee, too," Bobby said. "As long as it isn't too much trouble."

Tomorrow he'll be gone, Vivian told herself.

"No trouble at all."

She went to the kitchen to brew a pot of coffee. From the

kitchen, she could hear Bobby talking to Holt, trying to give him bits of uncle wisdom.

"You're the man of the house," he said. "Don't forget that. Women are emotional. You know what that means?"

"Sure," Holt said. "It means they cry at movies."

"It does. But not only that. They feel scared more than we do. Hard to believe, huh? You need to make sure you're brave. Protect your mother. Protect your sister."

"From Ruben?"

"From whoever!"

And as Vivian watched the coffee percolate, she grinned bitterly at Bobby's hypocrisy.

Vivian returned to the table with a cup of coffee for her and Bobby. They sipped the coffee and ate the brownies in silence, while Holt talked about Star Wars and Star Wars and Star Wars. After Holt had finished not one, not two, but three brownies, he left the table, and it was just Vivian and Bobby.

The two of them sat at the table, and neither of them said a word. Finally, after finishing his second cup of coffee, Bobby spoke.

"I wasn't always the best brother," he said. "Wasn't always the best anything."

"Leave it alone," Vivian said.

"She reminds me of you," Bobby said. "When you were her age."

"Who, Ophelia?"

"Yeah. She's got a big personality. Got a big soul. Just like you."

"She's lost," Vivian said. "Just like I was."

"Maybe a little bit. But she'll find her way. I know she will. You shouldn't worry about her. At least not so much."

Vivian picked at her brownie. "How come you never married, Bobby? How come you never settled down?"

Bobby laughed. "Why do you think?"

"I think you use music as an excuse. So you can keep running. I think you're afraid of being in one place."

"That's exactly what my shrink said."

"I'm being serious, Bobby."

"So am I. You should have been a psychologist. Listen, it sounds cliché, but music is my mistress. Maybe down the road, that will change. Maybe one day I'll find that woman that changes everything. But I doubt it. There are not too many girls like you, Vivian. Otherwise, maybe I would have settled down years ago."

"I'm no prize," Vivian mumbled.

"Listen. I told you before that you shouldn't worry about Ophelia, that she'll figure things out. But I can't help worrying about you. Can't help worrying that Ruben will come back and do you harm."

"You don't have to worry about me."

"I know I don't have to. But I do."

"I've got the gun."

"We both know you won't use it."

Vivian took a final gulp of coffee, and now it was her turn to smile.

"Yeah, but Ruben doesn't know that."

Later that night, Bobby finally went into Ophelia's room, trying his best to comfort her. Vivian pretended to go into her own bedroom, but instead she remained in the hallway and listened to their conversation.

Most of it was muffled, but at some point, she heard Ophelia saying, "You're just like my daddy, leaving me when I need you most."

And Bobby saying, "I'll be back. You can count on that. I'm not abandoning you. No way, no how."

"I guess I don't mean that much to you."

"Don't get overdramatic. You know I feel strongly about you. But I'm a hassle for your mama. I don't belong here. Not in this house. I'll figure out a way for you to come visit me."

"Promise?"

"Needle in my eye. And all the rest of that torture."

After that, there was a lot of crying. Bobby tried getting her to stop, but it was no use.

The next night, Bobby was gone. Vivian offered to give him a ride to the airport, but he turned down the offer.

"I've put you out enough," he said.

Instead, he called a taxi. The four of them sat in the living room, luggage and guitar case stacked by the door, waiting for his ride to show up. Ophelia didn't say much of anything. She didn't cry, and Vivian wondered if maybe she'd gotten it all out of her system the night before. When the yellow taxi pulled up in front of the house, Bobby sighed loudly and rose to his feet.

"I guess this is it for a while then," he said.

"You take good care of yourself," Vivian said.

"Bye, Uncle Bobby," Holt said. "I hope you get famous."

But Ophelia wouldn't speak to him. And when he tried hugging her goodbye, she shifted her body so that he was awkwardly hugging her sideways.

Bobby left the house and got into the taxi. Holt pressed his face against the glass and watched the taxi pull away from the curb, then watched as the taillights got smaller and smaller and then disappeared into the darkness.

CHAPTER 19

The day after Bobby left, Holt went missing.

It was a Sunday, and Vivian had decided that the family would skip church again that week. They'd stopped going while Bobby was in town, and she figured that God would understand if they missed one more week. Instead, they had stayed around the house, Ophelia locked in her room, moody as always, Holt playing with his Star Wars figures, and Vivian sitting in her room, reading a crime novel.

Vivian didn't notice that Holt was gone until she was preparing lunch. She called out his name, and when he didn't respond she began walking around the house, calling out his name over and over again. Nothing. She checked the front yard and then the backyard. He wasn't there, either.

She pounded on Ophelia's door. "Have you seen Holt?"

"No!" Ophelia shouted back.

Maybe, Vivian thought, Holt was playing hide-and-go-seek. She opened all the closets, all the pantries, all the places a five-year-old boy might be able to squeeze. He was nowhere to be found. Naturally, she went into a panic, her mind going to those same dark places that they'd been going over the past several weeks.

She rushed back outside, looking in every direction. She spotted one of their neighbors, Walt Handley, in his yard raking leaves, and she asked him if he'd seen Holt. He nodded and pointed toward Martin Street.

"Saw him about ten minutes ago. He went that way. Looked like he was on a mission."

Vivian didn't thank him. Instead, she began running. She ran and she ran and then, after about five minutes, she spotted little Holt a few blocks ahead.

She laughed in relief. A few more minutes and she caught up to him. He was wearing blue jeans and an *Empire Strikes Back* T-shirt, which was on backward. An oversized duffel bag was dangling from his shoulder. She grabbed his arm.

"Holt! You scared me. I didn't know where you went. Where are you going without telling me?"

Holt gazed at his mother with wide eyes. "I didn't want you to worry. I'm going to find the bad guy."

"The bad guy? You mean Ruben?"

"Yes. I brought a knife. And a gun that I made out of pipes. Just in case."

Vivian pulled him close and hugged him.

"Oh, Holt. You don't need to do that. You don't need to find the bad guy. He's not going to hurt you or Ophelia or Mommy. I promise."

"Uncle Bobby told me to protect you. So that's what I'm doing. I can do it. I can save you, Mommy."

Vivian stared at him for a long moment and then wiped away a single tear from her cheek.

"Do you know how much I love you?" Vivian said. "Do you have any idea?"

"Yes, Mommy. I know."

"Let's go home. You can be a superhero another day."

"I'm not a superhero like Superman."

"Maybe not like Superman. But you are a hero."

And together they walked home.

Over the next several weeks, Ophelia seemed to spiral. Vivian had seen Ophelia go into depressions before, but not like this. In the past when Ophelia had suffered disappointments—fights with friends, failed tests—she would simply go into her room, shut the door, and listen to music or draw pictures or write poems. In a couple of hours, sometimes a couple of days, the blackened clouds would always give way to a glimpse of sunshine.

But this time was different. It became difficult for Ophelia to get her up in the morning. It got to the point where Vivian nearly had to drag her from bed. Then Ophelia would stand in the shower for twenty, thirty minutes, while Vivian pounded on the door. No breakfast, no conversation, and when she got home from school—often an hour or two past her normal arrival time—her eyes were often swollen and glassy from what must have been recent tears. At dinner, too, she barely said a word, barely ate a bite. And on the rare occasions when she did eat, she would gorge herself and then quickly disappear to the bathroom, where Vivian could hear her retching.

Vivian knew about eating disorders, knew about bulimia, had seen more than one after-school special on the subject, but she hesitated to confront her daughter. She didn't know what, exactly, to say. When Ophelia would finally open the bathroom door, wiping her mouth with her sleeve, Vivian would only ask if she was feeling all right. Ophelia would merely shake her head in disgust and then march to her room and slam her door shut. When Vivian would stand outside her door, hands folded across her chest, she didn't hear Ophelia's music like she used to. Now, she only heard Ophelia's pathetic sobbing.

Holt, sweet Holt, sensed his sister's misery and often tried to comfort her by going to the store and buying her candy, or by offering to let her eat his ice cream, or by hugging her at the waist, but even his best efforts couldn't cheer her up.

"I appreciate you trying," she would say. "I really do. But I'm just too sad, little brother. The world is being mean."

Vivian tried not to panic, but she couldn't help but worry. She'd had an aunt, Esther, who'd lived in Des Moines and had suffered from depression and had eaten half a bottle of psychotropic pills in the bathtub. In the dark of the night, when Vivian lay awake in bed, she couldn't help but wonder if Ophelia had been infected with that same familial lunacy, if she might come home one day and find her own daughter dead by rope or blade or water.

Her friend, Joyce, tried comforting her over sips of whiskey in Joyce's kitchen and back porch.

"You're being overdramatic," Joyce told her. "I'm not saying things are easy for her right now, not after the mess with Ruben and Uncle Bobby leaving. But that's just the way teenage girls are. Moody as hell. One week they're talking about their latest love interest or the top they want to buy and you can't get them to shut up, and the next week their whole world has gone to shit when that boy won't return their calls or another girl says that their shirt makes them look fat. She'll be okay, Vivian. Just take a deep breath. And maybe another shot of whiskey."

"You and whiskey," Vivian said. "I'll bet you think it's a cure for cancer."

"Might be. Certainly a cure for the mother-of-a-teenage-girl blues."

Vivian laughed, and that felt good. Then she had that shot

of bourbon and that felt even better. Joyce grabbed the bottle of Jim Beam and poured Vivian another drink.

"Ophelia's a smart girl, a kind girl," Joyce insisted. "It'll take her a while, but she'll figure things out. Hell, when I was her age I was doing plenty of unfortunate things, most of them in the back seat of my father's Chevy."

"Believe me, I don't expect her to be perfect. I know she'll make mistakes. But to see her so sad, and to hear her vomiting. It's just hard, that's all."

"I know it is, sweetie. I know it is. Drink your whiskey."

Vivian touched her glass but didn't drink it.

"Maybe I should have convinced Bobby to stay. I mean, ever since her father left, she hasn't had that male presence. Neither has Holt. I think it was good for both of them to have Bobby around. Especially for Ophelia. Maybe things would have been better if he could have just stayed for a couple more weeks."

"I don't think so," Joyce said. "You told me yourself—he's immature. Self-centered."

"Yes. But Ophelia connected with him so deeply. Over music. Over books. Even over teenager drama. I hate to admit this, but he seemed to understand her better than I do."

Joyce finished her own drink and then, sensing that Vivian's lips were already whiskey-numbed, downed hers as well. She touched her friend's hand.

"You're just not giving yourself enough credit. It's fucking hard being a mother. Especially of a teenage girl. You want to know the truth? That's why I never wanted to have children. Too damn hard."

"I don't believe that."

"Well, it's true. That, and Mike's low sperm count." Joyce laughed. "Anyway. It's going to be fine. You just keep doing what you've been doing. Things are bound to change."

Vivian grabbed the bottle of whiskey. Maybe she would have just one more drink.

"You ever put a frog in a pot of water?" Vivian asked.

Joyce raised one of her eyebrows. "A frog? No. No, I can't say that I have."

Vivian stared at her own hands, scratched at the skin where her wedding ring used to be. Then she looked back up at Joyce.

"I read once that if you put a frog in water and then slowly raise the temperature, the frog will never jump. Its nervous system can't detect slight changes in temperature. Eventually, the water boils. Eventually, the frog dies."

"Well, that's fucking depressing."

"Yeah. Maybe I'm the same way. Maybe I need to jump from time to time."

A few nights later, as the snow whipped around outside, Vivian and Holt played Jenga on the wooden floor in front of a fire. It had been a long time since Vivian had stuck logs in that old fireplace, maybe not since her ex-husband ran off on her, but even though it took her a good thirty minutes to get it started, she was glad she did. The fire made the house feel like home, and that did her heart good. Holt's laughter also did her heart good, and there was a lot of it tonight. They played three, four games, and Holt won each time.

"My hands just shake too much!" Vivian said. "I get too nervous."

"Not me," Holt said. "I'm as cool as a cucumber."

The thing that was wonderful about playing games with Holt was that he wasn't particularly competitive. He just liked being with his mother. And that had especially been true over the past several weeks, what with the way Ophelia had been acting.

As she became more and more depressed, Ophelia had pushed Holt away, and so it seemed that Holt was clinging tighter and tighter to his mother.

Another Jenga tower collapsed. "Hey, Mommy, do you think we can have some hot chocolate? Since it's snowing? And that's special?"

Vivian smiled and pulled her son to her lap. "Hot chocolate? I didn't know you liked hot chocolate. I thought you preferred black tea. You know, the really bitter kind?"

"What are you talking about? I love hot chocolate!"

"Oh, I didn't know that. But what about marshmallows? You don't want any marshmallows in your hot chocolate, do you?"

"Of course I do!"

"Really? Are you sure you don't want Brussels sprouts instead?"

Holt crinkled his nose. "You're just kidding me, Mommy."

"I am. Yes, I'll make you hot chocolate with marshmallows inside. On only one condition."

"What?"

"That I can have a sip."

"You can have a sip."

Vivian squeezed her son tightly and kissed the top of his head. She thought it was scary to love somebody so much, scary to be so terrified of ever losing him.

Vivian was just about to rise to her feet, just about to head to the kitchen to make that hot chocolate, when Ophelia came storming out of her room. She wore an oversized sweatshirt, the same one she'd been wearing nearly every day the last few weeks. Her hair was a matted mess, her lower lip was quivering, and her eyes were bloodshot. She stood in front of her mother and her brother, and when she spoke, her voice was panicked.

"I need to talk to Uncle Bobby," she said. "I need to talk to him now."

Holt sensed his sister's desperation and pulled away from his mother's grasp. He managed to get to his feet and then stumbled out of the room.

"I need to talk to him now!" Ophelia repeated.

Vivian remained seated, the back of her hand accidentally swiping at the wooden Jenga blocks and causing them to clatter to the ground. She nodded her head slowly, her own anxiety rising.

"Okay, Ophelia. Just take it easy, sweetheart. Why do you need to talk to Bobby? What's this all about?"

Ophelia looked like a lunatic, the way her eyes darted back and forth in her skull, the way she scratched at an invisible rash, the way her voice cracked in panic.

"I'm not going to tell you what it's about. It's between me and him. Do you have his number?"

Vivian eyed her daughter, uncertainly. Then she shook her head.

"No. I don't have his number. He's not back in New York yet. You know that. He's on the road somewhere."

"Can't we find out the hotel he's staying at?"

"Darling, I don't even know what state he's in. California, maybe? Texas?"

And now Ophelia's legs gave way and she collapsed to the ground like some marionette doll. She was in bad shape, that much was clear. She hung her head and then the tears came, and they came hard. Vivian tried smoothing her daughter's hair to comfort her, but Ophelia slapped away her hand.

"He shouldn't have left me," Ophelia said, and there was anger in her voice.

"He didn't leave you. He needs to play concerts to make money. Otherwise, he would have stayed."

"We need to find out where he is. Somehow."

"You need to tell me what's happening here," Vivian said.

"You need to tell me why you need to speak to him. What happened? Why can't you talk to me?"

Ophelia startled Vivian with a cruel laugh. "I can't tell you because you wouldn't understand."

"Why don't you try me? I might understand. I'm your mother."

"Motherfucker is what you are."

Vivian didn't think. She slapped Ophelia, hard. "You don't say that to me."

"Can't take a joke, huh?"

"You don't say that to me," she said again.

It seemed to take a great effort, but Ophelia pushed herself up to her knees and then got to her feet. She towered over her mother and, for a second, Vivian feared she would kick her in the throat. But no, she just stood there, eyes on fire.

"I'm going to go live with Uncle Bobby, just so you know. Just as soon as I find out where he is, I'll be gone. You'll never see me again."

Vivian clenched her jaw and grimaced. She didn't want to say words she'd regret. Didn't want to, but she did.

"You might want to go live with Bobby, but Bobby wouldn't want to live with you. You're too emotional. Too cruel."

Ophelia's mouth opened as if she were going to respond, but she didn't. Instead she just stood there for a moment, looking down at her mother, and then she turned and walked back toward her room. She slammed the door hard.

At that very moment, little Holt appeared from his room, first just his eyes peeking out, then his whole body. His head was down and his face was devastated.

"Why is Ophelia so sad?" he said.

Vivian could only shake her head. "I don't know, Holt. I wish I knew."

Holt returned to the hearth and began picking up the pieces of the game. And as he did so, Vivian couldn't help herself. One tear leaked from her eye, and then another one. Soon the floodgates were opened, and there was nothing she could do. All the hurt and pain and sadness that had been building up over the past few months was too much for her. She had always tried to be strong—for Holt, for Ophelia—but now she felt so weak.

"Don't cry, Mommy," Holt said. "Everything's going to be okay."

Holt stroked her hair, just like she'd done for him many, many times, but all that happened was Vivian felt sadder and cried harder. She knew everything wouldn't be okay. Knew it from the bottom of her heart.

And now Ophelia appeared again, and she had her purple JanSport backpack on her back.

"I'm going," she said. "I don't want to be in the house tonight."

"Don't you leave," Vivian said, but her words sounded more desperate than authoritative.

"Goodbye, Mom. Goodbye, Holt."

Goodbye.

Vivian didn't say anything else. She watched as her daughter walked across the living room, watched as she walked out the door.

"Is she going to come back?" Holt said.

"Yes. She'll be back."

But Holt jumped to his feet and ran after his sister. "Ophelia!" he shouted. "Ophelia, come back!"

And then he, too, was outside, the door slamming shut behind him, and Vivian was all by herself. For a long time, she gazed at the fire until the flames were gone and there were only fallen embers and blackened wood.

CHAPTER 20

When Holt came home, he was by himself, and he was in tears.

"She made me come home," Holt said. "She said I was too young to be with her. Will I ever see her again? Is she gone forever?"

Vivian forced a laugh. "Don't be silly, she's just a little sad right now. A little angry. She needs some space. She'll be home soon, don't you worry."

Vivian tried calling the parents of Ophelia's friends, hoping she might have gone to one of their houses. Not that Ophelia had many friends. There was Emily. There was Rosie. But nobody had heard a thing from Ophelia. Vivian did her best to rationalize the situation, telling herself that teenage girls ran away from home all the time and that she'd be back before midnight and, if not, certainly by the following morning. But when she didn't come home that night, when she didn't come home the following morning, Vivian could no longer rationalize.

It was a Saturday, so she dropped Holt off at his friend Graham's house for a sleepover because she didn't want him to panic too. She thought about calling Joyce, but she was too embarrassed. The last thing she needed was for Joyce to tell Mike and then for him to file a missing person's report or something. No, she'd wait it out.

For most of the afternoon, Vivian stayed around the house. She tried watching TV and reading magazines, but every time she heard a car engine or a voice outside, her heartbeat would quicken and she would rush to the window, hoping Ophelia had finally come home. Each time she pressed her face against the glass and saw that it was just the neighbors coming home or the postman delivering mail or children playing ball, she felt a torturous disappointment. On a few occasions when she couldn't handle it anymore, she got in her car and drove, hoping she might see Ophelia wandering somewhere. But she never did.

At five o'clock, Vivian made herself a Salisbury steak TV dinner and drank a few Bartles & Jaymes wine coolers. Before she knew it, she was crying and moaning and then praying to a God she wasn't sure even existed. She slid from the couch and sat on the floor, and that only made matters worse. She was a pathetic old hag, and she'd never find love, and her daughter hated her, and—

And then she heard footsteps on the front porch, and the screen door creaking open.

She rose to her feet, feeling an intense jolt of joy. In those few seconds between when she first heard the footsteps and then saw her daughter, she made a multitude of promises: from now on she would go easy on her daughter; from now on, she would savor each moment spent with her, knowing that life was short and could be ripped away at any moment; from now on, she would be happy and thankful. She made all those promises, but they became meaningless as soon as Ophelia walked through the door, as soon as Vivian saw her torn clothes and bloody scalp and swollen temple. As soon as she saw her shivering and sobbing. In that instant, she knew that each of their lives had been irrevocably damaged.

"Ophelia. My God. Ophelia. What happened?"

But Ophelia only shook her head and used her hands to cover her devastated expression.

"Please," Vivian said. "Talk to me. Did somebody hurt you?"

And now Ophelia gasped and fell to her hands and knees. Another moment and she was lying on the hardwood floor, curled up in the fetal position, sobbing. She was bloody, and Vivian didn't know what to do. She never knew what to do. She got down on her knees next to her daughter, tried stroking her hair.

"Who did this to you?" she said, even though she already knew the answer to her question. "Who did this to you?"

"I'm so sorry," Ophelia said.

"Who did this to you?" and now Vivian was shouting.

"I don't want to, I'm scared that he'll—"

Vivian placed her face inches from her daughter's. "Was it Ruben Ray? Was that who it was? Did he hurt you?"

Ophelia nodded a single time.

Vivian felt a sharp pain in her gut, as if somebody had stabbed her with a paring knife. She tried speaking again, but the words wouldn't come out. Her vocal cords had tightened to the point of paralysis.

"I—I went to Mineral Lake," Ophelia said. "And he was there. Ruben Ray was there."

As her daughter spoke, Vivian had a hard time focusing on the words. She was consumed with guilt and regret. She should have known that Ruben would come after Ophelia. She should have protected her daughter. But she didn't, and now look at what he'd done.

Ophelia's voice was trembling. "He said that he'd been waiting for me. He said that it wouldn't do any good to scream, that nobody would hear me."

She should have protected her.

"I did scream, I did. But he was right. It didn't do no good."

Should have . . .

"The next thing I knew he was on me. I tried pushing him off, but he was too strong."

. . . protected her.

"I could feel his hands on my skin. He yanked down my pants. He yanked down my underwear."

Vivian pulled her daughter toward her. She wanted to comfort her. She wanted to tell her that everything would be okay. She wanted to tell her that the sun would shine again in the morning. But her own voice had vanished.

"I closed my eyes, Mom. It hurt so much. It hurt more than anything in the world. But I didn't cry. Not one time."

Why couldn't Vivian speak?

"Are you proud of me for that? He couldn't get me to cry."

What was wrong with her?

"And then he was finished, and he rose to his feet, and he towered over me. And he said, 'You're a whore. Just like your momma. Just like all of them.' He zipped up his pants. Then he turned and walked away. And it was like he was taking a stroll on the beach. Slowly. Enjoying every minute."

Finally, Vivian managed to speak, but only a single word.

"Ophelia." Her daughter's name. She could say that much.

"He raped me, Mother. He raped me."

"Shh," Vivian said. "Shh."

"I tried to run. It wasn't my fault. Mother, you've got to believe me. It wasn't my fault."

Vivian kissed her daughter's forehead. Her throat had loosened. "I know it wasn't your fault, Ophelia. I know that."

"He's a bad man. I told you he's a bad man. Why didn't you listen to me? Why the fuck didn't you listen to me?"

"I . . . I—"

"He raped me. Don't you understand?"

Vivian nodded her head. Yes, she understood. Ophelia was becoming hysterical. Her eyes were wild. Her hands were swinging around.

"What are we going to do, Mom? What are we going to do now?"

"We should call the police," Vivian said, but she said it so meekly that Ophelia didn't hear her.

"What did you say?"

"I said we should call the police. You need to tell them what happened. About what Ruben did to you. About how he raped you."

Ophelia's expression turned to terror. She shook her head. "No," she said. "Please. You can't do that."

"We need to, darling. They will arrest him. They will put him in jail."

"No, they won't!" And now it was Ophelia's turn to shout. "They'll make me testify in court. They'll make me face him. They'll make me talk about his hands. They'll make me talk about his breath. They'll make me talk about his cock. And then they'll let him loose. They always let him loose."

"Now, darling, that's not true. As long as you are telling the truth then—"

"I am telling the truth!"

"Yes, and so, that's why—"

"No police! Do you hear me? No police. Don't tell anybody. Please, Mother. Please. Promise me that. Don't tell anybody."

Vivian squeezed her eyes shut and then opened them. The room seemed to be spinning, and she felt like she would be sick. She should have protected her. But what now? What would she do now?

"I won't tell anybody," Vivian said. "I promise."

Ophelia looked at her mom, and in her eyes were gratitude, a gratitude that Vivian had never seen before.

“Thank you, Mom,” she said. “Thank you.”

Vivian nodded. She wiped away her daughter’s tears with her thumb, just like she’d done when Ophelia was a baby.

Remember those days? Remember when she was a baby? Snuggling her head against her chest? And when Vivian would put her down, when she’d place her in her crib, how her daughter would cry! Vivian would walk out of the room, let her cry it out because that’s what she’d been told she should do, but Vivian never lasted very long. A minute, sometimes less, and then she’d come back in the room and take the baby out of the crib. Vivian had loved her so much then. It was impossible to love somebody as much as she had loved Ophelia.

And wasn’t she still that baby? Somehow?

“Come on,” Vivian said. “Let’s get you in the shower. I’m going to take care of everything, darling. I promise you that I will.”

But Ophelia was adamant. She didn’t want to take a shower, didn’t want to be by herself.

“Even if I sit in the bathroom with you?” Vivian asked. “Even if I talk the whole time? Or sing you lullabies from when you were a baby?”

Ophelia shook her head. “No. No shower.”

“How about a bath? That way you can see me. That way we can talk.”

Ophelia thought things over for a few moments.

“Okay,” she said. “A bath.”

And so they went into the bathroom, holding hands, and Ophelia sat on the closed toilet while her mother started the water in the tub, checking the temperature with the back of her hand. Ophelia leaned forward and rested her chin in the palms of her hands, her expression despondent and defeated.

Vivian thought about how one person had taken everything away from her daughter, from her baby, and how it was possible that he might not ever be punished. How fair was that? How fucking fair was that? Then her thoughts shifted from Ruben to her ex-husband. She remembered the way he used to belittle her, calling her simple and stupid and fat. The way he used to make her feel worthless and disgusting. And how on that Christmas Eve—she was pregnant with Holt at the time—he'd gotten mad over something or another and hit her across the face with the back of his hand, and then, after she'd crumpled to the floor, stood over her as she sobbed and begged for forgiveness. Forgiveness for what? She never knew. And the worst part? She didn't leave him that night or the next day or the day after that. She let him stay. She let him get away with it, let him get away with being an abuser. He was the one who left, abandoned her and Ophelia and their unborn child. She'd let him get away with it because she'd been a coward.

She couldn't let Ruben Ray get away with a crime so much worse. No. Not this time.

As the bathwater got higher in the tub, as the steam slicked the mirror, Vivian decided what she was going to do. And as soon as the decision was made, there was no second-guessing, and she knew it was right.

Once again, she thought of Ophelia as a baby. With those heart-shaped lips. Those expressive brown eyes.

"When you were a baby," she said, "you hated baths. As soon as you heard the sound of the water, your eyes would fill with terror and you would begin to holler."

"I don't remember that, Mom."

"Babies are so helpless, but they sense things. You sensed that the water was dangerous, that the water could drown you. And maybe you didn't trust me. Maybe you thought I wouldn't hold you up with my hands, maybe you sensed that I would let you fall beneath the water. But I always held you tight, I always made sure your mouth was dry, made sure not a single drop of water touched your tongue."

When had she stopped holding her daughter tight? When had she stopped protecting her from the world?

"I used to dream about drowning," Ophelia said.

For some reason, that comment startled Vivian. "Drowning? You never told me that."

Ophelia lifted her head from her hands and nodded. "In my dream, I would be sitting in the bathtub, and the water was always high, up to my neck. And I would stare at the door, and then the door would open, and I could never see who it was. Dreams are strange that way. And he would hold me down so I couldn't breathe. I would slap at the water, but it was no good. Sometimes I couldn't breathe for real, and I'd wake up gasping for air. I had those dreams a lot. I'm surprised I never told you."

Vivian turned off the water. She stayed calm. "I'm sorry you had those dreams, darling. I'm so sorry."

"It's okay. Dreams aren't real."

"No. But they're still scary. Who was the person holding you down? Do you remember?"

"No," Ophelia said. "I could never see his face. I don't know. Or maybe it was a woman. Maybe it was you. I don't remember."

"I hope it wasn't me. Not even in a dream. That would make me sad."

"But I'm not scared of baths anymore. Is the water ready?"

Vivian nodded her head. "It's not too hot. You can get in. I won't leave you. Nobody's going to hurt you anymore. Not in dreams, not in life."

Ophelia rose to her feet. Slowly, she removed her shirt. There were welts on her belly and breasts. Vivian wanted to cry. But, no, not now. From now on, she had to be strong for her daughter. Ophelia removed her jeans. She wasn't wearing any underwear. Had it been torn away by Ruben? There was dried blood on her thighs.

"I should call the police," Vivian said again. Or maybe she only thought it. Ophelia didn't respond. She got into the bathtub, and the blood washed away. Vivian thought back to her own baptism, and Holt's, in Mineral Lake, and how Ophelia had refused the baptism then. So many sins still needed to be washed away.

"It was Ruben," Ophelia whispered. "It was Ruben Ray."

"I know, darling. But he won't bother you anymore. He won't hurt you. He won't touch you. When you hear the floor creaking, it'll be because the house is old, not because he's sneaking around. Use the soap to wash your body, use the shampoo to wash your hair. Clean away his sin. It'll be gone forever."

It was strange, but as she sat there on the edge of the bathtub with her daughter, Vivian felt a kind of peace. She loved Ophelia, she needed Ophelia, but now Ophelia needed her too, and that was the most important thing of all. Vivian watched as Ophelia rubbed the bar of soap over her traumatized body, watched as she submerged her head, her long hair swaying gently in the water. When she came up for air, Ophelia's eyes were pressed shut, and Vivian saw her again as an infant, the infant she had been so many years ago.

"It's a shame you had those dreams," Vivian said as Ophelia lathered her hair with shampoo. "Drowning is an awful way to die."

Though the words came from her own mouth, it sounded to Vivian like a stranger was speaking. Not only the words, but the intonation. Why was Vivian so calm, when she already knew what she was going to do?

Ophelia stayed in the bathtub for a long time, pulling her knees to her chest, occasionally sobbing. She stayed there until the water got cold, and even after the water got cold for a while longer.

"Let's come out of the bathtub," Vivian finally said. "Let's get you into bed. It's time for you to sleep away all this nonsense. Tomorrow, when you wake, when you see the sun shining, everything will be different."

And it would be different. Of that, Vivian was certain.

Ophelia slept on her side, her legs pulled up to her belly. Vivian sat at the foot of her bed, just watching her sleep.

When Ophelia had been a toddler, maybe two or three years old, Vivian would lie on the floor until Ophelia fell asleep. In those days, if she tried sneaking out of the room too soon, Ophelia would sit up in bed and stare at her mother, and sheepishly Vivian would lie back down, one of those little daily sacrifices of parenting. Tonight, it seemed to Vivian that Ophelia was just as vulnerable as her toddler self. And just like those days, whenever Vivian prepared to leave, Ophelia could sense it. Her eyes would open, and so Vivian remained. Finally, after sitting there for more than an hour, Ophelia was still and snoring softly, and Vivian managed to rise to her feet and tiptoe out of the room.

How many times had she made that walk from Ophelia's bedroom to her own? Ten thousand? More? But tonight was different. All of her movements felt preordained. Down the hallway, left foot, right foot, left. It seemed to take an hour. Finally, she stood in the doorway of her own bedroom, her reflection ghostlike in the far windows. Then she took a few steps into the room. When she was in front of her bed, she got down on her knees, reached beneath the mattress, and once again pulled out the little pistol that Mike Brandt had given her for protection. Then, just like that night when Ruben had been skulking around her property, she opened the nightstand drawer and took out six .38 Special bullets and placed them in the chamber, one after the other. Her hands remained steady, her breathing even. She raised the gun slowly and extended her arm.

Just a squeeze of the trigger. That's all it would take.

She lowered the gun, snatched her purse from off the bedpost, and placed the gun inside. On her way out of the room, she spotted her Polaroid camera, resting on her dresser. She grabbed it and placed it in the purse as well.

When she left the house, the sky was dark, the moon was missing, and the air was still. The streetlights glowed dully in the November night. She got into her car, slammed the door shut, and placed her purse on the passenger-side seat. She caught a glimpse of the camera, of the pistol, lying in the unzipped purse. Fate, she decided, was more powerful than morality. She hit the engine and drove slowly through the neighborhood, terrifying doo-wop on the radio.

She remembered what it said in the Bible: *Whoever sheds the blood of man, by man shall his blood be shed, for God made man in his own image.* But hadn't God killed over and over and over again Himself? The flood of Noah, the plagues of Egypt, Sodom and Gomorrah, just to name a few? Would He dare damn her for this single act of rebellion? She was only bloodying the heart of the wicked to save the soul of the innocent.

She drove east on Highway 66, and the whole time she drove, she didn't see another car, and a few times she wondered if she were dreaming or dead. The radio had somehow changed from doo-wop to ghostly gospel. Part of her wanted to get caught, wanted to have a policeman pull her over and find the gun and prevent her from forever bloodying her hands. And so she stepped on the gas pedal and got the car up to seventy, eighty, ninety. But there were no sirens whining. No lights flashing. She slowed down, gritted her teeth. And then off to the north she saw that old brick grange with the sign that read: "Liberty Hall: Service and Friendship."

She turned off the radio, and now she could hear the sound of the wheels and of her own breath. She drove down a dirt road for a mile or more, and then she saw Ruben's farmhouse, his car parked out front, the porch light flickering. It was the only house for miles around. Nobody would hear the gunshot. Nobody would hear him scream. She parked her car in what had once been the driveway, now overrun with buffalo grass and weeds. She sat in the car for a long time, unable to move.

Her thoughts turned to Ophelia. She imagined Ruben, a cruel grin on his face, pinning her to the ground. She imagined him ripping away her clothes. Imagined him pounding at her flesh. *Oh, Jesus.* She was fifteen years old. Think of what he'd taken.

Vivian didn't need God's forgiveness. This would be the first act of bravery in her life.

She killed the engine and stepped outside. Fate had only one path. She thought of all the other choices she was never going to take, never *could* take now. With the purse hanging from her shoulder, she walked toward the farmhouse, toward the flickering porch light.

The screen door was busted and hanging from its hinges. She pulled it aside and tried the front door. It was locked. But she still had a key from back when they were dating, back when she still thought he was some kind of tattooed savior. Despite her calmness, despite her certainty, her fingers trembled as she placed the key to the lock. She couldn't get the key in, not right away. She had to use her opposite hand to steady her fingers, and only then was she able to get the teeth lined up. She twisted and the lock clicked. She pushed open the door.

In the living room, the television was on, the sound of gunshots echoing against the walls. She shivered. *I don't need your forgiveness*, she thought. *I never have. You kill a thousand a day, at least.* She walked slowly toward the hallway which led to the kitchen, and then she stopped in the doorway.

Ruben sat at the table, which was decorated with cigarettes and booze. He was drunk. She knew he was drunk. He rose to his feet.

"I kind of figured you'd come back," he said.

"I guess you were right."

She didn't remember reaching into her purse. She didn't remember pulling out the pistol. She didn't remember firing the weapon, not once, or twice, or three times. But when she opened her eyes, Ruben Ray was on the ground, the wall behind him smeared with blood.

For a few moments, he stared at his killer, occasionally blinking, and Vivian was scared that he wouldn't die. But soon he stopped blinking, stopped moving. And eventually, stopped breathing.

Vivian looked down at her hands and was surprised at how steady they were. With a deep exhale, she placed the gun back into her purse. Then she fumbled for the Polaroid camera. Now she'd take a photograph, to remind herself of what she'd done.

To remind herself how she'd protected her daughter.

CHAPTER 21

In the weeks after she shot Ruben Ray, Vivian fell into a deep depression. She felt no remorse for what she had done, at least that's what she told herself. Still, she couldn't eat, couldn't sleep. When she came home from work, she would go into her bedroom, lie on the bed, and start crying. She would cry and cry, and she worried that the tears would never stop. When she closed her eyes, she was haunted by images, smells, and sounds. The explosion of the gun. The metallic stink of blood. The wheezing of his final breaths.

Holt sometimes entered the room and tried comforting her, but she didn't want him to see her cry, so she would tell him that she was fine and that he needed to go into his room, go into his room right now.

She also spent a lot of time staring at the photograph of the dead man. She studied his face, his wide eyes. What had he been thinking in those final moments? Had he experienced any remorse for what he'd done to her daughter? How much had it hurt? Not enough, as far as she was concerned. Not enough. Vivian felt profoundly alone and searched for comfort wherever she could find it. Sometimes it was in a pint of ice cream.

Sometimes in a bottle of gin. And sometimes she found comfort in the arms of Mike Brandt.

They only made love twice, but both of those times he told her that he loved her, that he'd always loved her. He held her for hours on end while she cried into his chest, wetting his shirt. She hated herself for doing it, hated herself for betraying her best friend.

But mostly, Vivian found comfort in the Lord.

Until she shot Ruben Ray, her faith had been fleeting and uncertain, moments of devotion interrupted by weeks of doubt. But killing him had somehow transformed her faith. She felt—no, that's wrong—she *knew* that God had a plan for her, and avenging her daughter was part of that plan. Now she only needed to listen to God, listen closely, to find out the rest of that plan.

And so she began going to church more frequently. She paid rapt attention to the sermons, cried during the hymns, and savored the blood and body of Christ at communion. At home and at work, she began memorizing lines from the Bible. She also began praying for hours on end, her knees becoming bruised and scabbed. She couldn't help worrying about her children and their lack of faith. Holt had been baptized, but he seemed bored at church, often dozing asleep. And Ophelia—well, Vivian wasn't sure that she believed at all. Eventually, Vivian forced her children to pray with her. She wouldn't cook dinner for them until they had said the proper words, closed with an "amen." She forced them to read passages from the Bible. She forced them to *believe.*

And then came that cold and dreary Saturday morning when Vivian's own faith was tested. She was sitting at her desk, reading Psalms and praying. There was a tentative knocking on the door, a pause, and then more knocking.

"Come in," Vivian said.

It was Ophelia. Vivian didn't turn around, not right away.

"Mom? Can you talk? I've got something to tell you. I've got something to show you."

No answer from Vivian. Her finger touched each word in her Bible as she read. "*Be merciful to me, Lord, for I am in distress; my eyes grow weak with sorrow, my soul and body with grief.*"

Ophelia: "I need you to listen to me."

Vivian turned to face her daughter. Ophelia was wearing a white nightgown and held a thin glass tube, the liquid inside bluish-gray.

"What do you need to talk to me about? And what is that in your hand?"

Ophelia shook her head and wiped a tear from the corner of her eye. "You're not going to like it. You're not going to like it one bit."

Vivian rose from her chair and walked toward her daughter. She felt that old sense of unease. "Tell me."

Ophelia extended her arm, the one that held the glass tube. Vivian eyed it, but made no move to grab it.

"It's a pregnancy test," Ophelia said. "It's called First Response. If the color turns blue, then . . ."

And now Vivian took the tube from her daughter. She studied it for a moment, her eyes narrowing into slits. "Where did you get this?"

"At the store. I've missed my period, and—"

"These home tests don't work," Vivian said, her voice feigning confidence.

"Mom, I—"

"You're not pregnant. It's impossible."

Ophelia's lower lips began trembling. "I'm sorry. I'm so sorry."

Vivian let the glass tube fall from her hand. It bounced on the hardwood floor, the blue liquid trickling at her feet. Vivian began chewing at the webbing of her fingers. Pregnant? No, not Ophelia. Not her daughter. She felt a wave of sadness come over her, but that wave was quickly washed away with another emotion. Something like rage.

"Who'd you sleep with, girl?" Vivian said. "Tell your mother. Don't lie to me."

Ophelia shook her head. "I haven't slept with anybody, Mommy. I swear."

Vivian grabbed her by the wrist. "You tell me the truth, Ophelia! I won't be mad. I'll be relieved. Who'd you sleep with? Who's the father?"

"Ruben," she whispered. "Ruben Ray."

Vivian slapped her across the face. Hard. "Liar!"

For a moment, Ophelia was paralyzed. She just stood there, staring at her mother, a madwoman. Then she turned and hurried down the hallway.

Vivian knew she'd made a mistake and called after Ophelia, but Ophelia slammed the door shut.

Vivian didn't see her daughter for the rest of the night or the next day after that.

After that, Vivian began praying harder than she'd ever prayed before, looking for comfort in the Lord, looking for answers. Deep inside, she knew it wasn't her daughter's fault, but still she felt something like rage toward her. If the child was born, she would despise him. Every time she would look at his face, she would be reminded of that devil, Ruben Ray. That couldn't happen.

She pored over the pages of the Bible, trying to find some reassurance, but one thing became obvious: God didn't approve of abortions. Not even a little bit. *From birth I was cast on you; from my mother's womb you have been my God.* But one night, as she sat on her bed in the moonlight, staring at the photograph of Ruben Ray, God whispered in her ear, and the words were clear. There was no mistaking His command.

His name was Dr. Yamamoto, and Joyce had told Vivian about him. His office, located on the edge of town, was small and a bit dingy. He had no receptionists or nurses, and that made Vivian nervous, but he had kind brown eyes and looked like a good man, a man of God. He would be able to save Ophelia, Vivian thought.

The first time she met with him, she did so by herself. Dr. Yamamoto sat down at a desk empty of all papers. Vivian sat across from him, scratching at the skin of her leg, praying for God's mercy.

"And how long have you been pregnant?" he said.

"No," she said. "Not me. My daughter."

He raised his eyebrows. "Your daughter?"

"Yes. Her name is Ophelia."

She told him about Ophelia, about how she was only fifteen and that was far too young to have a baby, about how her life would be ruined, how the baby's life would be ruined. And then Vivian started crying, uncontrollably.

Dr. Yamamoto tried comforting her, reaching across the desk to grab her hand. He told her that he understood, that he would be happy to help, that he dealt with this sort of thing all the time. But he needed to meet with Ophelia first. Ultimately, she needed to provide consent.

Vivian shook her head. "I don't know if she'll agree."

"I'm afraid that's the only way."

"Isn't she too young to make that decision? As her legal guardian, can't I make that decision for her?"

"No, ma'am. I'm afraid not."

Two days later, Vivian drove Ophelia to Boulder. She didn't tell Ophelia where they were going, only that they were going to see a man who was going to give her some options regarding her pregnancy. Ophelia was suspicious, of course, and asked questions, but Vivian was vague in her responses. This was something that had to be done. Once Ophelia arrived at the office and Dr. Yamamoto explained the process, she would certainly agree. But as soon as they entered the doctor's office, as soon as Ophelia saw Dr. Yamamoto, she understood what kind of doctor he was. Face turning red, she looked at her mother and screamed.

"No!"

Ophelia tried running from the office, but Vivian grabbed her arm.

"Calm down!" Vivian shouted. Then she softened her voice. "I know this is difficult. But it has to be done. Otherwise, your whole life will be ruined. You understand that, don't you? You're just a kid yourself."

Ophelia began kicking and screaming, her voice fiery red.

"No! Never! You can't stop me from having him! I love him! I'll always love him." Then she looked at the doctor. "And you! If you try and take him, I'll pound your skull in! Do you hear me? I'll pound your fucking skull in!"

Shocked, Vivian let go of her daughter's arm, and Ophelia ran from the office. Dr. Yamamoto wiped a bead of perspiration from his upper lip and then touched Vivian's shoulder.

"These are always difficult decisions."

Vivian glared at the doctor, her eyes full of anger and hurt. "Tell me this, doctor. Have you ever failed in your craft? Have you ever brought out a baby alive?"

"No. That's never happened."

"I'm glad."

She hurried out of the office and ran after Ophelia.

They drove without speaking, and the only sound was the tires on the asphalt and the rattling of the heater. Outside, the sun hung low in the sky, blurred behind a gray veil of clouds. Vivian tapped the steering wheel with her long and slender fingers, thinking about death and salvation. The afternoon was cold, and a light snow was beginning to accumulate on the highway. God had a plan for the world, and of course they were a part of that plan. But one thing Vivian knew: Ophelia needed the power of God, and the only way to gain that power was through surrender.

"We'll go to the lake," Vivian whispered. "We'll wash away your sins. Each and every one of them."

Ophelia buried her head in her hands. "I didn't do anything wrong." But her voice was without conviction.

"God makes no mistakes. And so maybe the baby—"

"A gift from God. That's what he is."

"I'll push your head beneath the water. I'll say the words of the baptism. It's what we have to do, Ophelia."

Vivian expected her to argue. She expected her to lose control. But, instead, Ophelia looked defeated, exhausted. She only nodded.

Sue Harding, the other kindergarten teacher, had been babysitting Holt. When Vivian and Ophelia arrived home, Sue met them at the door, and she was all in a panic.

"He has a nose bleed," Sue said. "A bad one. I can't get it to stop."

"It's okay, Sue. He gets them frequently. It's the dry climate."

"He's been bleeding for thirty minutes. Maybe more."

"Deep breaths, Sue. He'll be okay."

They entered the house, and Holt was sitting on the couch, pressing a tissue to his nose and tilting his head back. On the floor were dozens of bloody tissues. Vivian sat down on the couch next to Holt and smoothed back his hair.

"Bloody nose, huh?"

Holt nodded his head. "Bad one."

"Just keep the pressure on for a while longer. It will stop."

Sue took a few steps forward. She was rubbing her hands together nervously. "Do you want me to stay? Do we need to call a doctor, you think?"

"No, no. I can take care of this. Thanks for watching him. I'll see you at school tomorrow."

"I'm sorry about his nose, Vivian. Really I am."

"It's not your fault."

Sue blew a strand of hair from her eyes. Then she looked at Ophelia.

"I haven't seen you in a while. Your mother told me that you've been a bit under the weather lately."

Ophelia shook her head. "No. My mother got it wrong. I'm fine. I'm not sick."

Sue gazed at Ophelia a moment too long. "I'm glad to hear that."

Then she walked across the living room and toward the front door, stopping to wave goodbye. The door slammed behind her. As soon as she left, Vivian pulled the tissue from Holt's nose. The bleeding had stopped.

"See?" Vivian said. "Magic."

Holt touched his nose and laughed. "Yup. Magic."

Vivian went to the kitchen and wetted some paper towels. Then she returned to the living room and wiped the remaining blood from Holt's nose and face. She kissed him on the cheek.

"Guess what, Holt?" she said. "Now that you're all cleaned up, we're going to go on a little adventure. Just the three of us."

Holt's eyes lit up. "An adventure? Where?"

"The lake."

"The lake? Why are we going to the lake?"

"Remember when you and I were baptized, Holt? Remember when we were saved?"

"Yes, Mommy. I remember."

"Well, now it's your sister's turn."

Holt looked at Ophelia who stood in the middle of the room, rubbing her belly.

He said, "It's good that you're being saved, Ophelia. That way you can go to heaven. I'd miss you otherwise."

Twenty minutes later, Vivian, Ophelia, and Holt walked toward Mineral Lake. The snow was falling harder now, illuminated in the glow of the streetlights. Vivian squeezed Holt's hand tightly. Ophelia remained several steps behind. Her head was bowed and she stared at the sidewalk ahead of her.

"Mommy?" Holt said. "How does a baptism work?"

Vivian didn't know how to respond, and so she didn't, instead just quickening her pace. But Holt wouldn't let it go.

"Mommy? Did you hear me?"

"What, darling?"

"How does a baptism work?"

Vivian stopped walking. She bent down so that her eyes were level with his and squeezed his hand tighter.

"Magic," she said.

"Magic?"

"Magic."

They crossed the train tracks and walked past the storage lots and the car junkyard. And then the lake appeared, coal black and shimmering in the darkness.

"We're going to save Ophelia," Holt said.

Vivian nodded her head. "Yes."

"Is this the only lake where people can be baptized?"

"It doesn't matter the lake," Vivian said. "When it's time, every lake, pond, or river turns to the blood of Jesus. That's where you leave your sins. That's where you leave your pain." She hoped that sounded plausible.

"And what happens to your sins?"

"I don't know exactly. But I think they get washed away. Mixed with Christ's blood."

"Christ's blood . . ."

"He'll never fail you. Do you hear me, son? He'll never fail you."

Ophelia stared straight ahead. Then, mechanically, she removed her shoes and her jacket and placed them on the snowy ground. She wore only jeans and a Ramones T-shirt; she began to shiver.

"Holt," said Vivian. "I need you to sit on this rock. I don't want you to move. I'm going to take Ophelia out in the water. I'm going to dunk her head. I don't want you to move. Do you hear me?"

"Yes, Mommy."

"Believe in him," she said. And now she turned to Ophelia. "Not the devil."

And now, just as Ophelia had done, Vivian removed her own jacket and shoes. She looked up at the sky, and she could feel His presence. Whispering a prayer of gratitude, she grabbed Ophelia's hand and the two of them walked toward the water, the snow falling diagonally, the moon hidden behind darkened clouds. They stepped into the lake, and Ophelia gasped from the shock of cold.

"We'll clean your sins," Vivian said.

In the falling snow, they walked farther and farther into the lake until the water reached their calves and then their thighs and then their stomachs. Vivian stopped. Without warning, she released Ophelia's hand and grabbed the back of her head. Then, with a shriek, she pushed Ophelia underwater and said the words of the baptism.

"Just as Christ was raised from the dead, by the glory of the Father, so we too might walk in newness of life."

She kept her underwater for another ten, twenty seconds, and Ophelia began to slap desperately at the water. Finally, Vivian pulled her head out of the water, and Ophelia took a gasp of breath and then began coughing. She wiped the water from her face and eyes.

"Now you're saved," Vivian said. And after a moment: "But not the baby."

And that was it. Vivian started walking back to the shore, but Ophelia stayed where she was.

"The baby, too!" Ophelia shouted.

Then Ophelia bent down and placed her face in the lake and began drinking the water, as much water as she could swallow.

When they returned to shore, soaking and shivering, Holt wasn't at the rock where he was supposed to be. Vivian called out his name.

"Holt! Holt, where are you?" No answer. Vivian felt that familiar panic. "Holt!"

A moment later, she heard him call out, "I'm over here, Mommy."

She exhaled and walked toward the sound of his voice. She located him by the light of the moon. He was standing between two skeleton trees, his shirt and pants removed, his arms extended toward the branches, his ankles pressed firmly against one another.

"Holt! What are you doing? Where are your clothes? You'll freeze. You'll—"

She walked quickly to where he stood, and now she noticed that his nose was bleeding again, drops of blood mixing with the snow.

PART V

2018

CHAPTER 22

"The baby. Did she have the baby?"

It was early in the morning, not even seven o'clock, and Holt stood on Joyce's porch, his hands clenched at his sides. His vision was blurry from exhaustion, his hair an unruly mess. He hadn't slept the night before, not for a single minute; instead, he ruminated hour after hour about what he'd learned and what he still didn't know.

Joyce stood behind the screen door, trying frantically to tie her robe. Skin sagged from her jaw and neck, and without makeup her face was pasty white, eyes sunken beneath the fatty ridges. Her mouth opened as if she were about to say something, but nothing came out.

"Did she have the baby?" Holt said again.

She shook her head. "Holt, I don't know what you mean. What baby are you talking about?"

"Ophelia's baby."

"Ophelia? What do—"

His voice got louder. "No more bullshit. Not now."

Joyce glanced over Holt's shoulder, checking for neighbors. "Please. Let's go inside so we don't make a scene."

Holt's cheek twitched and his eyes narrowed. He followed her inside, and as he did he was filled with dread. In the living room, he glanced at the glass shelves with the knickknacks, glanced at the photo of Joyce and Mike from when they were young. He shouldn't have come back to Thompsonville. The truth never did anybody any good.

Joyce pointed to the couch and said, "Why don't we sit?"

Holt shook his head. "I'd rather stand."

"Suit yourself."

Joyce sighed deeply and sat down on the couch. She crossed her legs, revealing varicose veins on her calf and a jagged scar below her knee. "You went to see your sister, didn't you?"

"Yes."

"And she told you that she'd had a baby?"

"No."

"Then what?"

Holt closed his eyes and pictured his sister from long ago, young and smiling and beautiful. And then his sister of today, eyes wild, teeth missing. But sane, he decided. Still sane.

"This is what I think," he said, his voice raspy and desperate. "I think that Ruben Ray, the monster, raped my sister. That's why my mother went to his house that night. That's why my mother shot him dead."

Joyce stared at Holt for a long time, not responding. Finally, she spoke, and it was just a single word. "Yes."

Holt took a step forward and pointed his index finger at Joyce accusingly. "Why didn't you tell me? When I asked you, why didn't you tell me about what Ruben had done? Why?"

Joyce answered in a voice firm with conviction. "Because I made a promise to your mother to never tell you what happened to your sister. She thought it would be easier for you to live the rest of your life. Lies are sometimes the kindest words."

"He raped her and Ophelia got pregnant."

"Yes." Again, that single word.

"This doctor. Yamamoto. He delivered babies. He aborted them. Which one? I've been having visions, memories. Of her pushing the baby stroller around the house, of her rocking the baby to sleep. And of the baby crying. I remember. I swear that I do."

Joyce leaned forward in the couch and shook her head. "No," she said. "You've got it wrong."

"What do I have wrong?"

"The things you think you remember—they didn't happen. Ophelia didn't have the baby. She had an abortion. I promise you that. It would have been her rapist's child. What kind of a life would that have been for her? What kind of a life for the child?"

Holt began rocking back and forth, rubbing his face with his hands. And once again, he could hear a baby crying, crying, crying, but it was all in his head, all in his imagination.

Joyce again: "She didn't have the baby—"

Holt dropped his hands to his side. He began nodding his head slowly, and a bitter grin spread across his face. "I should stop digging," he said. "Before it's too late."

He turned and walked toward the front door. Joyce called his name, but he ignored her. He shouldered open the front door and stood in the morning light, his heart hammering in his chest.

"I remember," he muttered.

The Countryside Village mobile park was located on Collyer Street, just south of Mountain View Cemetery. Twenty or twenty-five mobile homes were scattered on a dirt lot. There were a bunch of beat-up old pickups and hatchbacks, but Holt was surprised that were also a handful of newer, expensive cars: an Audi, a Saab, and a BMW, cars that probably cost more than the trailer. Holt parked his car on a dirt path that led to nowhere. Then he stepped outside and stretched his body. It was cold this morning, and he could see his faint breath. He pulled up the collar on his jacket and started walking.

He thought that maybe he could knock on each door and ask for the elder Yamamoto, but then he decided that wouldn't be a good idea. This seemed like the kind of place with a lot of guns, a lot of resentment. Instead, he wandered around for a while, checking mailboxes, searching for Yamamoto's name. No luck.

Finally, he saw an old woman standing in front of her trailer holding a mop in one hand and a wrench in the other. Holt waved at her.

"Good morning," he said.

She didn't wave back.

"Can you help me? I'm looking for a Dr. Yamamoto. Do you know where he lives?"

She didn't answer.

"My sister was a patient of his a long time ago. I'd just like to talk to him."

The woman slung the mop over her shoulder and continued glaring at Holt.

"Okay," he said. "I'll keep walking around then. Hopefully I'll find him. Hopefully."

But he had just turned to walk in the other direction when the woman said, "Hey."

Holt spun around.

She nodded her head and spoke in a voice ragged from cigarettes or whiskey or heartache.

"He ain't home," she said.

"No?"

"I saw him drive away not so long ago."

"Yeah, well. I can wait for him."

There was a long pause as if she were thinking things over, and then she pointed at a trailer maybe fifty yards away.

"That's where he lives," she said. "He owes me twelve dollars. But that's where he lives."

"I can try to get the money for you."

She shook her head. "The old fucker won't pay me back. Not now. Not ever."

And then she turned and walked away, still gripping the wrench and mop.

Holt took a deep breath and walked toward the mobile home. It was rundown and in bad need of another coat of turquoise paint. What had once been a porch swing now rested on the dirt, the wood rotted. A pair of cracked and filthy windows were covered with yellow curtains.

Holt pulled open the screen door and noticed that the front door was open a crack. He knocked twice but nobody came. He glanced around to see if anybody was watching him. The woman was gone. Nobody else was around.

"Fuck it," he said, and pushed open the front door.

He stepped inside. It was dark and damp, and an acrid smell filled the air.

"Hello?" Holt called out. "Dr. Yamamoto? Are you here?"

No answer.

Next to the door was a standing lamp. Holt fumbled with the switch, turned it on. The place was a mess. Clothes and papers on the floor, dishes and cans on the table. In the corner of the room there was an old school desk, probably from the '50s, the desk itself laminated wood, a metal chair attached at the legs. Holt pulled the top of the desk up and looked inside the cubby. There were dozens and dozens of medical folders with patient names on the front. Holt flipped through the folders, but he couldn't find his sister's name. He closed the desk and wandered around the trailer for several more minutes, pulling out drawers, looking under the bed, and studying the scattering of papers on the floor. No evidence of Ophelia.

He needed to take a piss, so he went to the bathroom. When he was done, out of curiosity, he opened the medicine cabinet. In addition to the usual toiletries, it was filled with prescription vials, a dozen at least. Holt grabbed one and studied the label.

Prescription: OxyContin.

Patient: Ted Yamamoto.

Doctor: Ryan Yamamoto.

Holt grabbed a few more. All of them were the same. So that's how the younger Yamamoto was helping his old man.

Holt stuffed one of the vials in his pocket, returned to the living room, turned off the light, and sat down in a chair. And then he waited.

Afternoon turned into evening, and still Yamamoto didn't return. Sitting in the dark, Holt began to worry that maybe Yamamoto was gone forever. But just when he was getting ready to leave, the front door opened. An old man, who must have been Yamamoto, staggered inside. He turned on the light, took a few steps forward, and stopped.

He looked like an older version of his son, only he was gaunter, his skin more pallid. His gray hair was slicked back toward a bald crown. When he saw Holt sitting at the desk, he stopped, his eyes opening wide.

"Who . . . who are you?" Yamamoto said. "What are you doing in my house?"

Holt noticed that perspiration was forming on his brow. He lifted the vial and waved it at Yamamoto.

"Bet you're looking forward to your evening fix," he said.

"I have every right to take my medication. I had back surgery. It was prescribed. By a doctor."

"By your son."

"A doctor." Yamamoto remained where he was, his shoulders heaving up and down. "Who are you?"

Holt rose from his seat and took a few steps toward the elderly man. The floor creaked beneath his feet.

"The name's Holt Davidson."

"And am I supposed to know you?"

"You knew my sister. Ophelia."

A brief flicker of recognition, but then Yamamoto shook his head.

"No. I don't know an Ophelia. You've got the wrong guy."

Holt took another step forward. He was right in front of Yamamoto.

"C'mon, doc. Let's not make this harder than it has to be. I just need to know what, exactly, happened to her. And then I'll be out of your hair. Then you can swallow as many pills as you want. But until then . . ."

Yamamoto stood there for a moment, his lower lip quivering. Then, moving past Holt, Yamamoto walked over to the far wall and slid down until he was sitting on the floor, his knees pulled up to his slender chest. His face was now glistening in sweat, and his hands were trembling.

"Ophelia," he whispered. "Ophelia Davidson."

"Yes. You do remember her."

He nodded his head slowly.

"In a way," he said, "her memory has always haunted me." He paused for a long time. "Whatever became of her? Of your sister."

Holt cleared his voice. "Nothing became of her. Nothing at all."

"It seems like yesterday. It seems like a million years ago."

Holt leaned forward. "She'd been raped. Did you know that?"

Yamamoto's eyes rolled back into his skull. "I seem to recall that."

"And when she came to you—"

"She was very scared. I don't blame her. She came with your mother, of course."

"For what? For an abortion, or—"

"Yes. An abortion."

"Then why does her memory haunt you? I mean if—"

"Because your sister refused."

The words hung in the air. It took a long moment for Holt to speak. "She refused? But did she agree to later? Or did somebody else—"

Yamamoto shook his head. "No. Nobody else."

"But—"

"I didn't hear from your mom for a long time. Not for another seven or eight months."

Holt felt a sharp pain in his gut. He knew what was coming. He knew . . . "And then—"

"Your mother. She called me again. But this time not for an abortion. She had learned that, in my former life, I'd been an obstetrician. One who'd lost his license because of a terrible mistake. The kind of mistake that killed a mother and child both. Can you imagine what that's like? Killing somebody?"

"My mother. She—"

"—asked me to deliver Ophelia's baby."

Again, a baby crying. But only in Holt's imagination. *Only in his imagination.*

Yamamoto adjusted his legs until he was sitting on his haunches. He sucked in his breath, his neck cording.

"I told her that it wouldn't be a good idea. I told her that I hadn't delivered any babies in a long time. I told her that I'd once killed a baby, killed a mother. She didn't care. She offered money, a good amount of money, as long as I followed some conditions."

"What kind of conditions?" Holt's voice was soft, barely louder than a whisper.

"The delivery had to be done in secret. At my house. No other nurses or doctors. And I couldn't tell anybody, not a soul."

"And you . . . you agreed to this?"

Yamamoto eyed the vial of pills hungrily and nodded. "I did. I needed the money. Each week your mother would bring her to my office. To check on her. To check on the fetus. Ophelia. She was such a crumbling beauty. Her hair was always mess, her eyes hidden beneath. Sometimes she would whisper the same phrase, over and over again: 'Love, not sinfulness. Love, not sinfulness. Love, not sinfulness.' She hardly listened to my directions at all."

"And then—"

"And then, on the morning of August 8, Ophelia's water broke. Your mother brought her to back to my house and left Ophelia there with me. She didn't want to witness the birth. If you want to know the truth, I was more terrified than Ophelia, afraid that I would kill another life. But, no. That evening, I delivered the baby. A blood-soaked boy. Crying like he'd seen the devil. There were no complications."

"Bobby," Holt mumbled.

"She made me promise to never tell anybody. Don't you understand?"

Holt's head was spinning, and the room looked like a kaleidoscope.

"And did you keep your promise? Did you?"

Yamamoto hacked a few times and then spit on the floor. "Yes, I kept my promise. I never told anybody. Not until today . . ."

Holt nodded his head slowly. "I'm going to leave now," he said.

Yamamoto, the abortionist, the obstetrician, the addict, rose slowly to his feet.

"Wait," he said. "My pills."

Holt smiled but he wanted to scream. He unscrewed the vial and dumped the pills on the floor. Yamamoto's eyes opened wide, the muscles in his neck twitching like a horse stung by flies. He began frantically scooping up the pills and stuffing one, two, three into his mouth.

And so Holt left that trailer, and when he pushed open the door, standing not ten yards away, illuminated by the jaundiced moon, was the same woman from earlier, and she was still holding her mop.

"I talked to Yamamoto," Holt mumbled. "He told me some things." He reached into his pocket and pulled out his wallet. He handed the woman a twenty-dollar bill, his own money. "Here's the money he owes you. Now you're even."

Then he pushed past the woman and staggered toward his car. He thought of his mother, and he remembered her sitting next to his bed, the sun filtering through the blinds. He remembered her whispering in his ear: *We'll take him to the darkened well. Out by Ruben's farmhouse. Nobody will know.*

Nobody will ever know.

PART VI

1984–1985

CHAPTER 23

Mike and Joyce were the only people Vivian told about the pregnancy. But she couldn't bear to tell them that Ophelia had refused the abortion and was going to have the baby, Ruben Ray's baby. And so a couple of weeks after Ophelia's baptism, Vivian lied and told them that the baby had been aborted.

"It took days and days of near constant pressure," Vivian said, "but she finally gave in. She came to the realization that it would be too difficult to look into his eyes and see the echoes of her rapist. So that's that. It was traumatic, but not as traumatic as having the baby would have been."

At this, Joyce Brandt's eyes filled with tears, and she pulled her friend close and hugged her.

"It was the right decision, darling. It was the only decision."

Mike Brandt stared at his hands, seeing, perhaps, a thin coating of Ruben Ray's blood.

"Yes. The right thing. Now you can both move on with your lives. Nobody's going to know. Not about the abortion. Not about any of it."

And so after the baby was born, shortly after Ophelia's sixteenth birthday, Vivian didn't allow the Brandts—or anybody else for that matter—to come to the house. In fact, she didn't allow the baby to be seen at all.

"Not until we're ready to explain," she said to Ophelia. "Not until then."

That made Ophelia angry. "What's there to explain? I had a goddamn baby. I'm not the only one, you know. It happens a couple hundred thousand times a day."

Vivian sneered. "And when they ask who the father is?"

"Just say it was some guy who skipped town. No need to provide names."

"A perfect solution," Vivian said. "My daughter the sixteen-year-old slut."

"There are worse things to be called."

Vivian covered her eyes with her hands. She wanted to scream.

"The truth," she mumbled, "feels like a goddamn insult."

But she knew it was something more. The guilt from letting Ruben into her life, the shame of not protecting her daughter. The fear that the presence of baby would somehow lead to her own arrest. Vivian never mentioned Ruben Ray's name again, and Ophelia never once asked her mother about his death. Did she know that her mother had shot him dead? In a perverse way, Vivian hoped that she did. Then Ophelia would understand just how much she loved her, just how much she'd sacrificed for her.

Vivian set up Holt's old crib for Bobby to sleep in, but most nights the baby slept with Ophelia, usually right there on her chest. That meant that Ophelia didn't get much sleep, but she didn't seem to mind. She told Vivian that she loved lying there listening to him breathe, smelling his skin. Vivian had worried that Ophelia wouldn't be emotionally equipped to take care of another human being, but Ophelia surprised her. Vivian helped her daughter in the beginning with changing diapers and nursing techniques, but once Ophelia learned how to do things she was a natural.

Vivian was uncertain how much Holt knew. He was still in half-day kindergarten, old enough to understand some things but not old enough to understand most. Certainly he must have wondered how one day there were only three people in the house and then the next day there were four. They'd hid Ophelia's pregnancy from him—they'd hid Ophelia's pregnancy from everybody—and even though Holt mentioned that Ophelia was getting fatter ("You're eating too much pie!") he never seemed to comprehend that there was a baby growing inside of her. So when the baby appeared, he was surprised. He asked where it had come from. His mother wouldn't tell him.

"We're just taking care of him because nobody else will," she'd said.

She hated herself for lying, especially to her own son, but she was filled with such shame, such sadness, such resentment, that she couldn't bear telling him the truth. And there was a part of her that believed that if she said the lie enough, if she believed it enough, it would become true. Meanwhile, God had gone into hiding, leaving her to suffer alone.

"How long is he going to be here?" Holt said one day. "I don't like hearing him cry."

"I don't know. But he can't stop himself from crying. That's what babies do. Don't you know that?"

"Ophelia says she loves him."

"Yes," Vivian said. "She does."

"Will we baptize him?"

"I'm sorry?"

"So that he can go to heaven?"

Vivian nodded her head slowly.

"Soon," she said. "We'll baptize him soon."

When the school year began, choices had to be made. Ophelia told Vivian that she wanted to drop out of school and be a full-time mother, but Vivian was a teacher and she wasn't having any of it. She tried scaring Ophelia. "You know what happens to drop outs? Do you? They end up homeless. Needles stuck in their arms. You're going to school. You're graduating, you're going to college. Baby or no baby, that's the way it has to be."

They could have put the baby in day care, but Vivian still wasn't ready for the world to know. She was still too humiliated, too frightened. Mike could only protect her so much.

So she called in sick. She told Principal Bartlow that she was ill, very ill, and wouldn't be back for at least a month. Bartlow expressed sympathy and got a long-term substitute in place. Vivian had enough money saved up to last a little while, anyway. So she took care of the baby while Ophelia was in school.

Bobby turned three weeks old and then a month. He was a good baby as far as those things go. Even though he remained hidden from the world, he smiled a lot. He laughed sometimes. He slept through the night and ate when he was supposed to eat.

But taking care of a baby is hard work, especially when you thought your mothering days were through. Especially when you resent the baby's very existence. Were there times when Vivian looked at the baby and felt something like love, a desire to protect and nurture him? Of course. But were there times when Vivian shouted at the baby, told him to stop his fucking crying? That too. Were there times when, in frustration, she grabbed him a bit too hard? Also, yes. When Holt (who didn't go to kindergarten until noon each day) would see his mother seething (face reddened, eyes narrowed, mouth trembling), he would disappear into his room and close the door and play with his Star Wars figures, hour after hour.

As for Ophelia, she rarely showed frustration with the baby. She rocked him when he was sad and smiled at him when he was happy. She played peekaboo and blew raspberries on his belly. Vivian had to admit that Ophelia was a good mother. She had to admit that she'd never seen her so happy.

Baby Bobby had just turned five weeks old when he got sick. It was a Tuesday, and from the moment he woke up, he wasn't right. He was pulling at his ear and crying and screaming. Holt told Ophelia and his mother to make him stop, and then he went outside and sat on the swing set. Vivian checked the baby's temperature, and it was 101 degrees. Ophelia was worried.

"We need to take him to the doctor," she said. "He's sick."

Her mother only shook her head. "No. We're not taking him to the doctor. Not yet."

"But, Mom—"

"He's got a little fever. So what? I've raised two kids. You don't think I know when it's time to go to the doctor? He's got a little virus or maybe an ear infection. We'll just give him some baby Tylenol. He'll be fine by the end of the day. Now go to school."

But he wasn't fine by the end of the day. Bobby's fever was up to 103 degrees. He was crying less, but he'd become lethargic, just lying in his crib staring straight ahead. He wouldn't drink out of his bottle. Vivian gave him more medicine. The fever remained. When Ophelia got home from another miserable school day, she was in a panic.

"Something's wrong with him! Can't you see? Something's wrong."

Vivian kept her voice calm. "Babies get sick. They're building up their immune systems. He'll be fine. A virus is all."

"We need to take him to the doctor. Please."

Vivian touched her daughter's shoulder. "If it'll make you feel better, I'll call the doctor's office. If they want us to bring him in, we'll do so. Otherwise, we'll treat him at home. Just a little virus. Maybe an ear infection."

"Yes," Ophelia said. "Yes, please call the doctor."

Vivian sighed and smiled. "Okay. If that's what you want. Now you just take a deep breath and relax. Everything will be fine. Do you hear me? Everything will be fine."

Holt appeared from his bedroom, gripping the Millennium Falcon.

"Is the baby okay? Is he going to die?"

Vivian shook her head. "See what you've done, Ophelia? You've got your brother thinking crazy thoughts as well. Now both of you sit down. I'm going to call the doctor. I'm going to call him right now."

Vivian sat down on the couch and grabbed the phone off the cradle. She dialed a seven-digit number and then waited a few moments.

"Hello? Yes, this is Vivian Davidson. My children are both patients of Dr. Howard . . . No, actually this isn't about either of them. You see, we're taking care of a baby, and the poor guy isn't feeling well . . . That's right . . . Well, I just wanted to find out if we need to bring him in or not."

Ophelia rocked Bobby and watched her mother from the corner of her eye. Meanwhile, Holt meandered through the room, his prized Millennium Falcon soaring high above him.

"Oh, that's fantastic," Vivian said. "I hope I'm not pulling him away from another patient . . . No? Excellent . . . Yes, I'll hold."

Vivian nodded at Ophelia. "Dr. Howard is between patients. He's going to talk to me."

A minute or two passed. Ophelia was bouncing up and down, shushing little Bobby, who was pushing his head against her chest and whimpering.

"It's okay, Bobby," Ophelia said. "We're going to make you all better."

Vivian started speaking into the receiver again. "Oh, hello, Dr. Howard. Thanks so much for talking to us . . . Yes, that's right. It's my sister's baby. She's out of town for a couple of weeks and . . . Yes, he does have a fever. About 103 degrees . . . I guess this would be the second day now. Yesterday, he was very angry. Today, more tired . . . No, he doesn't have a cough. He has been pulling at his ear . . . No, I wouldn't say so."

The conversation lasted another five minutes or so. Vivian said, "Okay, that makes sense. Yes, we will set up an appointment if he doesn't feel better by Friday . . . Thank you so much . . . Yes, I feel better about things now . . . Okay, bye now."

Vivian hung up the phone. She looked at Bobby, who seemed pale, and then back at Ophelia.

"Good news," she said. "Dr. Howard doesn't seem too concerned. He says that there are a lot of viruses going around and—"

"How could he catch a virus if he never leaves the house?"

"—he thinks he should be all better in a day or two. If the fever hasn't come down by Friday, he'd like me to bring him in. Otherwise—"

"Dr. Howard is wrong!" Ophelia interrupted. "Look at him! Just look at him!"

Ophelia didn't want to go to school the next day. She wanted to stay home with Bobby, wanted to comfort him when he cried, rock him when he moaned. But her mother wasn't having any of it.

"No," she said. "You're going to school. If I've told you once, I've told you a hundred times. You're going to school. I'll take care of Bobby. He'll be fine. And Dr. Howard said—"

"Will you hold him when he cries?"

"Yes. Of course."

"Please, mother. Don't allow him to suffer. Please."

"Go to school. When you get back, he'll be better. I promise you that. I promise."

Ophelia stared at her mother for a long time. Then she handed over the baby. Vivian held the baby in her arms, but not with the same love as her daughter. She held him like the burden he was. Holt peered out from the hallway, his upper lip brown from sneaking chocolate milk. Ophelia leaned in and kissed the baby on the cheek, kissed him on the lips. The baby didn't respond, just stared ahead with glassy eyes.

"Go," Vivian said. "Or you'll be late."

"I love you," Ophelia said, and she was talking to her son, not her mother.

"Yes," Vivian said. "I love you too."

Ophelia pushed open the screen door and let it slam shut behind her. As she walked down the concrete steps, she stopped and took one last look at little Bobby.

CHAPTER 24

Ophelia's first couple of years of high school had been pretty shitty. Administrators leaning against walls, arms folded, faces grim, scolding students for laughing or talking a bit too loud. Teachers standing behind wooden podiums, droning on and on about "Shall I compare thee to a summer's day?" or "Four score and seven years ago" or "volume equals length times width times height." Buckets of worthless knowledge, ready to be dumped into the river of irrelevance. Classmates organizing into exclusive cliques, and her not pretty enough or smart enough or athletic enough or weird enough to be accepted into any of them. Not that kids were particularly cruel to her. They just ignored her, treated her like a piece of bland furniture.

But now, as a junior, things were different. Now Ophelia had a baby boy, and so none of that other stuff mattered to her. She didn't need to be validated. Didn't need to be invited to parties. Didn't need a boyfriend. Her perspective had transformed. The things that the other students were blathering about or worrying about seemed silly and inconsequential. The lessons that the teachers delivered day after day seemed equally ridiculous. If she were being completely honest with herself, she now looked at everybody else with a measure of condescension. The other students had no idea what it was like to feel a tiny life—your own skin and blood—pressed against your skin. And even those teachers who had experienced it hadn't experienced it the way she had, that she was sure of.

But today, her heart was full of ache and her mind full of worry. She tried rationalizing things, telling herself that Bobby was just fine, that her mother was right, that the doctor was right, but there was a persistent voice in her head that kept whispering the same thing over and over and over again.

He's dying, he's dying, he's dying.

She couldn't focus on anything in class. Instead of taking notes, she wrote Bobby's name over and over in her notebook. At lunchtime, she went to the front office and asked to use the phone. The secretary, Mrs. Powell, a heavy woman with too much makeup and a 1960s bouffant, quizzed her on why she needed this privilege.

"It's my baby brother," Ophelia said with full sincerity. "He's very sick. I want to check in with my mom. See if he's feeling any better."

The secretary's eyes narrowed, and she sniffed, as if she could smell deceitfulness on Ophelia's breath.

"Your baby brother, huh?" she said.

"Yes. He's only five weeks old. He has a high fever. I just want to check."

"I'm very sorry that he's sick." More contempt. "But I'm afraid we need to keep the line clear. We have school business we need to conduct. We can't be allowing students to use the phone whenever they feel like it. If we make one exception, then we'll be forced to make two and then three. You understand, don't you?"

Yeah, I understand, she thought. *I understand that you're a bitch whore.*

"Yes, I understand," Ophelia said.

She left the office, her stomach aching with worry, then went to her locker and grabbed her lunch. She sat by herself at the cafeteria. She tried eating, but she couldn't swallow without gagging. She tossed the lunch in the garbage, and then went to algebra, American history, and French. Just like a good girl.

Poor Bobby, she thought. Poor, poor Bobby.

As soon as the final bell rang, Ophelia rushed out the side doors, not bothering to grab her books from her locker, knowing full well that she wouldn't be doing any homework tonight. Usually, it took her about fifteen minutes to walk home, but today she was in her neighborhood in less than ten. She ran across the front yard (the grass yellow, probably dead), up the front porch, and through the front door, not noticing that her mother's car, usually parked crookedly in the driveway, was not there. As she entered the house, she didn't shout out in case Bobby was sleeping, but instead tiptoed from room to room, searching for her mother, searching for her son.

Nobody was there. Not in any of the bedrooms. Not in the unfinished basement. Not in the attached garage.

"Fuck," she said out loud. She checked the kitchen table, hoping for a note, but there was nothing. That voice inside her head returned.

He's dying, he's dying, he's dying.

Ophelia covered her ears, and somehow the voice quieted and then disappeared.

"Maybe they went for a drive," she said out loud. "Or maybe they went to the doctor. Just in case. Bobby is fine. Everything is fine."

But four o'clock passed, and nobody came home. Five o'clock. Six o'clock. She made macaroni and cheese and watched *The Cosby Show* on television. It wasn't funny, so she turned it off. At seven thirty, she didn't think she could take it anymore. She didn't know what to do.

She decided to call Joyce. Maybe her mother's friend would know where they were. The phone rang six times, seven, and she was afraid nobody was going to answer. But then there was a click, and a woman's voice. It was Joyce.

"Hello?"

"Hello? Mrs. Brandt?"

"Yes?"

"Hi, this is Ophelia. Vivian's daughter."

"Ophelia!" she said with a little bit too much excitement. "How are you? Are you feeling okay? I mean, now that—"

"My mother," Ophelia interrupted. "Is she over there?"

"Your mother? Why, no."

"Have you heard from her today? Do you know where she is?"

A pause. "I'm afraid not. I haven't heard from her in several months. Not since—"

"If you see her, can you please tell her to come home? I need her to be home."

"I can. What's going on? You don't sound so good. Is there anything that I can—"

"No. Nothing you can do. Just tell her to come home. Goodbye."

She hung up the phone.

She turned back on the television. *Cheers*. She liked *Cheers*, especially Carla, but no matter what she did she couldn't keep her mind on the show, and soon she was crying, her hands covered with disgusting tears.

It was shortly before nine, as the sky had begun to darken, that Ophelia heard the familiar sound of her mother's car pulling into the driveway. All her dread turned to hope. She leapt from the couch and ran over to the window, pressing her face against the glass. As her breath fogged the window, she stared at the car in the driveway, engine still running, doors still closed. After what seemed like an eternity, the front door opened and then the back one. Her mother stepped outside and then her brother. Ophelia waited for her to open up the other back door and take little Bobby from his car seat, but she didn't. The doors shut closed, and her mother and her brother, heads down, shuffled slowly toward the front door.

Where was Bobby? Where the hell was Bobby?

Ophelia rushed outside and met them on the porch. "Where is Bobby?" she said, and the words were hard to say in between her sobs.

Holt's head remained bowed. Her mother stopped on the first step and looked up at her daughter. There was something about her that was off. Ophelia couldn't put her finger on it.

"Bobby?" her mother said. "What Bobby are you talking about? Do you mean your Uncle Bobby?"

"No! Not Uncle Bobby. My baby. My son. Where is he? Where the hell is he?"

But her mother looked down at Holt and then back up at Ophelia. She took a few steps forward, brushing by her daughter, and stepping into the house. A moment later, little Holt followed. It was all wrong.

Ophelia followed them into the house. She closed the front door shut, and her mother stood there, eyes empty. Eventually, she forced a smile.

"I'm sorry we're late. Did you get something to eat? If not, I could make you a hamburger. Or sloppy joe."

Ophelia didn't know what to say. She didn't understand what was happening. "Is he dying?" she said. "Is he at the hospital? Is that where he is?"

Her mother shook her head. "Don't be silly. Nobody is dying."

Ophelia looked at her brother. "Holt?" she said. "Where's the baby? What happened to the baby?"

"A baptism," he said.

"What?"

"I'm going to bed. I'm tired."

And that's what he did. Holt walked right past Ophelia, down the hallway, and into his bedroom. The door shut and remained that way until the following morning.

Ophelia wondered if this was all some elaborate prank. She wondered if maybe she was dreaming. It seemed as if all of this were happening outside of her body, outside of her consciousness. That morning, twelve hours earlier, she had held her baby. Now the baby was gone.

"Sloppy joe then?" Vivian said.

"What?"

"Do you want me to make you a sloppy joe? I could also make tater tots. I know you like tater tots."

Ophelia shook her head. "Mom, what is going on here? What is happening?"

Her mother stood there for a moment, those blue eyes still blank as a summer sky. "I'm sorry, darling. What's happening with what?"

"Where is he?"

Another odd pause and then Vivian shook her head. "I'm going to go into the kitchen. Dinner will be ready in twenty minutes. I'm sorry it's so late. We were helping a friend."

"A friend?"

Vivian walked past Ophelia and into the kitchen. Ophelia stood there, staring at the place where her mother used to be. Then she started laughing. She laughed and she laughed. She laughed until her gut was hurting and her face was aching. Then she laughed some more. She wasn't sure why she was laughing, but she couldn't stop.

"Is something funny?" her mother called out. "Did you see something on television?"

Ophelia didn't answer. She pushed open the front door and stepped outside. She stared at the sky. Millions of stars, some already dead. She turned her attention to her mother's car. Maybe Bobby was still inside. Maybe her mother had forgotten to take him out. These things happened from time to time, mothers (or grandmothers) becoming distracted and forgetting the baby in the car seat. It was night and the temperature had cooled, so Bobby wouldn't be particularly uncomfortable. Ophelia walked across the lawn, her legs heavy. She peeked inside the darkened windows.

The car was empty. The baby was gone. So was the car seat.

Her panic becoming more acute, Ophelia started walking around the perimeter of the house, hoping that she might see her son safely nestled beneath a bush or in the bough of a tree. She called out his name, "Bobby! Bobby!" but there was no response. Of course not. Bobby didn't even know how to speak.

Eventually, she came back inside, downtrodden. As soon as she entered, she heard her mother's voice.

"Dinner!"

What the hell? Ophelia walked into the kitchen. She sat down at the table. She placed the napkin on her lap. And she started eating. Her mother sat down across from her. For a while, the only sound was Ophelia chewing.

"And how was school today?" her mother asked.

Ophelia didn't answer. Maybe he'd gotten pneumonia. Maybe he'd died that very afternoon. Maybe they'd buried him next to the dandelion tree.

"It seems as if you've turned over a new leaf. I haven't gotten any phone calls about you ditching class, anyway."

This was nuts. Completely nuts. Ophelia didn't know what the hell to do. Maybe she was crazy. Maybe her mother was crazy. Maybe the both of them were crazy. Ophelia rose to her feet. She leaned over the table and pointed into her mother's face.

"Where is Bobby?" she said. "Where is my baby?"

Again, that empty stare. Again, that empty smile. "Darling," Vivian said. "You're acting strange. You're acting crazy."

Crazy. With a spurt of rage, Ophelia picked up her plate and threw it on the ground. The china shattered, and food went flying across the floor. Her mother touched her hand to her chest, shocked, but remained seated.

"Why?" Ophelia said. "Why are you doing this?"

"Doing what?"

"Making it seem like I'm crazy."

Her mother shook her head. "I never said you were crazy. I only said you were acting crazy."

"What did you do with Bobby? What happened to him?"

She reached over and grabbed Ophelia's hand. "I want you to take it easy, darling. It's all been a bad dream. All of it. Don't you understand?"

"I'm awake. I've been awake."

"And if you believe hard enough, if you have enough faith—"

"Believe in what?"

Her mother's mouth spread into a grin, and her eyes were unblinking. "Why, that there was never a baby. Believe with all your heart. With all your might."

"But there was. Bobby. He—"

"And now it's time to go to bed. When you wake up, everything will be different. I promise."

"Bullshit! Where is he? Don't do this."

"I'm not doing anything."

"You are! Where is he? Where is he?"

"The sky is dark. It's time for bed."

Ophelia blinked a few times. "Okay," she said. "Okay."

And with that, Ophelia stepped over the scattered food and shattered china. She walked down the hallway and into her room. She stood in the doorway. The crib was gone. So was the changing pad, the diapers.

Still fully clothed, Ophelia lay down on top of her covers and crossed her hands on her chest, just like a vampire. She stared at the ceiling, noticing for the first time water damage that was shaped like a sinister grin.

She closed her eyes. Soon she was asleep, but she kept waking to sounds of Bobby, of her baby, crying.

CHAPTER 25

Her mother had lied. When Ophelia woke up, nothing was different. Bobby was still missing, the world was still diseased. Ophelia found her mother in the kitchen, drinking coffee and reading the comics.

Ophelia wasn't too proud to beg. She got down on her knees.

"Please," she said. "Just tell me what happened to him. Was it his sickness? Something else? I won't tell. Please."

Her mother stirred her coffee with a spoon. She smiled, but it wasn't right. She looked like a madwoman. She was a madwoman.

"Nothing like that happened. Now get off your knees. It's not becoming of a young woman."

"Please—"

"Just have faith, Ophelia. Just believe."

Meanwhile, Holt wouldn't talk at all. He just tiptoed around the house like a ghost. Most of the time his eyes were empty, his face blank. But every so often his expression turned to something like panic, and he would suddenly begin gasping for air. Then he would close his eyes, spread out his arms like a miniature Christ, and sway back and forth. Ophelia didn't know what was wrong with him. After one of these episodes, Ophelia grabbed him by the arm, got inches from his face.

"C'mon, Holt," she whispered. "Tell me what you know. Tell me what happened to the baby. Mom is hiding the truth, don't you do the same."

But Holt just stared at her, unblinking, and then turned away, returned to his room, and spent the next hour playing with his action figures.

The desperation was building. She wasn't crazy.

And then a thought. Dr. Yamamoto. The man who'd delivered the baby. She would go to his house, she would knock on his door, she would tell him what had happened. He would be able to help her. Later that morning, as her mother napped, Ophelia left the house. She rode her bike, something she hadn't done since junior high.

He lived on the other side of town, by himself, in the Meadowview Development. She didn't think to bring a water bottle, so by the time she rode through her own rundown neighborhood, crossed over Hover Street—stuffed full of car dealerships, gas stations, and strip malls—and entered the Meadowview Development, she was soaked with sweat and maybe a bit dehydrated. She'd written down his address—3143 Pinewood Circle—but all the houses here looked identical. It took her twenty minutes of riding through the sanitized streets before she finally found his.

She dropped her bike on the front yard and walked up the steps to the door. On the ground was a mat that said *Welcome.* To the left of the door hung an American flag. Ophelia rang the doorbell two times. Then she opened up the screen door and pounded on the front door with the palm of her hands. Then she waited.

She heard footsteps, and the door opened and a man's face peered out. It took Ophelia a moment to recognize Dr. Yamamoto, who she had last seen on the day Bobby was born. He wore jeans and no shirt. When he saw her, his face immediately tensed.

"What . . . what are you doing here?"

"The baby," she said. "You delivered him. Isn't that right? And when you delivered him, he was alive and healthy."

Dr. Yamamoto scratched at his face so hard that he drew blood just below his eyebrow. "Please," he said. "Go away. Leave me alone."

"Tell me that it happened. You see, my mother said that—"

"I delivered the baby. Yes. Healthy. Now go."

She felt a wave of relief when he said that. She wasn't crazy.

"He's gone missing. I don't know what to do."

"Missing? I'm sorry, but I can't help you. Call the police. I can't help you."

But Ophelia was desperate. She tried pushing open the door, but Dr. Yamamoto wouldn't let it budge. She stopped.

"He's missing," she said again. "The other day, he got a fever. My mother refused to take him to the doctor. Now I don't know where he is. He might have died. I need your help, that's all I'm asking for. Your help."

Dr. Yamamoto shook his head. "I feel terrible for you. But I met my end of the bargain. I can't get involved."

"But it's my baby!"

"It'll be okay. Believe me. Goodbye. Everything will be okay. Goodbye."

And now, Dr. Yamamoto pushed closed the door. Ophelia tried resisting, but he was too strong. She knocked again, rang the doorbell, but the doctor wouldn't answer, the doctor wouldn't help her. Hadn't he taken an oath? She took a step back. She felt sick to her stomach. She placed her hands on her knees and started heaving. Nothing came out, but she couldn't stop, dry heave after dry heave. She could barely breathe.

At some point, she looked up and saw Dr. Yamamoto peering through the window. As soon as she made eye contact with him, the curtain closed. So she left that place, and never saw Dr. Yamamoto again.

Ophelia rode her bike back to her own neighborhood, the day getting hotter and hotter, and the whole time she was crying. She didn't know what to do. Her mother was concealing information of the worst kind. And now the doctor was too. It seemed that the world had turned upside down.

What now? She thought about calling the police, but she didn't. She knew that they wouldn't believe her. They would call her a liar, and her mother would tell them that they were right. Instead, she went from house to house to house, pounding on doors and asking surprised men and women—most of whom she'd only ever known peripherally—if they'd seen a little baby named Bobby.

She wasn't crazy. Her mom was crazy. Bobby was dead. Bobby was alive. What the fucking fuck? She was only met with shaking heads and bewildered expressions and concerned responses.

"Are you okay?"

"You don't look so good."

"Where is your mother?"

Each house she went to, she became a little bit more panicked, and pretty soon her body wasn't her own. She was zigzagging from house to house, sobbing, while the neighbors watched the proceedings from behind their drawn blinds. Ophelia had been running around her own neighborhood for nearly an hour, but the sun still hovered high in the August sky.

Finally, she came to a door that she hadn't knocked on, and she recognized it, and it was her own.

CHAPTER 26

For a full week, Ophelia didn't go to school, and Vivian didn't force her to. Ophelia ate dinner with her family, but she almost never spoke except to ask them to pass something her way. She never spoke about the rape, never spoke about the baby. Holt, for his part, seemed to have forgotten about everything. He talked about things that kindergartners talk about: friends, teachers, television shows. He watched *Knight Rider* and couldn't get enough of it.

"Do you think we could get a talking car, maybe?" he asked his mother.

"I don't think so," she said. "I think KITT is the only car like that."

"Maybe we can get KITT then? Once Michael Knight is done with him, I mean."

"Maybe. I can ask."

And for a while, some normalcy returned to the Davidson household. Eventually, Ophelia did go back to school. She did her work and held it together. For a while.

But then something changed. It was a Saturday morning when Vivian saw her daughter go down to the unfinished basement, filled with boxes of old clothes and childhood toys. Ophelia was down there for a long time, and when she came upstairs she was holding a bald-headed doll that she used to play with when she was a child. She disappeared into her room. That evening, Vivian noticed that Ophelia was wandering aimlessly around the house, holding the doll like a baby, rocking it back and forth.

"It's going to be okay, Bobby," she whispered. "Everything's going to be okay."

On Monday, Ophelia brought the doll to school. She used a small basket for a baby carrier and kept it by her desk. Every five or ten minutes she would take the baby out of the basket and rock it for a minute or two and then place it back in the basket. The students and teachers initially thought that she was doing it for another class (Family Studies, for example—message of the class: don't have sex!). But Ophelia wasn't enrolled in Family Studies.

Her art teacher, Ms. Colette, bewildered, referred her to the counselor, Ms. Wibby. Ms. Wibby had been at the high school for nearly thirty years, and she'd seen plenty of strange things over that time. She'd seen one student bring a goldfish in a plastic bag to school every day for a month. Another student had worn a fake cat tail for an entire year. But she'd never seen anything like this. Ophelia seemed to think the doll really was a baby. She'd even given him a name: Bobby. She talked about his sleeping patterns. Talked about changing his diapers. Talked about how he recently said his first word: *Daddy*.

Ms. Wibby usually dealt with scheduling, applying for colleges, and the occasional relationship drama. Not full-blown psychosis. This was above her pay grade. She called Ophelia's mom and told her what was happening. Told her that Ophelia should see a psychiatrist. Vivian thanked her for her professional opinion, and then she told her to leave her fucking daughter alone and to never, ever tell her how to parent.

After school, Ophelia would take the doll, place him in an

old wheelbarrow, and push him all around the neighborhood, singing lullabies all the while:

Good evening, good night!
Wrapped in roses,
Covered with a small nail
Slip under the deck,
Tomorrow morning, if God wills,
Will you be awakened again?

When neighbors would stop and stare, Ophelia would hold a finger to her mouth and tell them to be quiet, tell them that the baby was sleeping. But they could tell that there was no baby, could tell that it was just a doll wrapped in blankets.

At first, it was only during the afternoons after she got home from school, but then it was after dinner. Then it was late at night. Pretty much anytime the neighbors looked outside, they would see that girl, Ophelia, pushing her fake baby in that wheelbarrow.

People didn't say she was crazy, not then.

The Potters lived at the end of the block in the big house with the wraparound porch. Ophelia only knew them in passing, but she knew that they'd recently had a baby. It was a girl, and her name was Claire. Claire was beautiful, just like Bobby. Ophelia missed Bobby, missed him so much. So one afternoon, after getting home from school, after taking the doll out for a walk, she decided to pay Claire a visit. Derek Potter was still at work (construction of some kind), and Mary was home with Claire. The baby was napping in her crib, and Mary was resting in her own bed. She'd left the front door unlocked, and Ophelia had walked right in to the house and into the nursery.

At first, she simply sat on the rocking chair and watched the baby sleep. But then, after five or ten minutes, she rose from the chair, reached into the crib, picked up the baby, and held her. At first the baby remained asleep, but then she woke and, upon seeing a stranger's face, began crying. Ophelia tried rocking and shushing her, but it didn't work. Mary came rushing into the room. Even after seeing the strange neighbor girl holding her baby, she didn't panic. She looked at Ophelia.

"Please hand me my baby," she said, quietly but forcefully.

Ophelia waited for just a moment and then handed the crying baby to her mother. Ophelia explained that she didn't mean any harm, that she just wanted to hold a baby, and she begged Mary not to call the cops. So Mary didn't, but she did contact Vivian and tell her what had happened.

That was when Vivian called the first psychiatrist and told him that Ophelia was sick and needed help. But it wasn't until psychiatrist number three, a hunchbacked woman named Dr. Goldfarb, that Ophelia finally told her story, or a version of her story. She told Dr. Goldfarb how she'd given birth to a healthy baby boy and had named him Bobby, and how that baby had gotten sick one day and now he was missing, maybe dead.

"Is that why you've been pretending?" Dr. Goldfarb asked. "Is that why you've been walking around with a doll? Is that why you've been pushing him in a wheelbarrow?"

Ophelia didn't respond.

"Do you think that doll is really a baby? Do you think that doll is really Bobby?"

Ophelia shrugged. "What do you think?"

"Your mother told me that you were never pregnant. Is your mother lying?"

"I don't know if she's lying. I think maybe she's crazy instead."

"I think it would be good," Dr. Goldfarb said, "if we gave you some medicine. Medicine for your brain. To help you feel better."

"I'm not sick. I've never been sick."

But Dr. Goldfarb had done her research. She hadn't spoken just to Ophelia's mother, she'd also called the Davidson family doctor, Dr. Howard, and asked if he knew anything about a pregnancy. He couldn't comment. He did say, rather slyly, that Ophelia had quite an imagination. She contacted the local public health department and asked for any official birth certificate of a Bobby Davidson born that year. There were no records of anybody by that name.

Dr. Goldfarb diagnosed Ophelia with delusional disorder. In her notes, she wrote:

> *Ophelia has developed the belief that she gave birth to a baby boy and that the baby was taken from her, perhaps by her mother. This delusion falls loosely into the persecutory category. While I have not ruled out schizophrenia, I am leaning toward the delusion diagnosis, as Ophelia's behavior is fairly normal outside of these narrow delusional themes. Most concerning is that these delusions about the baby and his disappearance seem to be fixed beliefs that do not change even when presented with conflicting evidence (mother, friends, school, county all denying the existence of the baby).*

She prescribed the antipsychotic drug chlorpromazine. Vivian asked her if she was sure it was going to work. Dr. Goldfarb shook her head.

"The biggest challenge is that Ophelia doesn't see these delusions as delusions. She doesn't recognize her own sickness."

At the beginning, Ophelia refused to take them. She'd just shake her head.

"I'm not sick. You're the one who's sick. Dr. Goldfuck is the one who's sick."

So Vivian turned to force. She'd pin her daughter down and stick the pill in her mouth, jam her mouth closed until she saw her swallow. She did that twice a day. The chlorpromazine caused Ophelia to feel nauseous and prevented her from sleeping. But it didn't stop the delusions.

"Because they're not delusions," Ophelia would say. "Because I had a baby and his name was Bobby. Because you took him away from me. Because you let him die, or something worse."

September turned to October. October to November. On some days she went to school. On most days she stayed home. She slept a lot, sometimes fourteen hours a day, but whenever she would wake up, she would ask the same question.

"What did you do with my baby?"

She wasn't getting any better.

"Let me see Uncle Bobby. He'll know what to do."

By this time, the wheelbarrow had been discarded. So had the doll. But sometimes at night, past midnight, she would still wake up from slumber and rise to her feet. She would lean into an imagined crib and pull out an imagined baby. She would rock the baby back and forth and whisper, "It's okay. It's going to be okay." While Vivian and Holt slept, she would walk through the house and toward the front door. She would push open the front door and place that imagined baby in an imagined stroller. Then she would push that imagined stroller up and down the streets. The whole time, she would have a smile on her face because Bobby was happy and healthy, and it didn't matter what everybody else said.

"We need to have her institutionalized," Dr. Goldfarb said. "You can't continue to care for her at home."

"How long?" Vivian said. "How long until she's better?"

"I don't know. These things are hard to know. If she won't come willingly, we'll have to transport her by force."

"Maybe she just needs a different medication. She was never raped. She never had a baby. It's all in her head. It's all—"

It's all in her head.

On November 15, 1985, they came. There were three of them. They all looked the same: short and stocky; dull gray eyes; blond buzz cut. They didn't knock; instead, they just pushed open the door and made their way inside. Vivian was sitting on the couch, reading a copy of *Entertainment Weekly*. Holt was on the floor, playing with his action figures. Ophelia was in her room, moaning through another nightmare. The men didn't say anything. They just looked at Vivian and nodded their heads simultaneously. Vivian nodded back and then returned to reading her magazine.

Holt looked up from his imaginary game. "Hello."

One of the men said, "Hello."

"Are you here to help my sister?"

A different man said, "Yes."

Holt returned his attention to his Star Wars figures. C-3PO was in trouble, and Chewbacca was trying to save him. The men were here to help his sister.

"She never had a baby," Holt said. "It's all in her head."

"That's what we hear," the third man said.

The men walked down the hallway toward Ophelia's room. Holt and Vivian remained where they were. Chewbacca killed a Storm Trooper with his bare hands, Vivian flipped the page of her magazine, and everything was quiet for a few moments.

Then there was a scream, and then another one. The men appeared again, and this time they were carrying Ophelia. Two of them had grabbed her by the arms and the other by her legs. She was kicking and screaming and lunging. The men remained calm. Vivian closed her magazine and rose to her feet.

"It's for the best. They're going to help you."

Ophelia screamed.

"Please forgive me," Vivian said.

Holt dropped his figures and darted toward his sister. He grabbed at her leg.

"Ophelia!" he shouted.

The men pushed Holt away and continued toward the front door. They'd almost reached it when Ophelia managed to lean forward and bite one of them. She got him good, right on the forearm, drawing blood. Instinctively, he loosened his grip, and the man holding her legs lost his balance. A kick and then another one and, for a moment, Ophelia was free. On her hands and knees, looking like some grotesque crab, she scurried back toward the hallway. But she hadn't gotten very far when one of the men grabbed her foot and then another man grabbed the other. With no gentleness, they dragged her across the floor, her fingernails scraping against the hardwood.

"Let me go!" she shouted. "Let me go!"

The third man kicked open the door, and the other two pulled her outside. A white van was parked outside. Ophelia was screaming and crying and kicking. Neighbors opened doors and watched the proceedings. They knew she was crazy, and they knew the men were taking her to the psychiatric ward.

Holt ran to the window. He watched as the men slid open the van door and pushed her inside. He watched the door close, watched as they got into the van and, just like that, drove away. His sister was gone. They'd taken her away. The baby wasn't real, and they were going to make Ophelia better. Vivian came up from behind Holt and kissed him on top of the head.

"I tried to baptize her," she said, "but it didn't work. They tried to baptize you, but I don't know if it worked either. We need to try again. Tomorrow, we'll go back to the lake. Tomorrow, I'll submerge you. Tomorrow, you'll be saved, and every day after."

For the rest of the evening, they sat on the couch together, staring out the window, watching as the sky turned from blue to orange to black.

Tomorrow he'd be saved.

Just like Bobby.

PART VII

2018

CHAPTER 27

Vivian Davidson sat by herself in the front row of the wooden pew, her blue-veined hands clasped together, her flushed cheeks wetted with tears, her thin lips moving in a repeated prayer. She looked older than her seventy-one years, with her deeply-creased face and her cotton-white hair and her sagging jowls. A bleeding Christ watched her from the cross. A stern-faced pastor watched her from the vestibule.

She hadn't always been such a believer. But after Ophelia got raped, after Vivian shot and killed that man Ruben Ray, after Ophelia gave birth, she didn't have a choice, not really. She needed to believe in God because she needed to believe that there was a plan for her. That the world wasn't just chaos and violence. And so she chose to believe. And God had comforted her. But after her daughter went away, taken by the men in white, Vivian's religiosity became more intense, more focused.

Every Sunday morning, she would fix her hair up pretty and put on a fancy dress, and then she'd go to church, a reluctant Holt by her side. And every Sunday afternoon, once the sermon had been spoken and the blessing conferred, she would take Holt back to Mineral Lake, the same place Ed Hawkey had baptized the both of them, the same place she'd baptized Ophelia on that snowy night, and she would once again submerge him in the water, hoping that this time salvation might take.

"I baptize you in the name of the Father, and of the Son, and of the Holy Spirit."

She would submerge herself, too, although she wasn't sure if you could baptize yourself. Sometimes she would stay underwater for too long. She wondered if Holt had panicked when she did this, worried that she'd never come up. But she always came up, she always breathed. She decided it was because of weakness, not strength. She did this every week until he was thirteen years old, and that's when he refused to go to the lake anymore—"If God hasn't saved me by now, He'll never save me"—so she went by herself. She would walk slowly into the lake until the water covered her shoulders, until the water covered her mouth, until the water covered her eyes.

I baptize you in the name of the Father, and of the Son, and of the Holy Spirit.

And even though her belief was fragile, she prayed every day. She prayed for her daughter, locked in that dreary institution. She prayed for her son, that the scabs of sin wouldn't reopen. But mostly, she prayed for herself. Salvation was what she longed for, though damnation was what she expected. Because she'd betrayed her daughter, betrayed her in the worst way possible. And for what? Lies. But wouldn't the truth have been much worse?

There had been many times throughout the years that she'd wanted to confess to the police about Ruben Ray, but she could never go through with it. She was a coward. There were an equal number of times throughout the years that she'd wanted to confess to Ophelia about what happened to baby Bobby. But again, the truth would have been worse. She was sure of it. And so here she was, an old woman, alone except for the promises of some mythic power.

She hadn't heard Pastor Boswell's footsteps, so she jumped when he placed his thick hand on her shoulder.

"'This is the confidence we have in approaching God: that if we ask anything according to his will, he hears us.'"

Vivian turned to him and smiled, but her smile couldn't hide the trouble in her eyes, the desperation in her soul.

"I need His answers," she said. "More than ever, I need His answers."

A kindly smile, as if he knew. But the pastor could only speak in biblical verse.

"'If we know that he hears us—whatever we ask—we know that we have what we asked of him.'"

"But I'd like an answer outside of scripture." She squeezed her eyes shut. Her lower lip trembled. "I'd like an answer from Him whispered in my ear."

Pastor Boswell gave her the same smile, only now it looked condescending, not kindly.

"If only He worked that way, Vivian. All I can tell you is that you must believe. You must trust. The answers you're looking for might reveal themselves in unexpected ways."

Vivian wiped the tears from her wrinkled cheeks. "I visited Ophelia yesterday. My sweet Ophelia."

Pastor Boswell's face turned somber. He cleared his throat. "And how is she? Has she found some peace with the Lord?"

Vivian laughed, and her laugh was harsher than she meant it to be. "There is no peace to be found, not for her. Because of God. Because of me."

"As I said, the answers might reveal themselves in unexpected—"

"Please. I don't need to hear that. Pastor Boswell, what

if there are no answers? Have you thought of that? Have you considered that possibility? What will we do then? What will we do if, ultimately, there is no meaning? If there is no God? If it's all one big lie? I think I'll continue to believe, continue to cry in the pews, continue to scab my knees in prayer, because lies, the big ones and the small ones, are what keep us sane."

"No. Belief in God is not a lie. Belief in God is the truth."

Vivian rose to her feet. "The truth, the only truth, is that I'm tired. I may have done some bad things. I miss my daughter so much. I miss my son. I miss when the world was a little sweeter, a little less vicious."

He again placed his hand on her shoulder, and kept it there for a long moment. "You're a good woman, Vivian. God has plans for you."

"Maybe," she said. "Maybe."

And then she left.

It was late autumn, and the leaves were falling, death conquering life again and again. Vivian had walked to the church and now she walked home, hands buried in her jacket pockets, eyes fixed on the ground instead of the horizon. These days, she always seemed to feel lonely. Her job, teaching children to read, teaching children to share, didn't bring her any joy, not anymore. Her friendships didn't fulfill her, not rehashing the same gossip, the same politics. And her romantic relationships were non-existent—she hadn't been intimate with a man in more than a decade, and that man was Dan Parker (who had died from a stroke three days after they'd made love, and please don't blame her for his demise). But even her lack of connections didn't fully explain the profound isolation, and every few minutes she would imagine being buried not six but eight feet under, pounding on her casket, screaming for a rescuer, knowing there was none, knowing that her breath would run out.

She arrived home, but she didn't go inside right away. Instead, she stared at her house and marveled at how commonplace it looked. Someone walking down the street, looking at that house, wouldn't think anything extraordinary had happened there. It looked like a house where normal people ate normal dinners and talked about normal things. That's what it looked like.

She walked up the pathway and came to her front door. She placed the key in the lock. It made her arthritic hands ache to turn the key. There wasn't a single good thing about getting old, no matter what those bastards at AARP said. She stepped inside and sighed deeply. It was always so quiet. That's what loneliness was. A silence that caused agitation and, occasionally, rage.

She went to the kitchen and fixed herself a ham-and-cheese sandwich, an apple, and some potato chips. She didn't cook anymore, not really. It was a waste of time and money cooking for one person—better to eat a sandwich and finish it quickly. Better to not sit in one place for too long because then the dark thoughts would come. She ate all of the chips, some of the sandwich, and none of the apple. She rinsed her plate and placed it in the dishwasher. Holt used to love ham-and-cheese sandwiches. Ham and cheese and mustard on Wonder Bread. She probably made that for him every single day of elementary school.

Holt. She hadn't talked to him in such a long time. He probably hated her. That was okay, he had every right. She'd forced him to believe lies, the biggest ones imaginable, the same lies she'd forced Ophelia to believe, the same lies she'd forced herself to believe. She walked slowly down the hallway, back stiff from age and stress. She peeked into Holt's room, now just a glorified storage room filled with boxes.

Then she walked a few steps toward Ophelia's room. Her

heart began beating faster, as it was bound to do. She'd never really changed Ophelia's room. Maybe a few old school notebooks thrown away, but otherwise the same. It was sort of a shrine. But to what? Most of the time, of course, she'd walk right past the room; it was too painful to step inside and imagine her presence. But today, for some reason, was different. Today she went in. Today she climbed onto the bed, got under the covers, and pulled herself into a fetal position. She stayed like that for a long time.

"I'm so sorry," she said. "I'm so very sorry."

Vivian pressed her face against the pillow—the same pillow Ophelia had slept on thirty-three years ago—and inhaled deeply, trying to get a whiff of her memory. Thirty-three years. Jesus. Forever and yesterday. If she could go back in time, would she? Outside, a train whistle blew, sounding muted and melancholy. Vivian straightened her body. This was no good. She needed to leave this bed, needed to leave this room.

As was usually the case when she came in here, she told herself that she needed to throw away Ophelia's things. After all, Ophelia wouldn't be coming back tomorrow or any day. Vivian got out from under the covers and back to her feet. Yes, one day she would clear away Ophelia's things, but not today. Instead, she worked on remaking the bed, hospital style as Ophelia had liked it.

As she was doing so, she glanced under the bed and spotted that old plastic box, the one that was filled with Ophelia's childhood toys and knickknacks. She hadn't looked inside in years. She got down on her knees and pulled the box out from under the bed, unsnapped the lid and glanced inside. There were teddy bears and Cabbage Patch Kids, horse figurines and coloring books. There was also her old pink ballerina music box, the one that Ophelia's father had given her when she was seven or eight.

Vivian pulled out the music box and stared at it for a few moments. She remembered Ophelia opening the box and watching the little ballerina spin—dreaming, perhaps, of becoming a ballerina herself. Hadn't they put her in ballet lessons for a few weeks? She hadn't lasted because she refused to wear the shoes, refused to wear the tutu. She had always been her own person.

This type of nostalgia wouldn't do Vivian any good, but she couldn't help herself. She opened up the box and smiled as the skinny little ballerina popped into position. She reached around to the back and wound the key tightly and then watched as the ballerina danced jerkily to a warped version of Beethoven's "Für Elise." And if Vivian had tears in her eyes, so what? Didn't she deserve to mourn, even if it all happened thirty-three years ago? Hell, didn't she deserve to mourn for the rest of her life? Mourn for what had happened and what might still?

Behind the ballerina was a small oval mirror, and in front of her was a small compartment covered with pink cloth.

Why on this particular day did she choose to open it? Why not all the other times she had wound up the box? There was no real reason. There was no real reason for anything.

Inside there was an old piece of paper, folded, yellowed with age. She removed the paper with her thumb and forefinger, but she didn't open it, not for some time. Instead, she just sat there, staring at it, hands trembling—but from what?

And then she got up the nerve. She opened the paper and flattened it on the floor in front of her. She read it once, she read it again. As her slender fingers traced the letters, she began shaking, the room spinning around her.

My love,

I'm not a poet, but I know these things to be true: a heart can only ache so much until it ruptures. Eyes can only cry so much until they're blinded. A soul can only long so much until it withers and dies.

I wonder: do you have any idea how much I want to tell the world about us, about how I feel about you? Any idea how much I want to stand on rooftops and shout at the top of my lungs? But I know that the world would not allow it. Because they wouldn't understand. Because they mistake love for sinfulness.

And so, I will wait in quiet. In the darkness of my room. But know that you are the first thing that I think of when I open my eyes in the morning. You are the last thing I think of when I close them at night. And you are all that I dream of as the sky stays dark. I know that your heart aches as much as mine. Just know that someday we'll be together. This I promise you. Someday I'll take you far from this pathetic little town, and we'll never look back. I love you. I love you more than you know.

The handwriting. She recognized the handwriting. It was unmistakable, because who but he had such lovely handwriting? Who but he?

She rose to her feet. In one hand, she held the music box. In the other hand, she held the letter. Outside, thick clouds drifted over the sun, causing the room to darken. The wind began to howl, shaking the windows. Hadn't Ophelia been raped by Ruben Ray on an evening very much like this? No. She'd never been raped. But then maybe Vivian had always known this, even when she pointed the gun at Ruben Ray, even when she shot him dead. Even when they came and took Ophelia away.

She recognized the handwriting.

Vivian walked slowly toward her bedroom. She felt a painful urge to look at the photo, something she hadn't done in many years.

When she had done it, when she had killed Ruben Ray, she

had decided to take the photograph as a kind of souvenir. She was aware how memories changed, how narratives changed, and she wanted to remember the anger and hurt forever. She wanted to remember what Ruben had done to Ophelia and wanted to remember that she had stood up for her daughter—that she had killed him, that she had played God and shot him in the chest and the stomach. In the months following the killing, whenever she looked at the photograph, she felt not regret but exhilaration. After all, it was the first time in her life that she'd truly been brave, coming face-to-face with the demon and not blinking, firing that weapon and seeing his smug expression change to shock and then horror. He deserved to die, she believed. She'd done the right thing, she believed.

One of the bedroom windows was open, and the curtain whipped in the wind. She shivered, and she wasn't sure if it was from the cold or the dread. She placed the music box and the letter on her desk, walked to the back of the room, opened the closet door, and grabbed a metal box from the top shelf. Then, just like she had done in Ophelia's room, she sat down cross-legged on the floor and placed the box in front of her. She snapped it open.

Inside were dozens and dozens of old photographs, most beginning to fade. She'd never gotten around to making a photo album, and for that she felt ashamed. A better mother would have made several albums, would have sat her children on her lap and showed them the pictures. *See*, she would have said, *here you are after you found the first ripe tomato of the season. Look at how happy you were. And here you are after you saved up and bought that Dave Winfield glove. You loved that glove. Slept with it for a few months, if I remember correctly.* And her children would have smiled because they loved to recall those childhood days.

But for Vivian, the past had never been something she wanted to relive. It had always been something she wanted to exorcise. Now she knew that even if you somehow managed to banish your past, you couldn't always prevent yourself from resurrecting it.

She went through the photos slowly. She studied each one closely, trying to remember the day, the moment, it had been snapped. A few times she remembered, like the photo of Ophelia in her blue and yellow two-piece swimsuit and Holt in his Spider-Man trunks. They'd gone to Union Reservoir that day. Vivian had sat on the sand in her chair reading a Nora Roberts book, watching her children swim and splash and laugh. But most of the photos—of Ophelia, of Holt, of herself—were mysterious moments that Vivian had no recollection of at all.

And there, buried at the very bottom of the box, was the picture she was looking for. She placed all the other photos back in the box and picked up the photo of Ruben Ray, taken moments after his death. Now, so many years later, there was no pleasure, no exhilaration. There was only dread and desperation. She sat on the floor for thirty minutes or more. The universe had played the worst possible trick on her. God was either cruel or indifferent.

She finally rose to her feet and placed the box back in the closet, but she kept the photograph of Ruben in her hand. She returned to her desk, a wooden antique that had once been her mother's, and removed an envelope from one of the slats. She put the letter and the photograph into the envelope and sealed it. She grabbed a red sharpie, and on the front of the envelope she wrote *Each little world must suffer.* Ophelia's world, Holt's world, and now her world too. She placed the envelope inside the music box and shut it closed. Then she sat there staring at that music box, now filled with secrets of the worst kind.

What should she do with it? Burn it? Toss it in the landfill? No, she would hide it beneath the floorboards, in the same place where she'd once hidden the gun. Maybe somebody would find it. Maybe.

And then she knew what she would do next. She wiped a wisp of gray hair from her face. She squeezed her eyes shut.

"Each little world must suffer," she whispered. "And so, me too."

PART VIII

2018

CHAPTER 28

Holt slept in his mother's room, on the floor. His sleep was filled with nightmares from which he had difficulty waking. In one of the nightmares, he was swimming across a lake, Mineral Lake, and he felt somebody grab his ankle. He looked back, and it was his mother, only her face was hidden by a black veil. He tried to speak, but his mouth was filled with lake water, and she pulled him deeper and deeper beneath the surface, the sound of laughter muffled by the water—

In another nightmare, he was back in Tacoma, back in the fiery apartment, and he opened the closet door, and there was the mother and the child huddled in the corner, only this time the mother was Ophelia, old Ophelia, and the baby was dead, his head lolled to one side. Ophelia began rocking him back and forth, singing him Brahms' Lullaby. A smile spread across her face. Then the fire reached the closet and caught her foot and her leg and her torso. She screamed in agony. Holt tried reaching for her, but she and the baby were already lost to the flames—

Holt opened his eyes. His hair was wet with sweat. He blinked for a few minutes, gritted his teeth. The nightmare faded, leaving him to face the unease of now.

He got dressed and walked downstairs, listening to his own footsteps, to his own breath. He felt lonely, so damn lonely. He had the sudden urge to call Michelle, the woman he'd almost married, someone he hadn't talked to in a decade. He imagined her voice, a voice of compassion, somebody who would tell him that the world wasn't so dark, that a new day was always just hours away. But he didn't have her number, and even if he did, he knew she wouldn't answer his call. It was too late for that.

He made a cup of coffee and sat at the kitchen table, sipping it. He kept returning to his conversation with Yamamoto. And, in particular, he kept returning to a phrase the doctor had said. *Love, not sinfulness.* When Ophelia had been in Yamamoto's office, she kept repeating the phrase. *Love, not sinfulness.*

Holt had heard something like that before. But where? He kept sipping on his coffee, chewing on his fingernails. Outside, the sun was shining through the curtains, and the light in the kitchen was turning golden. He heard the distant moan of a train.

Love, not sinfulness. Love, not sinfulness.

Holt's eyes narrowed in concentration, his lips tensed in a frown. And then, just like that, he remembered. He slapped the table with his hand. He stood up and rushed out of the kitchen, back to his mother's room. He sat down at her desk, removed the revolver from the top of the music box, and placed it at his feet. Then he opened the music box, and the ballerina started to dance. With trembling hands, he removed the love letter and unfolded it. He quickly skimmed through the letter until he came to that phrase he was looking for: *Because they mistake love for sinfulness.* He stared at it for some time. And suddenly, he started to feel lighthearted. Because now he understood.

The letter hadn't been for his mother, it had been for Ophelia. He rose from the desk and walked across the room to where his suit jacket was lying in the corner. He reached into the pocket and pulled out the copy of Bobby's speech that Joyce had given him on the day of the funeral. He read the first sentence: *Vivian was my sister. Not only that, she was my best friend in the world.*

Right away, he knew. Bobby's handwriting hadn't changed with age. The same broad, heavy strokes; the same high and pointed *t* bars; the same exaggerated loops. And the same odd letter placement—some slanted to the left, some slanted to the right.

Bobby Hartwick had written the love letter. And he had written it to Ophelia.

Holt squeezed his eyes shut and inhaled deeply. He held his breath for a long time, until his lungs burned and his head ached. Then he exhaled. An overwhelming sense of grief enveloped him. He thought of his mother, hanging from a tree. She'd tried to make things right, but she'd killed the wrong man. She should have killed her brother instead.

Holt pulled out his phone and called Joyce.

"Holt," she said. "How are you?"

"Bobby. Where is he? Is he still in New York?"

A long pause. "What do you want to know about Bobby for?"

"Because I want to see him."

"Oh, darling, I don't know if that's such a good idea."

"I didn't ask if you thought it's a good idea. I asked where he was."

Joyce sighed. "I don't know for certain."

"He mailed you his speech. You must have looked at the envelope. The return address."

"Holt. Listen to me. I—"

"The return address. Where is he living, Joyce?"

Holt could hear Joyce breathing heavily on the other end. It took a few moments, but Joyce finally answered.

"Denver. He's living in Denver."

"You're fucking kidding me."

"I'm not."

"And he couldn't bother coming to her funeral? Couldn't bother contacting me?"

"No. I guess he couldn't."

"Okay, fine. Denver. Fuck. And do you have his address?"

"I'm sorry. I don't."

"Phone number?"

"No. But I know he plays music at a place called Angie's. Wednesday evenings."

Holt bent down and picked up the revolver. It felt cold in his hand. He closed one eye and aimed the gun at nothing.

"Today's Wednesday," he mumbled.

"Yes. It is."

"Guess I'll go listen to some music then. I'd like to thank you, Joyce, for all your help."

A long pause. Then: "Okay. You're welcome. But I don't like the way you're talking. I don't like the way you sound."

"I can't help how I sound."

"What are you going to do, Holt?"

He squeezed the trigger. Click.

"I don't know. I guess I'll decide when I see him."

Angie's was located on East Colfax, sandwiched between Popeyes Louisiana Kitchen and Lucero's Bail Bonds. There were bars on the windows and a drunk on the pavement. Muted country music was playing inside, probably from a thirty-year-old jukebox. Holt stepped over the drunk and pushed open a heavy steel door.

Two men, one white, one Hispanic, sat at the bar, both

staring at the television, which was turned to the World Series of Poker. The bartender, a bleach-blond woman with both arms covered in pin-up-girl tattoos, wiped the counter with a rag. Holt took a seat at the bar in between the other men. The bartender smiled; she was missing a few teeth, and the rest would probably be gone soon as well.

"Hey, sweetheart," she said. "What can I get for you?"

"Let me try a pint of Bud. And a shot of Beam."

She nodded and winked and grabbed a hazy mug from beneath the counter, pouring the beer until it was spilling over the top. Then she located a nearly-empty bottle of Jim Beam from the middle shelf and dumped a shot and a half into a wineglass.

"Six dollars," she said.

"Cheap."

"What did you call me?"

"Not you. The drinks."

She winked again. "Just giving you a little shit."

He handed her a ten and told her to keep the change. Then, after taking a long slug of beer, said, "I understand you got some live music tonight."

"We do. A band called the Mountain Hellions. Rockabilly. They start playing at eight. Maybe word of mouth will bring a few people in here, eventually."

"The guitar player. I might know him from a few years back. His name Bobby Hartwick?"

"It is. Bobby's sweet."

The way she smiled and spoke, Holt guessed the two of them had kept each other warm on a few occasions.

Holt slammed back his whiskey and chased it with the Budweiser. He left the empty wineglass and brought his beer to a corner booth, the seats yellow plastic. He sipped at his drink slowly, and pretty soon boredom overtook him and he was watching the poker match as well. At five minutes until eight, the door creaked open and two men entered. One, lugging an upright bass, looked to be in his midtwenties and had dozens of piercings (ears, nose, mouth, eyebrows). The other man was older and more grizzled. He wore a battered porkpie hat and had a white goatee that stretched to his clavicle.

Holt took another swallow of beer, eyes narrowing to slits. He hadn't seen Bobby in more than three decades, but he recognized him at a glance. The two musicians sat at the bar and both ordered whiskey. The bartender flirted with Bobby, grabbing one of his hands with both of hers and bending down so he got a good look. Holt sat in the booth and drank his beer. Every so often, he pawed at his left pocket where his mother's gun was buried. As he sat there drinking, he realized that all these years Bobby had been just a few dozen miles away from where his niece was rotting in psychiatric hospitals and halfway homes.

Holt could take out the gun and shoot him right here and now, watch him die the way his mother had watched Ruben Ray die. But no. Not yet, not now. Not until he talked to him, not until he made sure.

The duo didn't get on the makeshift stage until close to eight thirty. The white man who'd been sitting at the bar had left, so the audience was just Holt, the bartender, and the Hispanic man. Holt didn't make any attempt to shield his face. He was pretty sure Bobby wouldn't recognize him, not in this context, anyway.

On the stage, there was a microphone, an amp, and a single speaker. The pair spent about thirty seconds checking the mic and tuning strings, then Bobby stared at nobody and introduced them.

"We're the Mountain Hellions."

The bassist slapped and plucked, and Bobby hit the swampy

4/4 rhythm of Gene Vincent's "Be-Bop-A-Lula." His voice was deeper and harsher than Holt remembered, but he still sounded pretty good.

Well, be-bop-a-lula, she's my baby.
Be bop-a-lula, I don't mean maybe.
Be-bop-a-lula, she's my baby.
Be-bop-a-lula, I don't mean maybe.
Be-bop-a-lula, she's my baby doll.

When they finished their first song, Holt was the only one who clapped, although the bartender hooted a bit. Holt ordered another beer and watched as his uncle played "Train Kept A-Rollin'," "Twenty Flight Rock," and "Bottle to the Baby." At one point Bobby had opened for Elvis Costello in New York, and now he was playing rockabilly covers in a shithole Denver bar. Different circumstances, and Holt might have felt sorry for the old man.

Holt drank some more, and his clapping and cheering got louder and louder. The Hispanic man left the bar, so soon it was only Holt and the bartender. The Hellions played until nine thirty, and then, after a rockabilly version of Dylan's "Don't Think Twice, It's All Right," announced they were taking a short break.

Holt was drunk, and so he hollered, and Bobby never looked at him, not once. The bassist went outside to smoke, so Bobby sat at the bar and drank another whiskey, chatting it up with the bartender. Holt rose from his booth, stumbled across the floor, and took a seat next to his long-lost uncle at the bar. Bobby glanced at him without making eye contact, then went back to his drink.

"Don't get much live rockabilly these days," Holt said.

Bobby sighed, said, "Nope. Not too much."

"You play here every week?"

"We do."

"I live down in Thompsonville. Drove down just to see you play."

And now Bobby turned and looked at Holt. His eyes narrowed, but he showed no recognition.

"Is that right? Thompsonville?"

"Yes, sir. I saw you play years ago. Can I buy you another drink?"

Bobby shrugged. He swallowed down the last of his whiskey. "I never turn down a drink. Not unless it's from an ex-girlfriend or an ex-wife. Figure they might be trying to poison me, you know?"

Then he smiled and Holt saw it was that same mischievous smile from so many years ago. Holt waved down the bartender with the missing teeth.

"Two more whiskeys," he said. "Give us the good stuff this time."

She winked. "We don't have good stuff here."

"Then give us more bad stuff. One ice cube in each."

She poured two more Jim Beams and dropped in the ice cubes. Holt paid, and the bartender went into the back to wash dishes. Soon it was just the two of them. They clanked glasses, and Bobby Hartwick didn't know that his nephew was sitting right next to him and that he had a pretty little gun in his pocket.

"So where'd you hear me play?" Bobby said.

Holt swallowed half of his Jim Beam, and his head was spinning. "Where? Funny you should ask. I saw you play in my living room."

Bobby blinked a few times but didn't say anything. He still didn't recognize Holt, his own blood.

Holt continued. "You played for me, my mom, and my sister. You remember her, don't you? Ophelia?"

And now Bobby understood. His mouth fell open, and the blood drained from his face. He studied Holt for a few moments and then nodded his head. A smile came to his face slowly.

"Holt Davidson," he said.

"Yes, sir."

Bobby reached out to embrace Holt, and Holt let him do it, although it was awkward because of the bar stools.

"Goddamn," Bobby said. "It's been an awful long time."

"It has been. My mother died a few days ago. I kind of figured you might come to the funeral, especially since you're just an hour away."

The smile faded from Bobby's face. "I should have come," he said. "But I couldn't bring myself to. These things are complicated."

"Yes. I guess they are."

The bassist came back into the bar. He nodded at Bobby, said, "You ready, brother?"

"Yeah. I'm ready." Then Bobby turned back toward his nephew. "You going to stick around for the second set? You want to catch up afterward?"

Holt finished his drink. "Yeah," he said. "That's why I drove down here. There are some things I'd like to talk to you about."

Holt placed his hand on his pocket, where the gun was, and smiled.

CHAPTER 29

The Mountain Hellions played for another hour. A few more people entered the bar, but they came just to drink, not to listen to music. The longer the duo played, the less energy they had. Bobby stood in front of the microphone, not moving at all, and his singing became muffled and slurred.

By the time they closed with a halfhearted version of "Rock This Town," Holt had had enough. He was tired and drunk, and he wasn't sure if he could muster the anger to kill anybody. For several minutes, Holt leaned against a dartboard as Bobby packed up his guitar and said goodbye to his bassist and thanked the bartender for her hospitality. As he met Holt at the door, Bobby shook his head and grinned.

"Little Holt Davidson," he said. "Not so little anymore. Goddamn. Hard to believe I'm talking to you."

"Yeah, it's a strange old world, isn't it?"

"That it is. So what are you thinking? You want to grab a bite to eat? There's a breakfast joint just off Humboldt. Serve eggs and oysters all night."

Holt shook his head. "Nah. I'm not all that hungry. You live nearby? Maybe we could talk there. Have some privacy."

Bobby raised an eyebrow. "What do we need privacy for?"

"Can't tell you. Not until we have it."

Bobby laughed. "Fair enough. I've got little shithole two-bedroom not far from here. Ten-minute walk. Unless your drunk ass thinks you can drive."

Holt pulled up the collar of his jacket. "Let's walk."

And that's what they did. They walked down East Colfax, drunks leaning against worn brick walls, skittish women in too-tight black skirts, heads down, walking hurriedly home, neon signs advertising all you can eat or drink or imagine.

"It's a shitty town," Bobby said. "Filled with shitty people."

"Then why do you stay?"

"I've got my reasons."

"Like what?"

Bobby looked up at Holt and then back at the dirty street in front of him. "I've got my reasons," he said again.

It took longer than ten minutes to make the walk, but Bobby wasn't lying about his house. He really did live in a shithole. Sandwiched between a couple of low-rent apartment buildings—one called the Manor, the other called the Vista—his house was a tiny 1950s ranch with a small dirt yard protected by a dilapidated metal fence. A handful of beer cans and a broken shovel lay dead in the yard. There was a concrete porch, and on the porch were a couple of potted plants. Both were dead.

"Fixer upper," Bobby said.

"I know a guy," Holt responded.

"That's okay. I like it the way it is."

Holt followed as Bobby walked up the concrete steps and pushed open the cracked red wooden door, which he'd left unlocked. The front door opened directly to the kitchen, which was outdated, cramped, and filthy. Dishes and beer cans were piled in the sink, cereal and frozen meal boxes on the counter.

There was no table, but there was a litter box, and a mangy-looking cat stood next to it, snarling.

"That's Jeepers," Bobby said. "He's never liked me. He's never liked anybody."

They walked through the kitchen and into the living area, where Bobby rested his guitar against the wall. More filth here, with clothes and books and magazines strewn over the floor, furnished only with a couch and a wooden chair. Hanging on the wall were a few photographs of Bobby when he was young and handsome, posing with various musicians, some of them recognizable. Bobby pointed to one of them.

"Me and Joe Strummer," he said. "I played rhythm guitar for him once at a show in Boston. Generous guy."

Holt nodded. "Lead singer of the Clash, right?"

"That's right." He pointed to another photo. "See her? That's Donna Summer. Didn't play for her, but I met her at a party once."

"You must have been big time."

Bobby laughed. "Not really. Just hung out with some big-time people. I knew how to strum an ax, so they let me stand on the stage sometimes."

"Don't sell yourself short."

Bobby gestured at the surroundings. "No need for me to do it. My house makes it pretty obvious."

"Yeah, well. Success comes and goes, I guess. Just like everything. You got any beer? My buzz is waning."

"No beer. But I do have PBR." Bobby smiled.

"Close enough."

Bobby went back to the kitchen and returned with a six-pack of Pabst. He tossed one to Holt and grabbed one for himself. Bobby sat down on the couch and Holt on the chair. They both cracked open the beers and toasted. Holt took a long slug. The beer was warm and tasted like piss.

"It's funny," Holt said after a while.

"What's funny?"

"Toasting with a guy like you."

Bobby looked offended. "A guy like me? What do you mean by that?"

"Ah, nothing." Another slug and a long pause. "It's just that ever since I arrived home for the funeral, I've been digging around. Trying to make sense of things. Trying to understand why my mother killed herself."

"And? Did you get it all figured out?"

"Maybe. I think so."

At this, Bobby removed his hat and placed it on his lap. His head was shaved bald. He scratched at his goatee. "Okay," he said. "I'll bite. What did you discover?"

"A gun, a photograph, and a letter."

Bobby didn't respond, not right away; instead, he just drank his beer, stared straight ahead. Holt studied his face, looking for any tells, but there weren't any. He looked old, so damn old. For a brief moment, a sense of doubt settled over Holt, but he quickly shook it off. Holt knew what had happened. He knew the truth.

"What kind of a photograph?" Bobby finally said. "What kind of a letter?"

Holt squeezed his can, causing some of the beer to spill on his hand.

"A photograph of a dead man. A letter from a lover."

"I don't understand. What exactly are you talking about?"

Holt reached into his shirt pocket. He unfolded the letter, the letter that Bobby had written to Ophelia so many years ago, and handed it to him. He watched as his uncle read it, his eyebrows raising, his cheek twitching.

Bobby looked up. "What is this?"

"You don't remember?"

"No. What should I remember?"

Holt finished his beer and placed the can on the floor. "Here's what I think, Bobby. I think you wrote this letter. I think you wrote it to Ophelia. And I think, not too long ago, my mother found it. That's what I think."

But Bobby only laughed. "You're a fool, Holt. You always were."

Holt could feel his heart pounding and his fingers trembling. "You're saying you didn't write this? Is that what you're saying?"

"I'm saying you're not smart enough to be a detective."

Holt rose to his feet. He didn't know what he was going to say until after he said it. "I'm smart enough to know that you fucked Ophelia."

In response, Bobby threw his beer can on the ground. Beer went everywhere. "You dumb piece of shit," he said.

"And I'm smart enough to know you got her pregnant."

"A liar or an idiot. That's what you are."

"And smart enough to know that you and Ophelia convinced Mom that this fellow Ruben Ray had raped her. Convinced her to kill the poor bastard."

At this, Bobby rose to his feet and charged at Holt. He swung his fist wildly, but he missed. He was too old, too slow. Holt grabbed him by the arm and twisted it behind his back.

"Easy now," Holt said.

"What gives you the right?" Bobby said. "What gives you the right?"

With a quick jerk, Holt flipped his uncle to the ground. He pressed his knee against his back, and Bobby groaned in pain. Holt moved his hand to his pocket, pulled out the gun, and pressed it against the back of his uncle's head.

"I could kill you," he said. "I could kill you right now."

"Jesus, Holt. Come on, man. Let's talk."

Holt kept the gun there for a few moments and then yanked it away and rose to his feet. He kicked his uncle's leg. "Fine. Let's talk."

Bobby was wheezing, and it was a struggle for him to get to his feet. Holt motioned with his gun for Bobby to sit down on the couch. As Bobby sat there, shoulders heaving, filth all around him, Holt noticed how defeated the old man looked. He let his gun hand drop.

"Let's do it this way. I'll ask a question. You answer. If you lie, I kill you. Understand?"

Bobby nodded. "Yeah. I understand."

"All right. First question. Did you fuck her? Did you fuck my sister?"

Bobby paused for a moment, and Holt aimed the gun again. This time he pulled the hammer back.

Bobby raised his hands, pleadingly. "Please," he said.

"Answer the goddamn question."

Bobby covered his face with his hands as if they could protect him from a bullet. When he spoke, his words were garbled.

"What did you say? I can't hear you."

Bobby looked up, and his eyes were filled with tears. The son of a bitch was crying, and that only made Holt hate him more. "I said that I sinned. I sinned in the worst possible way."

"So the answer is yes? The answer is yes, you fucked my sister."

Bobby nodded his head. "I didn't mean for it to happen—"

"Fuck!" Holt shouted.

"We'd been spending a lot of time together. I should have understood that her feelings weren't healthy."

"Don't blame this on her. Don't you fucking blame this on her."

"No . . . I'm not. I just—I'll tell you. I was staying with you guys for a few weeks. Like I said, we'd been spending a lot of time together, me teaching her how to play the guitar, and then just talking. This one night, we were in her room. Your mom was gone. It was the same evening Ruben Ray came to the house and scared you. The same evening, goddamn it. We were sitting too close together. I'm so sorry for what I did. Please believe me. But she placed her hand on my leg. I should have pushed it away. I should have—"

Holt felt like he was going to be sick. The room was spinning. All he had to do was squeeze the trigger. And then the right man would be dead.

"How many times did you fuck her?"

Bobby quickly answered. "Just the one time. I swear. Oh, God. I've had to live with it for my whole life and—"

"You've had to live with it?" Holt shouted. "Fuck you. Just fuck you."

"Nobody knew. Through all these years. Nobody but her. And me. And now you."

Once again, Holt let the revolver fall to his side. He began pacing back and forth across the room, stepping over the cans and clothes and filth. The past was catching up to the present, and anything could happen.

Holt took a deep breath. He couldn't lose control. He needed to know for sure.

"When did you find out that she was pregnant?"

"Not until later. Months later. I was on the road. I called, just to see how she was doing. And that's when she told me."

"And did she say that the baby was yours?"

Bobby didn't answer.

Again: "Did she say that the baby was yours?"

Bobby's voice was barely louder than a whisper. "She did. But that doesn't mean that it was true. I mean, she could have—"

"And the story about Ruben Ray? About him raping her?"

Bobby shook his head and again covered his pained face with his hands.

"You've got to understand. I pleaded with her to have the abortion. I told her that her life would be ruined if she went ahead with it. But she wouldn't listen to me. She told me that she was going to have the baby, and she was going to name him Bobby. She was the one who came up with the idea about Ruben. To protect me, she said. To protect us. She hit her temple with a rock, used a paring knife on her stomach, her inner thighs. Made it look like she'd been raped. It was her idea."

"And you never thought to tell my mother the truth?"

"I was a coward, Holt. I've always been a coward."

"My mother killed Ruben for what she thought he'd done. She killed herself when she found out that it was you."

"I wish I could change the past. You've got to believe that I do."

"The past," mumbled Holt, "tortures the present."

Bobby eyed the gun still dangling from Holt's hand.

"So what are you going to do? Are you going to kill me? I might deserve it."

"I don't know. I don't—"

"There's something else you should know," Bobby said. "Before you make up your mind."

"What? What else should I know?"

And now the agonized expression on Bobby's face changed to something lighter, almost giddy.

"It's about the baby."

The baby. Strange, but even now, even after Dr. Yamamoto had told him that he'd delivered the baby, Holt had refused to acknowledge his existence. It was too painful to think about. Holt pulled back his hair with his hand. He shook his head.

"What about the baby?"

Bobby leaned forward in his chair. "After the birth, I called again from the road. Ophelia wanted me to come visit; she wanted me to meet the baby. My great-nephew, my son. I told her that I would come, of course I would come, but deep inside I knew that I wouldn't. I was too big of a coward. Plus, I was afraid that Vivian would figure everything out. Discover the awful truth. So I never met him. Never. Regrets, so many of them."

"The baby—"

"For many years, I didn't talk to your mother. I didn't talk to Ophelia. I didn't even know she had been hospitalized, I swear I didn't. Otherwise, I would have . . . done things differently. But I didn't know. Sometimes, I thought about the baby, wondered what he looked like. Wondered what kind of music he listened to."

"What happened to him? What—"

"Many, many years later, I did visit your mother. She was hostile, resentful. But still we ate dinner together. Then we got drunk in her kitchen. She told me about Ophelia, how she'd lost her mind. But she didn't say a thing about the baby. Not a thing. She didn't know that I knew. We drank more tequila. I confronted her on it. I'm not sure why, exactly. Told her that Ophelia had called me and told me about the baby. At first, she denied it. She denied everything. I lost my temper, told her to stop the lying. She sobbed more tears, said lying was the only thing she knew how to do anymore. I grabbed her wrist and squeezed. And then, just like that, she told me. She told me everything. And it might have even been the truth."

Holt could hardly move. His skin seemed to be tightening around his bones and muscles.

"What happened to the baby?" he said, and his voice was only a whisper.

"The baby. My son. Several weeks after he was born, he got sick."

"Sick?"

"You sure you don't remember this, Holt? You sure?"

Holt only shook his head.

"He had a bad fever. He was lethargic. It could have been pneumonia. It could have been something else. Ophelia wanted to take the baby to the doctor, but your mother refused. You see, she didn't want anybody to know about the baby. She thought that maybe she could keep it secret forever. So she sent Ophelia off to school."

"And the baby died?" Holt mumbled. "He died from pneumonia?"

Bobby shook his head. "He died. Yes. But not from pneumonia."

And now Bobby rose from the couch. He didn't look defeated anymore.

"Don't you wonder," he said, with a gleam in his eye, "why you're consumed with guilt?"

"I saved the baby from the fire. They wrote an article in the newspaper. They—"

"Your mother was sleeping. She didn't hear you go into the bedroom. Didn't hear you take Bobby from the crib."

"Stop. Please."

But Bobby wouldn't stop.

"You took the baby and you—"

Bobby's voice sounded faraway, and the room began swaying from end to end. Holt couldn't listen anymore. He gripped the revolver and pointed it at Bobby's chest. His hand was shaking with rage.

"Fuck you!" he shouted. "You're a goddamn liar!"

"You pretend like you don't remember, Holt. But you do."

Tears began leaking from Holt's eyes. Just a twitch of his finger and it would be over, just a twitch. Everything was very quiet, and he could hear his own breath. And then something strange happened. His rage began to dissipate, and his hand steadied. The ever-present dread changed to something he couldn't name: resignation, maybe.

With the back of his hand, Holt wiped the tears from his cheek. Then he lowered the gun slowly, stuck it in his pocket.

"You remember," Bobby whispered.

Holt dropped his head to his chest, nodded slowly. Then he turned and walked out the front door.

PART IX

1985

CHAPTER 30

This is how it happened.

The baby wouldn't stop crying. Ophelia could have comforted him, maybe, but she was at school. The doctor could have given him medicine, maybe, but Holt's mother had refused to take him to the hospital. Why? Because he was a secret, because he was a sin. Each time Vivian held him, rocked him, shushed him, the crying got worse.

Holt could tell that his mother was getting more and more agitated. "What's wrong with him?" Holt asked. "Why won't he stop crying?"

His mother didn't answer. She tried singing a lullaby, but little Bobby wasn't having any of it. His face turned bright red, and a bubble of snot appeared on both nostrils. More sobbing, only taking a break to sneeze and cough.

"What's wrong with him?" Holt asked again.

Vivian looked at Holt and then back at the crying baby, and now there was contempt in her eyes.

"What's wrong with him? He's sin incarnate. That's what's wrong with him."

Holt knew what sin meant, but he didn't know what

incarnate meant. He didn't ask.

"He hasn't been baptized. Maybe things would be better if we submerged him. If the sin was scrubbed from his soul."

The way she spoke scared Holt. She sounded like the men at church, the ones who wore the long white robes. He could tell that his mother was sad, could tell that she was depressed. He didn't want her to be sad. He thought about what she'd said. *Maybe things would be better if we submerged him.*

Vivian tried feeding Bobby formula from the bottle, but he pushed it away. She tried sticking a pacifier in his mouth, but he spat it out. He began to gnaw at his fist and pull his legs toward his stomach.

"Sin," she said under her breath.

Holt followed her as she brought the baby to Ophelia's room. That's where the crib was, where the baby slept. She placed him in the crib and covered him with a blanket, but he only screamed louder.

"You need to sleep," she said. "You need to fucking sleep."

Vivian left him there, and when she came out, Holt noticed that she was crying, too, although she quickly wiped away the tears.

"It's a shame," she said, talking to herself, not Holt, "that this world was created."

She walked down the hallway and went into her bedroom. Holt watched as she grabbed a vial of pills from the nightstand, dumped a few into her hand, and stuck them on her tongue. No water, so she swallowed hard. Then she curled up on her bed, and Holt could tell that she was praying. God should help.

Holt stayed in the doorway for several minutes, and he was relieved when she finally stopped crying and fell asleep. He tiptoed into her room and stood over her, then he leaned down and kissed her on the forehead.

"I love you, Mommy," he said. She didn't stir.

He left the room, closing the door quietly behind him.

It's a shame that this world was created. Holt went into his own bedroom. He took out a new Star Wars coloring book and some crayons. Then he sat on the floor and began coloring, careful not to go outside the lines, all the while babbling to himself. "It's okay, Mommy. Don't be sad. I'll help you. He's sin in-car-nate. He hasn't been baptized. It's a shame. Don't cry."

He colored a picture of C-3PO and R2-D2. The colors weren't right (C-3PO ended up blue instead of gold), but he didn't mind. When he was done with them, he colored a picture of Darth Vader. He tore out the pages and placed them on his pillow. "Don't cry," he said, and he was talking to his mother and the baby.

He left his room and walked toward Ophelia's room. Just like his mother, the baby wasn't crying anymore. Just like his mother, the baby was asleep. Holt leaned over the crib.

"Hi, baby," he said and smiled.

The baby didn't move.

"You haven't been baptized," he said. "That's why you're sin in-car-nate."

He wished Ophelia were here. Or the other Bobby, the real Bobby.

"I'm going to help," he said.

Holt reached into the crib and grabbed ahold of the baby. The baby's eyes opened, but he didn't cry. "Shh, shh," he said, just like his mother. He pulled the baby from the crib and held him the way he'd seen his sister and mother hold him. The baby was watching him. "I'm going to help," Holt said again, and he knew he was doing the right thing.

Holt didn't say goodbye to his mother, because she was sleeping. He carried the baby through the house, and the baby was being so good, so quiet, he must have liked Holt the best of all. But even though he was small, he was still pretty heavy for Holt. Holt worried that he wouldn't be able to carry him all the way there, so he found the baby stroller. It was in the corner of the living room and hadn't been touched in a long time. His mother had told Ophelia a hundred times not to push the baby, especially during the day, but Holt put him in the stroller and strapped him in. He opened the front door and pushed the stroller through, and he was very proud of himself.

Outside, the sun was already blazing low in a blank blue sky. Holt thrust the stroller down the steps, and it was hard to keep his grip, but he didn't let the baby fall out. Then he pushed the stroller down the walkway and along the sidewalk. It seemed like nobody was outside, and that was a good thing, because they might ask why a little boy was pushing a baby in a stroller. Holt didn't want to tell them about the secret, didn't want to tell them that he needed to submerge him to save his soul.

Holt walked as fast as he could, but it still took about twenty or thirty minutes before he finally came to Hover Street and then 3rd Avenue. The baby was starting to make some noises, not crying but whimpering. Holt pushed the stroller along the train tracks and past the storage lots and car junkyard. Soon he spotted the small lake, Mineral Lake, where he had been baptized, where his mother had been baptized, where Ophelia had been baptized.

The air was still, and the cottonwoods and junipers hovered over the glistening lake. Holt unsnapped the stroller and grabbed the baby. He held him over his shoulder, and now the baby began crying. As Holt walked slowly toward the lake, the baby cried louder and louder. Nobody else was here. Nobody but him and the baby and God.

What's wrong with him?

He hasn't been baptized.

"It's okay, baby," Holt whispered.

Holt removed his tennis shoes and socks waded into the water. The baby was squirming in his arms, and he had to hold him tighter so he wouldn't fall. The water got to Holt's calves and then his waist. The baby was crying louder than before. He needed to do it, before it was too late.

He remembered what the old man and woman from church had done, how they had carried Holt into the water and then pushed him beneath the water, how his mother had done the same thing to Ophelia. They had all said the same words. Now Holt placed both his hands under the baby, so that the baby was lying flat, and then submerged him beneath the water. Holt made sure to grip him tightly, knowing that if he let go, the baby could float away. As soon as he went under the water, the baby started kicking and flailing, but Holt held him there for a few seconds as he said the words.

"I baptize you in the name of the Father, and of the Son, and of the Holy Spirit."

He pulled the baby out. His face was red, and he was coughing, trying to breathe. He looked the same. He didn't look baptized. Holt needed to try again. So, once again, he submerged the baby. And, once again, he said the words. He did this again and again, but each time he was unsure if the baby was fixed.

"I baptize you in the name of the Father, and of the Son, and of the Holy Spirit."

Finally, after he'd done it five or six times, the baby stopped crying. The baby was still, and Holt was pretty sure it had been baptized.

"It's okay, baby."

Holt walked the baby out of the water, placed him in the stroller, and secured the latches. The baby's head lolled to one side.

The sun had disappeared behind some low clouds. Holt tried

putting on his socks, but his feet were too wet and he couldn't get them on. He put on his shoes barefoot and thought about leaving the dirty socks behind, but he was worried that his mom would get angry. So he stuffed his socks in his pockets and began the long walk home.

Cars drove down Hover, but there was no one on the sidewalk. It was hot outside, and Holt's legs and shorts dried quickly. He felt thirsty. When he got home, he would have a Coca-Cola. He wasn't supposed to have Coca-Cola, but his mother would be asleep, so she wouldn't know. The whole way home, he sang songs that he'd heard on the radio. "When Doves Cry," "Dancing in the Dark," "Girls Just Want to Have Fun," "Take On Me," "One More Night."

Soon Holt would tell his mother what he'd done. She would give him a big hug, and things would be better from now on. She and Ophelia wouldn't fight anymore. The baby wouldn't cry anymore. The family would be happy again.

When Holt got home, he was surprised that his mother wasn't asleep. Usually, when she swallowed her pills, she was asleep for hour after hour. But not today. He was also surprised that she started shouting.

"Where have you been? Jesus Christ! I thought you'd been kidnapped! You and the baby both!"

But he hadn't been kidnapped. He'd taken the baby to Mineral Lake. He'd placed him in the water. He'd baptized him. His mother took the baby out of the stroller, saw that the baby wasn't crying. The baby was still. The baby was fixed.

"Oh, my God!" she shouted. "What have you done? What have you done?"

Holt left his mother with the baby. He went to his room and got into his bed. He felt very tired. From outside of his room, he could hear his mother screaming and crying and saying things he didn't understand. He closed his eyes. It took him a few minutes, but soon he fell asleep. Sometimes he would awake, and he could still hear his mother.

"What have you done? Oh, Holt, what have you done?"

"I baptized the baby," he said to himself. "I saved him."

He slept for two or three hours, occasionally rolling over or scratching at his skin or moaning in a nightmare. Outside, lightning flashed in the darkened sky, and a low grumble of discontented thunder followed. A few dogs barked, and from somewhere there was music playing.

At some point, Holt's eyes flew open wide and he sat up in bed. He was surprised to see his mother standing there. For a moment she didn't say anything, but then she got down on her knees and whispered in his ear.

"We'll take him to the darkened well. Out by Ruben's farmhouse. Nobody will know," she said. "Nobody will ever know."

PART X

2018

CHAPTER 31

After Holt left Bobby's house, the bullets still tucked safely in the gun's cylinder, he wandered alone through the desolate neighborhoods, dogs howling and drunks staggering, until he found his car parked outside of Angie's. He nodded at a man smoking a cigarette, his tie undone, and got into his car. He sat there for a long time, squeezing the steering wheel, staring at the dark and cold street. Finally, he hit the engine and drove. There was static on the radio, but he didn't change the channel. He was shivering, so he turned the heat up to full blast.

He didn't know where he was going (yes, he did; yes, he did). He drove down Colfax Avenue, all desperate neon lights and tired streetwalkers and narcotic gloom. He passed by Mel's (pigs-in-blanket, a buck fifty), Tiny's (shots of Jägermeister for an even two), and a Sinclair gas station, asphalt empty, the pumps looking like tombs. A few miles until Downing Street, and he hooked a right, and then another one and another one, and he couldn't stop his hands from trembling.

He parked his car in front of the trilevel house and stepped outside. For several minutes, he stood on the sidewalk, hands buried in his pockets, eyes gazing at the blackened windows of the Balsam Halfway House. He felt for the gun in his jacket pocket, the same gun his mother had used to kill Ruben Ray, the same gun he'd almost used to kill Bobby Hartwick, and then started across the lawn, dead leaves crunching beneath his feet.

He stood on the porch, pulled open the screen door, and rapped on the front door twice. All quiet, so he leaned forward and rang the doorbell. A minute passed, but then he heard the sounds of footsteps pattering on the floor and voices echoing against the walls. The porch light flashed on, and a moment later the door opened a crack. Holt could see a sliver of Dr. Tom's face, his eyes bloodshot and his hair disheveled from sleep.

"What is it?" he said. "Who are you?"

"It's me, Holt Davidson. Ophelia's brother. Remember?"

"It's late. Why are you here?"

"Something has happened. I need to see Ophelia."

Behind Dr. Tom, Holt could see Doris, the woman who had first greeted him at the Balsam Halfway House, the woman who had offered him an unlit cigarette. She was tearing at her hair, trichotillomania. And then a man he hadn't seen before, wearing nothing but long underwear, rubbing his hands together as if he were trying to light a fire.

"I'm sorry," Dr. Tom said. "But we have visitation policies. Now is not the time. Ophelia is sleeping."

"It's important."

"I'm sorry."

And Dr. Tom was about to push shut the door when Holt pulled out his gun and pointed it at the doctor's left eye.

"It's important," he said again.

For a long moment, Dr. Tom didn't move. Then he pulled the door open.

"Okay," he said. "I'll get Ophelia for you. Just put the gun away. Please."

Holt stepped inside and shut the door behind him. Then he stuck the gun back in his pocket.

"I'm not going to hurt anybody. I just need to see my sister."

By this point, several of the patients—or as Dr. Tom referred to them, tenants—had appeared from their rooms and were milling around the house, moaning and laughing and crying. One of them, an exceptionally tall man with an exceptionally long beard, wouldn't stop shrieking.

"I'm not going to hurt anybody," Holt said again.

Dr. Tom disappeared into the hallway and then reappeared a minute later holding Ophelia by the arm. She was wearing flannel pajamas and was holding a stuffed animal, a rabbit. Her mouth was open wide, and her eyes showed only terror.

"Ophelia," Holt said. "Ophelia."

It took her a few moments before she showed recognition. Then she mouthed the word, "Brother."

He didn't know what he was going to say until he started speaking.

"I've come to take you with me," he said. "I'm going to take you far away from here. We'll drive south, toward Mexico. It'll be just you and me. Nobody's going to hurt you, not ever again."

The other patients had quieted. Dr. Tom still held Ophelia's arm. She opened her mouth as if to speak but nothing came out.

"I've got some money saved up," Holt continued. "Enough to live on. All those years, they're gone, sand sifting through our fingers. But our future. It can still be lived. Just say yes. I'll take you away from here."

Dr. Tom said, "You can't just take her from here. You have to—"

"Just say yes," Holt said again.

Ophelia pulled away from Dr. Tom's grasp. She moved

toward her brother. A single tear fell down her cheek. Then she shook her head.

"I can't."

"Please, Ophelia."

From behind him, the moaning resumed. The laughing. The crying. The shrieking.

"You heard her," Dr. Tom said. "Come back another day."

"I could take care of you," Holt pleaded.

Then she said something that surprised Holt. "I know what you did," she said. "I've always known. But it's okay. I forgive you."

The tears filled Holt's eyes, and he started crying. He didn't know what for exactly, but soon some of the other patients were crying too. Ophelia reached for Holt and pulled him toward her, and now he was sobbing even harder and she was shushing him, telling him that it would be all right.

"I killed him," he said. "I killed the baby."

She rested her head on his shoulder. She whispered in his ear.

"I forgive you. I forgive you. I forgive you."

Holt pulled away from the embrace. He tried wiping away the tears, but soon his cheeks were wetted again. He needed to leave. He needed to say goodbye forever. He took a step backward and then another one. From somewhere, he could hear the sound of a wounded dog yelping.

Ophelia closed her eyes for just a moment and then reopened them.

"Thank you," she said, "for visiting me. I always missed you, Holt. Always."

"I always missed you, too."

It was time to go. But before leaving, Holt took one last look at his sister, and he thought that she looked just as lovely as when she was a child.

It was strange for him to be here again. Three in the morning, and Holt stood at the shore of Mineral Lake. The full moon reflected off the darkened water, the wind was blowing cold, and Holt shivered. He removed the gun from his jacket, let it rest in the palm of his hand for a few moments. Then, without really thinking, he reached back and threw it as far as he could. There was a splash, and the gun was swallowed up by the water. Holt squatted on the ground and stared at his hands. They were trembling, and he figured they might stay that way forever.

Along the shore there were pebbles and stones and rocks. Holt began gathering some of them and stuffing them in his pockets, jeans and jacket both. By the time he was done, he could feel his pants and jacket sagging. He leaned down and grabbed one more stone, a flat one. And this one he placed it in his mouth. He rose to his feet and walked slowly toward the water.

The world hadn't treated Ophelia fairly. The world hadn't treated his mother fairly, either. Remember what she'd said on that day so many years ago? *It's a shame that this world was created.* He removed his shoes and socks, just like he'd done when he was a child.

"It's okay, baby," he said out loud, and he didn't know why.

His mind was made up. He took a step into the water and then another one. Nothing was left in the world but the moon, the rocks, and the water. He walked farther and farther into the water. The same lake where he'd baptized the baby.

Soon the water reached his chest and then his shoulders. Each of the rocks in his pocket was a single sin. But what about the one in his mouth? Which sin was that?

He closed his eyes and took another step forward. An odd memory appeared in his consciousness. Of him as a small child, no more than three or four years old. He was walking down Main Street with Ophelia, and the snow was falling. They were on the way to the store to get a Christmas present for their mother. The snow was deep, nearly up to his waist. Holt gripped a ten-dollar bill in one hand, Ophelia held his other hand, but at some point she let go. She began walking faster. Holt tried catching up to her, but she kept getting farther and farther away. She turned around.

"Hurry," Ophelia said. "Before you're swallowed up by the snow."

Before you're swallowed up—

Holt took another step forward, and the water covered his mouth. Another one, and it covered his nose. He couldn't breathe. The baby couldn't breathe.

He relaxed his body. The roar of the water covered him.

His lungs burned, and his head pounded. Soon, he'd be dead. Not saved, but dead. He bent his legs, and his knees hit the floor of the lake. The weight of the rocks held him there. He counted in his head. Sixty seconds. Ninety. A hundred. He saw his mother's face. And then his sister's. A hundred and twenty seconds.

He didn't make a conscious decision to empty his pockets. He didn't make a conscious decision to rise to his feet. But the next thing he knew, his face was bobbing above the water, and he was coughing and gasping for breath. The stone was still in his mouth, and he spat it into his hand. He looked up at the moon, now covered by filthy clouds.

"I baptize you in the name of the Father, and of the Son, and of the Holy Spirit," he whispered, but he knew that nobody could hear.

He placed the stone back in his mouth and walked through the darkened waters toward the shore.

ACKNOWLEDGMENTS

First and foremost, thank you to my lovely wife, Tobey. She knows me and loves me anyway.

Thank you to Haila Williams, who fought for this novel before floating off to retirement. Every author needs a champion, and she was mine. I'm eternally grateful.

Thank you to my editor, Andy Kifer, for his sensitivity and wisdom. He cleaned up messes, called me on my bullshit, and forced me to be a better writer.

Thank you to Megan Bixler, Josie Woodbridge, Hannah Ohlmann, Kathryn English, Ember Hood, and the rest of the incredible staff at Blackstone Publishing. Their professionalism and passion made this trip a joy.

Thank you to my agent, Chip MacGregor, for his constant positivity and emotional support. He was able to talk me off the ledge, drink a cocktail at his own whiskey bar, and then come back and talk me off the ledge again.

Thank you to Micah Holmes for educating me on firefighting life before leaving me with the tab.

Thank you to the students and staff at Longmont High School, especially my principal and good friend, Jeff

McMurry. I'm forever proud to be a Trojan.

Thank you to my friends and loved ones. There are too many to mention here.

Thank you to my enemies. Also, too many to mention here.

And finally, thank you to my parents and my sister, Leah. The older I've gotten, the more their love means.